FEB 0 8 2011

30.99

A Time to Love

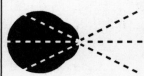

This Large Print Book carries the
Seal of Approval of N.A.V.H.

QUILTS OF LANCASTER COUNTY
SERIES, BOOK 1

A TIME TO LOVE

BARBARA CAMERON

THORNDIKE PRESS
A part of Gale, Cengage Learning

GALE
CENGAGE Learning™

Detroit • New York • San Francisco • New Haven, Conn • Waterville, Maine • London

*LP
CF
Cameron*

Copyright © 2010 by Barbara Cameron.
Thorndike Press, a part of Gale, Cengage Learning.

LIBRARY OF CONGRESS CATALOGING-IN-PUBLICATION DATA

Cameron, Barbara, 1949–
    A time to love / by Barbara Cameron.
       p. cm. — (Thorndike Press large print clean reads) (Quilts
    of Lancaster County series)
    ISBN-13: 978-1-4104-3320-6
    ISBN-10: 1-4104-3320-X
    1. Amish women—Ficton. 2. Amish—Fiction. 3. Lancaster
County (Pa.)—Fiction. 4. Large type books. I. Title.
PS3603.A4473T56 2011
813'.6—dc22   2010044218

Published in 2011 by arrangement with Abingdon Press.

Printed in the United States of America
1 2 3 4 5 6 7 15 14 13 12 11

*Dedicated to journalists who risk their
lives to pursue the
truth around the world.*

ACKNOWLEDGMENTS

This book — this series — would not be possible without Barbara Scott, an editor with vision who helped take the series to an even higher level than I'd envisioned. Barbara, you demonstrate your faith with such graciousness and inspire me as a writer and as a person with each contact we have. I feel blessed that we have been able to work together.

Laura Lisle also helped improve the manuscript with her editing suggestions.

Thanks to my agent, Mary Sue Seymour, for introducing my work to Barbara. You told me how much I would love working with her and you were so right!

Linda Byler, an Old Order Amish writer, was once again invaluable for her willingness to check the manuscript for accuracy. Linda, I am so grateful to you for your help. Good luck with your own writing endeavors!

Judy Rehm, friend and prayer partner, you

7

are always there with just the right Biblical quote and encouraging word when I need it. Thank you!

None of my Amish books would have been written if it hadn't been for Mary Cameron taking me to visit the Amish years ago when I visited her in Pennsylvania. Thank you so much, Mary.

A big thank you goes to my family for their love and support. You are first and foremost the heart of my world and I love you. No one knows better than you how bumpy and unpredictable the pursuit of a writing career can be. I thank you for always being there for me and encouraging me.

I am forever grateful to God for setting me down in a newspaper office when I was a teenager just out of high school. There I discovered how much I loved writing and learning about the world and its people. I am also grateful for His guidance to pursue inspirational fiction several years ago. I truly feel I am writing the stories I'm meant to write.

1

Jenny woke from a half-doze as the SUV slowed to approach a four-way stop.

"No!" she cried. "Don't stop!"

"I have to stop."

"No!" she yelled as she lunged to grab at the steering wheel.

David smacked her hands away with one hand and steered with the other. The vehicle swerved and horns blared as he fought to stop. "We're in the States!" he shouted. "Stop it!"

Jenny covered her head and waited for the explosion. When it didn't come, she cautiously brought her arms down to look over at David.

"We're in the U.S.," he repeated quietly. "Calm down. You're safe."

"I'm sorry, I'm so sorry," she whispered. Covering her face, she turned away from him and wished she could crawl into a hole somewhere and hide.

He touched her shoulder. "It's okay. I understand."

Before he could move the SUV forward, they heard a siren. The sound brought Jenny's head up, and she glanced back fearfully to see a police car.

"Pull over!" a voice commanded through the vehicle's loudspeaker.

Cursing beneath his breath, David guided the SUV to the side of the road. He reached for his wallet, pulling out his driver's license.

A police officer appeared at David's window and looked in. Jenny tried not to flinch as he looked at David, then her. "Driver's license and registration, please."

David handed them over. "Officer, I'd like to explain —"

"Stay in your vehicle. I'll be right back," he was told brusquely.

When the officer returned, he handed back the identification. "Okay, so you want to explain what that was all about — how you started to run the stop sign and nearly caused an accident?"

"It's my fault," Jenny spoke up.

"Jenny! I —"

"Let her talk."

"You can't stop at a four-way," she told him in a dull voice. "You could get killed." She drew a quilt more tightly around her shoulders.

"You look familiar," the officer said, studying her face for a long moment. "Now I got it. You're that TV reporter, the one who was reporting from overseas, in the war zone —" he stopped. "Oh."

He glanced at David. "And you're that network news anchor. What are you doing in these parts?"

"Taking her to recuperate at her family's house."

The officer glanced back at Jenny. "Didn't know you were Amish. Thought they didn't believe in television."

Jenny fingered the quilt. "It's my grandmother," she said, staring ahead. "She's the one who's Amish."

She met the officer's gaze. "Please don't give David a ticket. It was my fault. I freaked and grabbed the steering wheel. I didn't want him to stop. But it won't happen again."

The officer hesitated then nodded as he touched the brim of his hat. "I have friends who've been through the same thing. Be careful. You've been through enough without getting into a car accident."

She nodded. "Thank you."

After returning to his patrol car, the officer pulled out on the road and waved as he passed them.

Jenny looked at David. "I'm sorry. I just had a flashback as I woke up, I guess."

"It's okay," he told her patiently. "I understand."

She sighed and felt herself retreating into her cocoon.

He glanced in his rearview mirror and got back onto the road. They drove for a few minutes.

"Hungry yet?"

She shook her head and then winced at the pain. "No."

"You need to eat."

"Not hungry." Then she glanced at him. "I'm sorry. You must be."

He grinned. "Are you remembering that you used to tease me about being hungry all the time?"

"Not really," she said. "Lucky guess, since we've been on the road for hours."

He frowned but said nothing as he drove. A little while later, he pulled into a restaurant parking lot, shut off the engine, and undid his seat belt. "It'll be good to stretch my legs. C'mon, let's go in and get us a hot meal and some coffee."

"I don't —"

"Please?" he asked quietly.

"I look awful."

"You look fine." He put his hand on hers. "Really. Let's go in."

Pulling down the visor, she stared into the mirror, and her eyes immediately went to the long scar near her left ear. It still looked red and raw against her too-pale skin. The doctor had said it would fade with time until she'd barely notice it. Later she could wear extra-concealing makeup, but not now, he'd cautioned. The skin needed to heal without makeup being rubbed into it.

"Jenny?"

She looked at him, really looked at him. Though he was smiling at her, there were lines of strain around his mouth, worry in his eyes. He looked so tired, too.

"Okay." With a sigh, she loosened her hold on the quilt and rewrapped her muffler higher and tighter around her neck. Buttoning her coat, she drew her hat down and turned to reach for the door handle.

David was already there, offering Jenny her cane and a helping hand. When she tried to let go of his hand, he tightened his.

"The pavement's icy. Let me help," he said. "Remember, 'Pride goeth before a fall.'"

Her eyes widened with amusement as she grinned. "*You're* quoting Scripture? What is the world coming to?"

"Must be the environment," he said, glancing around. Then his gaze focused on her. "It's good to see you smile."

"I haven't had a lot to smile about lately."

His eyes were kind. "No. But you're here. And if I said thank God, you wouldn't make a smart remark, would you?"

She thought about waking up in the hospital wrapped in her grandmother's quilt and the long days of physical therapy since then. Leaning on the cane, her other hand in David's, she started walking slowly, and her hip screamed in pain with every step. Days like today she felt like she was a hundred instead of in her early thirties.

"No," she said, sighing again. "I think the days of smart remarks are over."

The diner was warm, and Jenny was grateful to see that there were few customers. A sign invited them to seat themselves, and she sank into the padded booth just far enough from the front door that the cold wind wouldn't blow on them.

"Coffee for you folks?" asked the waitress who appeared almost immediately with menus. She turned over their cups and filled them when they nodded. "Looks like we're gonna get some snow tonight."

"What are you going to have?" David asked.

14

Jenny lifted her coffee cup but her hand trembled, spilling hot coffee on it. Wincing, she set it down quickly and grabbed a napkin to wipe her hand dry.

David got up and returned with a glass of ice water. He dipped his napkin in it and wrapped the cold, wet cloth around her reddened hand. "Better?"

Near tears, she nodded.

"She filled it too full," he reassured her.

Reaching for an extra cup on the table, he poured half of her coffee into it. "Try it now."

Jenny didn't want the coffee now, but he was trying so hard to help, she felt ungrateful not to drink it.

"Better?"

She nodded, wincing again.

"Time for some more meds, don't you think?"

"The pain killers make me fuzzy. I don't like to take them."

"You still need them."

Sighing, she took out the bottle, shook out the dosage, and took the capsules with a sip of water.

"So, what would you like to eat?" asked the waitress.

Jenny looked at David.

"She'll have two eggs over easy, bacon,

waffles, and a large glass of orange juice," he said. "I'll have the three-egg omelet, country ham, hash browns, and biscuits. Oh, and don't forget the honey, honey."

The waitress grinned. Then she cocked her head to one side. "Say, you look like that guy on TV."

David just returned her grin. "Yeah, so I'm told. That and a dollar'll get me a cup of coffee."

She laughed and went to place their order.

Growing warm, Jenny shed her coat and the muffler. She sipped at the coffee and felt warmer. When the food came, she bent her head and said a silent prayer of thanks. Then she watched David begin shoveling in food as if he hadn't eaten in days, rather than hours.

She lifted her fork and tried to eat. "I like my eggs over easy?"

He frowned and stopped eating "Yeah. Do you want me to send them back, get them scrambled or something?"

"No. This is okay."

"How did you eat them at the hospital?"

She shrugged. "However they brought them."

Deciding she might have liked eggs over easy in the past but now they looked kind of disgusting, half raw and runny on the

16

plate, she looked at the waffle.

"I like waffles?"

"Love them."

Butter oozed over the top and the syrup was warm. She took a bite. It was heaven, crispy on the outside, warm and fluffy on the inside. The maple syrup was sweet and thick. Bliss. She ate the whole thing and a piece of bacon, too.

"Good girl," David said approvingly.

"Don't talk to me like I'm a kid," she told him, frowning. "Even if I feel like it."

He reached over and took her free hand. "I'm so proud of you. You've learned to walk again, talk again."

"I'm not all the way back yet," she said. "I still have memory holes and problems getting the right word out and headaches and double vision now and then. I have a long road ahead of me."

David looked out the window. "Speaking of roads . . . as much as I hate to say it, I guess we should get back on it as soon as we can."

Jenny turned to where David was looking and watched as an Amish horse-drawn carriage passed by slowly. The man who held the reins glanced over just then and their eyes met. Then he was looking ahead as a car passed in the other lane and the contact was broken.

He looks familiar, she thought . . . *so familiar.* She struggled to remember.

David turned and got the waitress's attention. As she handed him the check, she noticed Jenny, who immediately looked down at her hands in her lap.

"Why, you're that reporter, the one who —"

"Has to get going," David interjected. "She needs to get some rest."

"Oh, sure. Sorry."

She tore a sheet from her order pad and handed it to Jenny with a pen. "Could you give me an autograph while I go ring this up?"

She hurried off, sure that her request would be honored.

"Could you sign it for me?" Jenny asked David.

Nodding, he took the paper and quickly scrawled her signature, then added his in a bold flourish.

"Here you go, two for one," he told the waitress when she returned. He tucked a bill under his plate and got up to help Jenny with her coat.

The SUV seemed a million miles away, but she made it with his help. Once inside, she sank into the seat, pulled the quilt around her again, and fastened her seat belt.

"It'll take just a minute to get warm in here," David told her.

Jenny stroked her hand over the quilt. "I'm not cold. . . . I hate those pills," she muttered and felt her eyelids drooping. "Making me sleepy. The waffles . . . lots of carbons."

She opened her eyes when he chuckled. Blinking, she tried to think what could be so funny.

"Carbs," she corrected herself carefully after a moment, frustrated at the way the brain injury had affected her speech. "Lots of carbs. Don't think I used to eat lots of carbs."

"So take a nap," he told her. "You talk too much anyway." He grinned to prove he was teasing.

Smiling, she tried to think of a snappy comeback. They were always so easy for her, especially with David. But then she was falling into a dreamless sleep.

Sometime later, she woke when she felt the vehicle stop. "Are we there?"

"Stay here," she heard David say, then she heard his door open and felt the brief influx of cold air before it closed. She couldn't seem to wake up, as if her eyes were stuck shut. The door on her side opened, and she heard the click of her seat belt, felt arms lift her.

"I can walk," she muttered.

He said something she couldn't quite grasp, but his voice was warm and deep and so soothing that she relaxed and let him carry her. And then she was being laid on a soft bed, covers tucked around her.

Home, she thought, *I'm home.* She smiled and sank deeper in dreamless sleep.

Jenny woke to find herself in a bed, the quilt spread over her. Bright sunlight was pouring in through the window.

The walls of the room were whitewashed and plain. There were few furnishings: an ancient, well-polished chest of drawers was set against one wall, a wooden chair beside the bed. A bookcase held well-worn volumes and a Bible.

She sat up and saw someone had propped her cane on the wall near the bed. Grasping it, she walked carefully to the chest of drawers. When she caught a glimpse of herself in its small mirror, she grimaced. Reaching into her purse on top of the chest, she pulled out her hairbrush and drew it through her short, ash-blonde hair. Her face was too thin, the circles beneath her eyes so pronounced she felt she must look like a scarecrow. Even her eyes looked a faded gray.

Leaning heavily on her cane, huffing from exertion, she moved back to the bed and climbed into it. Pulling the quilt over her, she waited for her breathing to level.

It was so quiet here, so different from her apartment in New York City, which over-looked a busy street.

There was a knock on the door. "Come in," she called.

The door opened and her grandmother peeked around it. "I heard you moving about."

She smiled. "Yes. *Guder mariye, Grossmudder.*"

Phoebe's austere face brightened. "You remember some of the language?"

"Some."

Jenny found it interesting she could remember even though she struggled to find the right word in English right now. She held out her arms and her grandmother rushed to embrace her. They sat on the bed, wiping away tears.

"You got it," Phoebe said, looking at the quilt that covered Jenny.

Jenny's fingers stroked it. "I woke up in the hospital and it was tucked around me," she said quietly. "I said your name before I could say mine."

Phoebe's lined face crumpled, and she bent her head, searching in the pocket of her dark dress for a handkerchief.

"God brought you through it." She wiped at her tears and straightened her shoulders. "There is no place He is not."

I'd been in the valley of death, thought Jenny. She knew how close she had come. Maybe one day she could tell her grandmother how she had seen her grandfather and her parents shortly after she'd been injured. Jenny hadn't been particularly religious before, but she had to admit that her near-death experience had made her look at her life — what was left of what had been her life — in a new way.

A note had arrived with the quilt, a nurse had told her. She gave it to Jenny and then had had to read it because the head injury had left a lingering problem with double vision.

The words inside had been simple and direct: "Come. Heal." It had been signed "Your *grossmudder,* Phoebe."

Jenny studied her now. Phoebe's face was more lined and the strands of hair that escaped her *kapp* had more silver. But somehow she didn't seem any older than the last time Jenny had visited.

"You didn't come for so long after I wrote that I didn't think you would."

"I was doing physical therapy."

"David told me. He's a good man."

Jenny smiled briefly and then looked at the window. It was starting to snow. "I should get up and say good-bye so he can get on the road. I don't want him to get caught in a snowstorm."

"It's time to get up," Phoebe agreed, standing and lifting the quilt away from Jenny. "But he left last night."

"Left? Without saying goodbye?"

"There's a note for you. He spoke of something called 'e-mail' that's in a computer?"

Her lined face lit briefly with a smile. "I asked him if the machine he brought with your things ran on sunlight. He'd forgotten we have no electricity."

Jenny's lips curved. "A solar battery, hmm? Good idea but mine doesn't have one. And that would still leave the problem of how to access the Internet."

"Internet?"

"Don't ask me to explain how it works," Jenny told her, sitting on the side of the bed. "I interviewed someone about it once, but it's still a mystery to me."

She sighed. "I haven't had time to get a

new phone. Maybe that should be first on my to-do list."

Phoebe handed her the cane. "First let's get you up and ready for this day we were given."

A sharp pain shot through Jenny's hip as she got to her feet, and she had to bite her lip to keep from moaning. She stood still for a moment to gear up for her next move. Phoebe held out her hand, work-worn, dry, and warm.

Jenny shook her head. "I don't want to hurt you."

"I'm stronger than I look. I lead a simple life, but I work hard. You remember from the two summers you came to visit."

Jenny nodded. It had been one reason she had told her father she didn't want to go back. She wanted to stay home, be with her friends and have fun, not work so hard harvesting summer crops and baking bread and scrubbing the kitchen.

And laundry. It was bad enough to have to scoop dirty clothes up and throw them into the washer and dryer back home. At her grandmother's house, laundry was a daylong chore. Who wanted that?

Instead of television there had been singing, and the songs weren't the latest pop hits — no, these were church hymns! It was such a drag, too, to hitch up a buggy instead of jumping into the car and having Dad drive her someplace.

Later, as she'd grown older, she'd regretted her youthful laziness, but it was too late then to visit. She was immersed in college, an internship at a TV station, and then her demanding job that took her everywhere but Lancaster County, Pennsylvania.

Her grandmother was older, a little more bent, but the bright light in her eyes was still there, reminding Jenny of the bird she was named after. And her spare frame looked strong beneath the simple dress and sparkling white apron she wore.

The medication had worn off long ago. Jenny wanted to just sink back into bed, but she couldn't. She needed to get moving. She saw Phoebe glance down and a quiet gasp escaped from her lips.

The pant leg of her sweats had ridden up as she moved to the edge of the bed and stood. The light faded from Phoebe's eyes as she glimpsed the scars that ran down the length of one.

Bending, Jenny pulled the leg of her sweats down to cover them.

"I didn't want to move you too much when we put you to bed," she told Jenny. "So I left your clothes on you." She cocked her head to one side. "Is that what the *En-glisch* are wearing these days?"

"When they want something comfortable to relax in," Jenny told her with a grin.

With one hand, she pulled the tunic down over her hips and smoothed its wrinkles.

"Let's get you some breakfast and then you can take a bath and get fresh clothes on."

"Sounds wonderful."

Walking to the kitchen was a major obstacle. Jenny insisted that she needed to walk without her grandmother's help and took the short journey slowly.

"I can't believe David carried me into the house."

"He didn't," said Phoebe, following a step behind.

Jenny stopped and turned to look at Phoebe. "You didn't."

Again there was a ghost of a smile on Phoebe's face. "*Nee.* It was Matthew."

Images flitted through Jenny's mind as she started to navigate the way again. She remembered strong male arms, a deep voice that had sounded comforting when she'd sleepily insisted she could walk.

"Matthew?" she repeated. There was something about that name, but she couldn't quite remember . . . one of the

26

lingering effects of the head injury.

"He lives on the farm next to mine. He came to see if I needed any help."

"And I'm sure David was grateful for his help." She laughed. "David is a nice man, but he doesn't lift anything heavier than his wallet."

Wallet. Jenny frowned as she thought about what was going to happen to hers. The network was covering her salary, but how long would it do that? Disability payments would be less whenever they started. She didn't want to dip into her savings, but she knew it might be months before she could go back to work.

And who knew if she'd ever be able to do the overseas reporting she'd become known for?

Her grandmother's kitchen hadn't changed. There were simple counters and wooden cupboards, practical pottery bowls set on a shelf. A propane stove filled the room with warmth, and the scent coming from its oven promised something delicious would emerge soon. A hand-carved wooden table was big enough to seat an army. Jenny sank into one of its wooden chairs.

Jenny hadn't had much appetite for a long time, but her mouth watered when she smelled the bread baking and the coffee. Oh, the scent of the coffee!

Her grandmother sliced a loaf that had just been pulled from the oven a few minutes before. She placed it on a plate, setting out a bowl of churned butter, wild blueberry preserves, and a dish of hard-boiled eggs.

Jenny bent her head and gave thanks for the meal. When she looked up, Phoebe was smiling.

"I'm glad that you still say your prayers."

"Dad left the Amish, but he didn't forget God," Jenny told her. "We visited a lot of churches until he found the one he liked, but having a spiritual relationship with God was always important in our home."

Phoebe patted her hand. "I know. He wrote me once that he did a year of missionary work in Haiti while you were in college. I just wasn't sure if you remembered God after you left home."

"Oh, I surely did."

As her grandmother turned to stir the soup pot already simmering on the stove, Jenny felt a pang of guilt, remembering how often lately she'd questioned God about what had happened to her — questioned Him about how He could let innocent children suffer as she'd witnessed so often in her work.

There was a knock at the door. Phoebe crossed the room to answer it and greeted a tall man who looked about Jenny's age. The morning light coming in the kitchen window caught at his blond hair when he took off his wide-brimmed black hat and hung it on a wooden peg.

When he removed his winter coat Jenny saw his plain shirt and pants that showed off his muscular physique. His blue eyes sparkled as he greeted her grandmother and then he glanced over at Jenny.

She stared at him, searching her mind for his name when he continued to stare hard at her. He knew her. She could tell it from the way his expression looked hopeful, then disconcerted when she didn't immediately respond. *Why can't I remember his name?*

"Jenny, this is Matthew," said Phoebe as she poured his coffee.

She felt so awkward sitting there, painfully aware of the scar on her cheek, of her rumpled sweats.

He pulled out a chair and sat at the table with the air of a guest who was frequent and welcome. His eyes were filled with a quiet, thoughtful intensity. "I thought you might need help this morning," he told Jenny.

"My grandmother said you carried me

inside last night. Thank you. But I could have walked."

He smiled. "Perhaps. But you were sleeping so soundly."

Jenny found herself staring at his large, strong hands as he cupped his mug and drank the coffee her grandmother had poured. When Phoebe pushed the plate of bread and preserves toward him, he grinned and took a slice, spreading it thickly with preserves. He bit into the bread with relish.

"Nothing like your bread," he told her.

"I have a loaf in the oven for you," she said.

"*Wunderbar.* I'm going into town. Annie has her appointment. Do you need anything?"

When she shook her head, Matthew turned to Jenny. "You?"

"A new back and hip," she wanted to say. But she didn't want to call attention to herself, didn't want to make her grandmother worry. She shifted in her chair, wishing she'd taken her detested pain pills to the kitchen with her. So she shook her head and thanked him again.

"Ah, Matthew, I've thought of something," Phoebe said suddenly. "I'll get the money."

"No need to give me money —"

But with her usual spryness, she'd already

hurried upstairs for it.

Jenny liked the sound of Matthew's voice. She watched as he took another slice of bread and spread it with more preserves.

"You should try some," he said, pushing the jar toward her.

There was something on the edge of her consciousness, something that tugged and tugged at her memory. The preserves . . . what was it about them that made her think there was a link between the man and her?

She looked up and found him watching her with unusual intensity. It was almost as if he were trying to use telepathy to make her search her memory.

But for what? she asked herself. *For what?*

2

"Raspberries," said Jenny, then she stopped, shaking her head. "No, strawberries." Frustrated, she rubbed her temples. "No, that's not the word."

Tears sprang to her eyes, and her lips trembled. Unable to look at him, she stared at her plate, feeling humiliated. Days like this, she wondered if she would ever get better.

"It'll come," he said quietly. "Don't force it. Give yourself time to heal."

She looked up at him, saw the kindness in his eyes, then looked away. "It's like wires get crossed in my brain and I can't get the right word out."

"Give yourself time to heal," he repeated.

"Easy for you to say," she muttered.

He smiled. "Did you know what my Annie calls them? *Boo* berries."

"Annie?"

"My youngest. She's had some trouble

talking."

"It's taking forever." Frustration warred with despair. "I can't go on camera looking like this, talking like this. Having trouble with my memory."

Matthew got up to get more coffee for them. She caught the scent of hay, of horses, of the outdoors. It was a pleasant, familiar smell of man and work.

"You look fine to me," he told her.

Her hand went to her cheek before she could stop herself. She shook her head. "You're just being nice."

"Eat," he said. "You're as tiny as a sparrow. Frail, too."

I've never been described that way, she thought, stirring her tea. A memory came to her, a cloudy one, of being carried through the cold and dark night. There had been movement and a voice she couldn't quite place and yet she had felt safe.

Looking up, she found he was watching her. "I'm sure I was heavier than a little bird when you carried me in."

He shook his head. "You don't weigh much more than my older daughter Mary."

"David could have helped me."

"The *Englischer* wanted to, but he had on city shoes. The walkway was slippery. I feared he'd take a fall and hurt you both."

"You should have woken me. I could have walked," she repeated. Then she bit her lip. "I'm sorry. I must sound ungrateful. Thank you for helping last night."

Matthew nodded. "Sometimes we need to let someone care for us."

He glanced in the direction of her grandmother's bedroom, hesitated, then looked at Jenny. "Phoebe has faith that God is watching over you, but it's good that you came. I think she needs to take care of you."

Her grandmother hurried back then and gave Matthew a list and some money. She insisted on filling a metal thermos with hot chocolate for him and Annie, saying it was a cold morning and they might want a hot drink.

He got to his feet and put on his outdoor things. As he opened the door to leave, he glanced back at Jenny. And then he was gone.

"You haven't eaten much," Phoebe said when she came to sit at the table again.

"Oh, it's not your cooking," Jenny said quickly. "I just haven't had much of an appetite."

Making an effort, Jenny spooned some of the preserves on her bread and bit in. The sweet taste of blueberries flooded her mouth, flooded her memory.

A hot summer day. Her fingers stained blue and dripping juice from picking the bucket of berries in her hand. A young blond man, his eyes as blue as the berries, standing there looking at her and laughing.

Matthew.

And her first kiss, so innocent and so sweet.

No wonder he had looked at her the way he had, as if he wanted her to remember something. She hoped she hadn't hurt his feelings.

Her grandmother was speaking. Jenny pulled herself back from the memories that once started, wouldn't stop. "I'm sorry. What did you say?"

"You're looking pale. Maybe after breakfast you should lie down on the sofa before the fire."

Her back was aching, and the headache was beginning to be one she couldn't ignore. "I just hate being like this. I want to get back to normal."

"Patience, Jenny. This will take time."

"I wish I had your faith that everything is going to be all right," Jenny said as she walked slowly toward the sofa in the living room.

With a grateful sigh she sank down onto it and smiled as Phoebe pulled a new quilt over her.

"Warm enough?"

Jenny covered her yawn and nodded drowsily. "Wonderful. Thank you. For — for anything." She opened her eyes. "Everything."

Phoebe's smile was grave. "I knew what you meant. Rest, *Grossdochder.* Rest, dear one."

Exhaustion weighed down on Jenny like a soft, warm quilt. She slept.

Their eyes.

This was the first thing Jenny noticed on her first visit to the war-torn country. The children were so thin, so listless, their eyes vacant and staring. Mothers held them, their eyes desperate. No words were needed to communicate their fear they'd lose their children before they got them food.

She could barely keep the tears from her voice as she spoke on camera of the plight of the children, the innocent victims of warfare.

Then there was a movement, the cameraman catching her eye as he looked past her, over her shoulder. As the camera moved she glanced in the direction he looked and saw the car hurtling toward them.

Turning back, she screamed a warning

and the mothers and children scattered. Then, miraculously, the car stopped just feet from her. A man burst from it and ran.

Instinct made Jenny spin on her heel and run, but she wasn't fast enough. There was a deafening explosion and she felt herself lifted, thrown, and slammed into the ground.

Jenny screamed and woke. Terrified, her heart pounding, she sat up and stared around her.

A man rushed into the room, and she nearly screamed again before she realized it was Matthew.

"Jenny?"

Tears rushed out of her eyes as her fingers clutched at the quilt. She was shaking, shaking so hard she felt she'd fall apart at any moment.

"Bomb!" she whispered.

Matthew knelt beside the sofa and took her hands in his. "Jenny, you're safe. Look at me, Jenny. You are safe. I promise."

Her breath hitching on a sob, she stared at him, her eyes wide with fear.

Her grandmother appeared in the doorway. "Jenny?"

"She's all right," Matthew told her, not taking his eyes from Jenny. "She must have had a bad dream." He pulled the quilt up around her shoulders. "You're here, at your *grossmudder's.* You're safe."

"Daedi? Is the lady *allrecht?*"

Jenny turned her head at the sound of the childish voice. Phoebe held the hand of a little girl of about four who wore a simple, long navy dress. Her eyes were the same blue as her father's, full of concern like his. Her pink cheeks were rounded, the picture of health and well-being, her blonde hair carefully brushed and drawn into two pigtails. She looked nothing like the children in Jenny's dream.

Gradually, Jenny's racing heart settled down and her breathing evened. "Bad — bad dream."

Her doctors called it post-traumatic stress syndrome. But Jenny doubted either Matthew or Phoebe knew the term or what it meant.

The child watching her with big eyes didn't look like she even knew what a bad dream was. She put her hands on Jenny's cheeks and frowned. *"Fiewer.* Lady has a *fiewer."*

Phoebe stepped forward and placed the back of her hand on Jenny's forehead. She frowned. "Jenny, you're awfully warm. Maybe I should get the thermometer."

"I'm just warm from the fire," Jenny said,

38

but she knew it wasn't true. She'd experienced fevers several times since she'd been injured, but they always went away.

Phoebe looked doubtful, but she didn't insist. She turned to Matthew's little girl and took her hand. "Annie, come with me. I baked cookies today."

"I hope I didn't scare her," Jenny said as Phoebe left the room with Annie.

He shook his head and stared at her, his expression sober. "Do they come often, these bad dreams?"

She shrugged. "Less often these days. It must have been because I was so tired from traveling."

Annie came back into the room, carefully holding a glass of water. She held it out to Jenny. "Wasser."

Jenny searched for how to say thank you. *"Danki,"* she pronounced carefully and the little girl smiled.

"Annie? Will you come help me put some cookies in a bag for your brother and sister?" Phoebe called from the kitchen.

The child looked at Matthew, and when he nodded, she ran from the room.

"You'll be all right now?" he asked her.

She nodded, avoiding his gaze, and drank some water.

"Jenny? There is no need to be embarrassed."

Lifting her eyes to his, she looked for pity and found none.

"From what your friend said, you have been through a lot."

"David talks too much."

Matthew grinned. "He's a good friend. When you were hurt, he came all the way here to tell Phoebe what had happened."

Wrapped, cocoon-like, in the quilt, Jenny stared at him. "He never told me that."

She'd wondered how he'd seemed to know how to get to her grandmother's last night with nothing more than the address. He hadn't used the GPS in the SUV. But David was a terrific investigative reporter. She'd assumed he'd looked it up somehow.

"We'll be going then," Matthew said.

She nodded. "Thank you."

"Du bischt willkumm."

Getting stiffly to her feet, she walked into the kitchen behind him. He carried his little girl out to the buggy, set her on a seat, then climbed inside. *The Amish love children, and Matthew obviously adores his little girl,* thought Jenny. She smiled as he kissed Annie on the forehead before he tucked a blanket around her.

Jenny stood at the window, watching the

40

buggy roll down the road until she couldn't see it anymore.

When she turned, she saw that her grandmother was watching her.

"What is troubling you, Jenny?"

"I was remembering the last time I saw Matthew. I had a crush on him."

Jenny gazed at the winter-bare landscape, the trees void of leaves, their branches black against the gray sky. *Barren,* she thought, *like me.* She wrapped her arms around her waist, suddenly cold.

Her grandmother touched her shoulder. "Why are you so sad?"

"His little girl is so beautiful."

Phoebe pulled a clean handkerchief from her pocket and gave it to Jenny. She stared at the snowy square, not sure when she'd last seen such a thing. For a moment she didn't know why her grandmother handed it to her, then realized that she had tears on her cheeks.

"Talk to me, tell me what's wrong, *liebschen.*"

"I don't want to burden you."

"Why should talking burden me?"

Her legs were shaking from standing so long. Jenny walked slowly to a kitchen chair and sat. "You've been so kind to have me stay —"

"I haven't been kind, Jenny. You are my *grossdochder*."

"One who hasn't been the best at keeping in touch."

Phoebe's eyes were kind as she spoke. "Sometimes there is distance in families."

Jenny knew she meant more than the physical miles. Once her father had decided not to be baptized when he turned sixteen, he'd left the Amish community and never looked back. He'd only visited after his father died, and then he let Jenny come during those two summers years ago.

"I loved your letters, especially the ones from overseas. You described everything so that I could see it."

Not everything, thought Jenny. There had been a desire to protect this woman who lived the Plain life, as the Amish called it, from the terrible things she saw over there.

And yet, from the brief time she had visited here, she knew that life in an Amish community wasn't idyllic. Life was still life. Bad things happened, like when a farmer's tractor overturned and crushed him or a hit-and-run driver had killed a little boy walking a country road to school. Matthew's wife had died young; she remembered that Phoebe had written to her that the woman had been a victim of cancer. Not even the best treatment from the local Englisch hospital had been able to save her.

Life was life, after all, wherever it was lived.

"Jenny?" Her grandmother's voice was gentle but determined.

"The doctors say I might not have children. I had infernal —" she stopped, searching for the right word — "internal injuries."

Actually, she thought bitterly, *I might have gotten the word right the first time.*

Phoebe took her hand. "If it's God's will, you'll have them," she said simply.

"You say that a lot." Jenny wiped her eyes. "God's will."

Phoebe squeezed the hand she held. "It's simple but true. Now, eating something warm on this cold day will make you feel better."

"It's lunch already?" Glancing at her watch, Jenny saw that she'd slept nearly four hours.

"*Ya.* Hungry?"

"Not really."

She hadn't thought she was, but when Phoebe lifted the lid of the pot simmering on the stove, she discovered the smell of the vegetable soup was enticing.

"Well, maybe a little."

"A good bowl of hot soup on a cold day,"

her grandmother said, serving it up with slices of bread.

Comfort food, thought Jenny. She needed it.

Matthew walked into his house, letting in a blast of cold air. He stamped his feet on the doormat and pulled off his gloves, tucking them into his coat pockets. Shrugging off the coat, he hung it and his hat on the pegs on the wall by the door. He rubbed his hands together. "Cold out there."

His sister Hannah hurried over to take Annie's hat and coat off. She picked her up and gave her a big kiss on her cheek. "Your cheeks are cold, Annie. Go wash your hands, and we'll eat."

Obediently, Annie ran from the room. Hannah turned to Matthew. "How did her session go?"

"The therapist feels her speech is coming along fine," Matthew told her, washing his hands at the kitchen sink.

As he dried his hands, he watched her move about the kitchen, stirring the pot of hearty split-pea soup with chunks of ham, then getting out soup bowls and setting the table. She'd been sixteen when his wife had died three years ago and had moved in to help him take care of his *kinner.* The two of them were separated by twelve years, but they agreed on most things as a rule, so the arrangement had worked out well.

"You took longer than usual."

"I stopped by Phoebe's with some things she needed from town."

"Ah, I see."

Matthew settled into a seat at the kitchen table and Hannah put a bowl of soup before him. "You see what?"

"I heard that Phoebe's *grossdochder* is visiting."

Matthew nodded. He smiled when Annie ran back into the room and held out her hands for his approval. Smiling, he patted the seat of the chair beside him. "Your *Aenti* Hannah has prepared some nice warm soup for us."

Hannah set a bowl of soup at her own place, then a smaller one at Annie's. "That should warm you right up. Then it's time for a nap before Joshua and Mary come home from school."

The three of them bent their heads to ask a blessing for the meal before they began eating. Hannah buttered a piece of bread for Annie, took one for herself, and passed the plate to Matthew.

"The lady had a bad dream," Annie said suddenly.

"Lady?" Hannah looked curiously at Matthew.

"Jenny, Phoebe's *grossdochder*."

Hannah waited but Matthew didn't say more. *Men!* she thought. Well, there was more than one way to get information. She smiled at Annie. "What happened?"

"She was taking a nap, and she had a bad dream." Annie stirred her soup. "And *Daedi* held her hand."

Her eyes wide, Hannah turned to her brother. He looked a little embarrassed but said nothing as he reached for a slice of bread and buttered it with unusual care.

"He told her she was safe," Annie told Hannah.

"Annie, eat your soup."

"*Ya, Daedi.*" She put a spoonful into her mouth, then swallowed. "She says some words funny, like me."

"Matthew?"

He looked up from his soup.

"Do I have to pull it out of you?" she asked, exasperated.

"The Amish grapevine isn't working well enough to get information about Jenny?"

She frowned. "It's not wrong to be curious."

"If you say so."

"I remember how you felt about —" she

46

stopped as she caught Matthew's warning look.

Glancing over, he saw Annie drooping over her empty bowl. "Time for a nap, Annie. Sweet dreams."

Annie slid down from the chair and stood by her father. She stared up at him with big blue eyes. "*Daedi,* you should have told the lady to have sweet dreams."

He nodded solemnly. "You're right. Next time I will."

When she held out her arms, he reached down and hugged her.

Hannah smiled as she got a hug, too. "She is such a loving child." Getting up, she poured her brother a cup of coffee and set it before him. "Pie?"

"Of course."

She cut him a piece and smiled as he forked up a bite and sighed as he chewed it. He loved her baking. "It's time you thought about getting married again."

Matthew choked on the pie and took a gulp of coffee. "Where did that come from?"

"It's been three years. You need a wife. Your children need a mother." She sat again at the table. "Amelia would want you to be happy, for the children to have a mother. You know that."

Leaning back in his chair, Matthew regarded his sister thoughtfully. "You've been a wonderful sister, coming here to help —"

She waved away his words. "Family helps family."

"But you've put aside your own life. It's time you did what you wanted. Time you got married."

Standing, she gathered the bowls to wash them. "I have been doing what I wanted. And you're trying to change the subject."

He hid his grin by taking another sip of coffee. She knew him well. "How is Jacob?"

"I'm sure he's fine," Hannah told him. "But he's not the right one for me." She sat again. "I remember how you felt about Jenny."

"That was years ago."

"And now she's back."

"She's back to heal, Hannah, not to look in my direction again."

"But it could happen."

Taking a last sip of coffee, Matthew stood. "I have work to do."

She swatted at him as he passed her to reach for his coat. "Think about it," she told him.

"Did you forget she's *Englisch?*" he asked her gravely, settling his hat on his head. "She's not part of our world."

"No? Then why did she return?" Hannah

wanted to know.

Matthew stared at her for a long moment. "Because Phoebe is her family. Jenny needs to recover, to have someone watch out for her. That is the only reason."

Hannah tilted her head as she watched him pull on his gloves. "Maybe. Maybe not. All I'm saying is you should think about it."

"I have work," he repeated. "And so do you. No more romantic daydreaming, Hannah. Idle hands, remember?"

Exasperated, she threw a kitchen towel at him, but she missed, and he walked out the door, laughing. Another blast of cold air, then he shut the door.

Matthew thought about what Hannah had said as he moved about doing his chores. She'd shocked him when she'd said it was time for him to get married again. He hadn't thought about such a thing since Amelia died.

And he hadn't thought enough about what her living at his house, caring for it and his kinner, had done to her own life. He'd been selfish.

It was true that he'd been in shock from the day his Amelia had died after six months of desperate attempts to save her. He'd walked and talked and taken care of his children and his farm, but he'd been lost in his grief.

Then one day he woke up and realized that for two years he'd just existed.

Now he realized his children were his responsibility and it was time to see that Hannah found a life beyond his home. Time she found the happiness she deserved so much.

As he forked up hay for his horses, he thought about Jenny, too. If Hannah had seen Jenny as he had today, she'd have known that Jenny hadn't returned hoping to rekindle their relationship. She'd come at her grandmother's invitation to heal here.

Jenny. She was so fragile, reminding him of a bird with a broken wing, a broken voice. Her eyes had looked so lifeless. The long blonde hair he remembered had obviously been shorn for her surgery. And the scar on her face. . . .

His hand tightened on the bucket of feed for his horses. How his heart ached at the way she'd been so self-conscious about it. She was still beautiful, but it was obvious that she didn't feel that way. She was so different from the bright, happy, carefree teenage girl he remembered and not just because she was older and she was struggling to talk and to move. No, it was obvious that Jenny was experiencing so much inner pain. He'd been getting a box from his buggy when he'd heard her scream as if monsters were chasing her. She'd been shaking so hard her teeth chattered when he reached her.

He hadn't told Hannah that Jenny didn't remember him. Shame came over him again now as he thought of how his pride had been hurt. Then he'd realized how badly Jenny was injured and he knew it would be very small of him to tell her about his hurt feelings.

Their worlds were so different and so much time had stretched between them, so many experiences. Once, they'd been friends. Once, they'd almost been more.

Then Matthew and her father had talked. The older man had shown up several weeks before the time Jenny was due to leave. He found Matthew out in the field and insisted they had to talk. Somehow the man had found out that his daughter was seeing Matthew. He said the relationship was over, that he'd left the Amish community behind, and he wouldn't allow her to be married to someone from it. He insisted she deserved a chance to go to college. He'd wanted her to have more than she'd have in the Amish community.

And that was that. Matthew was forced to

agree there was no future for him with Jenny. It was all he could do. He had to respect her father. Respect for the head of the household came first in the community.

He never got a chance to talk to Jenny again before her father took her away later that day. He never knew if her father told her they'd talked. But she never answered the two notes he sent to her — even sent them back unopened.

Matthew tried to force away the painful memories. God hadn't meant for them to marry, he told himself, and he'd worked hard to forget her and married another.

He'd be a friend to Jenny now if she wanted one. He'd help her in any way that he could, for he'd discovered that he still cared so much for her.

And he'd pray that God would keep His gentle hand on this child of His and help her to heal.

3

Dreams were funny things.

Even before she opened her eyes Jenny knew she'd been dreaming. She'd been running barefoot through the grass on the farm, laughing, feeling free and joyful. The sky had been so blue, the sun so warm.

She wanted to stay here forever.

The pain was the first clue it had been a dream. She came awake feeling it in so many places that it became one big ache. The awkwardness of movement was next — her limbs moving like they were filled with molasses when she tried to roll over.

Still, she said her morning prayer of thanks for the day, just as she'd done every day for so many years. She was grateful for a day to be alive, no matter how pain-filled, no matter how disappointing.

And it was one day closer to getting better. Even if she often complained that it was taking too long. *God's time definitely isn't the same as mine,* she thought with a sigh.

Lying here thinking about it wasn't getting her anywhere. A glance at the clock on the bedside table showed her that it was 8 a.m. Her grandmother would have been up for hours.

Jenny winced as her body registered aches and pains that seemed to have grown worse through the night. She supposed she should have set the alarm to take her pain medication during the night, but she was trying so hard to wean herself from it. Too often she'd heard of surgery patients having problems with addiction after being on painkillers.

Kicking back the covers, she began the exercises the physical therapist instructed her to do each morning. Determined, she forced her body to work harder, pushing herself to add a few more to each prescribed set.

Panting, exhausted, and sweating, she finished and lay back, trying to catch her breath.

A warm bath helped to soak away more of the aches and pains. As usual, as she soaped and scrubbed, she avoided looking at the scars, the visual reminder of why her body hurt.

Her grandmother looked up from the kitchen table as Jenny limped into the room.

"You look like you're moving more easily," she remarked after they said their good mornings.

"If you say so," Jenny told her. "My body doesn't say so."

She poured a cup of coffee and moved carefully toward the table. Setting her cane beside it, she lowered herself into the chair. "Mmm, something smells good. Cinnamon rolls?"

Phoebe raised a brow as she served her scrambled eggs. "Cinnamon rolls?" She sniffed the air. "I don't smell cinnamon rolls."

Jenny grinned. "Yeah, right. What are you baking?"

She glanced toward the oven, watching as her grandmother pulled out a pan of warm cinnamon rolls and set it on the table before her. They looked perfect, but then her grandmother was spooning out vanilla-scented frosting that melted and oozed all over them.

"My favorite. I'm going to be so fat," Jenny complained.

But she had to try one. She bit into it, not caring that it was still a little too hot, and it melted on the tongue, all rich dough and cinnamony, sugary goodness. Licking the frosting from her fingers, she pulled the pinwheel roll apart and popped it bite by bite into her mouth.

"I bet I've gained five pounds in two weeks."

"And could stand to gain a lot more," Phoebe told her. "You're still skin and bones."

"Not for long," Jenny mumbled around a full mouth. Her appetite was coming back. She finished the roll and eggs, then found herself looking longingly at a second roll. Sighing, she took it. She could never resist her grandmother's cinnamon rolls.

After she helped with cleanup, Jenny stood to look out a kitchen window.

"Feeling restless?"

Jenny glanced over her shoulder and nodded.

"Join us this afternoon. Even if you don't like quilting, I think you'd enjoy meeting the women, especially the ones your age."

Her hand went to her cheek. "I'm not ready to see anyone yet."

Phoebe regarded her with steady eyes. "Jenny, can you show yourself to others only if you think you look perfect?"

Jenny laughed ruefully. "No, I never thought I looked perfect before. But — this!" She gestured at her face and shook her head. "I'm just not ready yet."

"Jenny, there is something we must speak of."

"That sounds serious."

"It is." Phoebe squeezed her hand. "Sometimes a parent — a grandparent — must push the baby bird from the nest so she can fly."

"Oh, I'm sorry. Have I overstayed my welcome?"

"No," Phoebe rushed to say. "But you have been hiding here and I have let you. And it's not the best thing for you."

Jenny sighed. "I know."

"The physical therapist left a phone message. I was going to talk to you about it later but perhaps now is the time."

"Called?" Jenny looked around for a phone, wondering why she hadn't heard it ring, and then realized it was in the shanty outside. "I wonder how she got my number here?"

"Your therapist at the hospital called her to do a follow-up." Phoebe stared at Jenny, her forehead creased in a frown.

"I do the exercises she gave me." Jenny heard the defensiveness in her voice and fidgeted as her grandmother continued to stare at her.

"I'm not going to say you're not. You're an honest young woman. But maybe they're

57

not enough."

Sighing, Jenny nodded. "Okay, I'll call her right away. Therapy isn't the most pleasant thing, but it helps."

In fact, it had helped enough that the doctors had decided to take a wait-and-see attitude about whether Jenny would need more surgery on her hip.

As Jenny reached for her coat, Phoebe did the same. "You don't need to come with me," she said hurriedly.

"I'm not coming to check up on you," Phoebe told her. "I want to help you on the steps so you don't slip."

"I'll be fine. And I don't want to worry about *you* slipping and breaking a hip."

Phoebe made a harrumphing sound. "Are you saying I'm old?"

Jenny made a face. "I didn't know I could get my foot all the way up into my mouth."

"I know how to be careful."

Putting her hand on her hip, Jenny just stared at her. "And I don't?"

Tucking her hand in Jenny's arm, Phoebe started walking toward the door so Jenny had to follow. "We'll be careful together."

Her tone brooked no protest.

"I'd like to take you for the appointment," her grandmother said as they stepped outside into the cold, crisp air.

"I don't want to put you to any trouble," Jenny said. "I can call a taxi or something."

"It's no trouble."

Jenny hesitated and then she nodded. "That would be nice. *Danki.*"

Phoebe smiled. *"Gem gschehne."*

"I was afraid of this."

Tears ran down Jenny's cheeks. "Me, too. It *hurts!*"

"You should have made an appointment as soon as you got here," Sue, the physical therapist, told her.

"But I've done my exercises."

"You need more for a while. I know they explained this to you." She looked at Jenny. "Right?"

Jenny had never been able to tell the smallest untruth. "Right." She wiped away the tears with the heels of her hands.

The therapist, a woman not much older than she was, patted her arm. "So take a deep breath, and let's do some more work. Okay?"

Nodding, Jenny took the deep breath and began again. *As soon as I get back home, I'm taking a warm bath,* she thought. *Climbing into bed. Doing nothing for the rest of the day. Maybe not even climbing out of bed to eat.* Then she remembered how her grandmother had put a pot roast with winter vegetables in the oven before they'd left.

Well, maybe she could make it to the kitchen table. It wouldn't be right to let it go to waste, especially since her grandmother had worked so hard to cook it! And she was right — Jenny knew she was too thin.

"Let's set up a schedule of appointments," the therapist said at last.

She helped Jenny to sit up, then stand, and handed her patient her cane. They walked to an office where Jenny sank down gratefully into a chair. The therapist took a seat at a computer and worked out a several-times-weekly schedule of appointments, then printed it out and handed it to Jenny.

"I've seen you on television," the therapist said, leaning back in her chair. "I watched you go to all those countries where war is making the lives of children so horrible."

Jenny nodded. The woman spoke of it in past tense. And it was, after all.

"Sometimes I wondered how you could stand what you were witnessing, what you were making sure we saw was happening," the woman said quietly. "But it was so clear how much you cared about the children."

"Thank you." Jenny looked away, uncomfortable with the praise. "But anyone would

60

have done it."

"That's not true," the other woman said. "No one's rushed in since you were hurt to take your place. I'd like to help you get back in shape to return if that's what you want."

"I —" Jenny didn't know what to say. "Thank you."

Nodding, Sue stood. "See you Friday."

"How was it?" her grandmother asked when she joined her in the waiting room.

"Okay." She kept her head down so her grandmother wouldn't see that she'd been crying.

They walked outside and got in the buggy. "Would you like to have something to eat while we're in town?" Phoebe asked her.

"Would you mind if we didn't today?"

Her grandmother patted her hand. "Of course not. I wondered if you'd be tired afterward."

Tired wasn't the word. She felt like her limbs were filled with lead. Depression threatened to overwhelm her, but she smiled when her grandmother glanced her way.

The ride home in the buggy seemed longer than the ride to therapy. By the time she climbed the steps to the house, Jenny was miserable. She offered to help put the horse and buggy in the barn but was secretly grateful when her grandmother refused her help. Somehow she'd make it up to her later.

"Well, if you don't mind, then, I think I'll take a warm bath and soak for a while."

"Let's eat first."

Jenny shook her head. "I'm not hungry. You go ahead and eat."

Phoebe frowned. "If you're in pain, perhaps you should take one of your pills."

"I might." She leaned over and kissed her grandmother's cheek. "I'll be fine. I just need to soak and I'll be fine."

But as she pulled off her clothes and started the tub filling, she felt the tears coming.

They slipped down her cheeks and tasted salty on her lips. Once she started crying she couldn't stop. Afraid her grandmother would hear, she reached for a washcloth to cover her face.

Drained and gasping for breath, she leaned back and soaked until her fingers and toes were wrinkled. She was miserable. Totally miserable.

There was a knock on the bathroom door. "Jenny? Are you all right? You haven't slipped down the drain, have you?"

"N— no. I'm getting out now."

"Good. You need to eat something."

"I will."

When she emerged from the bathroom,

she was surprised to see her grandmother sitting on the wooden chair in the bedroom.

Startled, Jenny tucked the towel more securely around her.

"You've been crying," Phoebe observed. "Maybe I shouldn't have pushed you to go to therapy."

Sinking down on the bed, Jenny reached for her robe and drew it on. "No, you should have. I *was* hiding here. And I need the therapy."

"But? I hear a 'but' coming."

Jenny shook her head as if she didn't know what her grandmother was talking about. Then she just couldn't hold it in. "It's just that she said — she said something —" her lips trembled.

"Did she hurt your feelings?"

"No." Jenny swallowed. "She said nice something . . . something nice," she corrected herself, hating the way expressing herself came so hard. "She said she'd watched me on television and I — I cared so much about the children."

Phoebe came to sit beside her and put her arm around Jenny. "Why did that make you cry?"

"She said no one else had rushed in to do my job since I was hurt." Jenny took a shaky breath.

Her grandmother sighed and put her arm around Jenny's waist. "Ah, now I see what makes you so sad. You're worried about the children."

Her throat was choking with tears. "Someone will. I have to tell myself that someone will do something now that they know."

"God is looking out for all His children, even when it seems He is not."

"I know." Jenny pulled a tissue from the pocket of her robe and wiped her eyes. "I know."

"Pray for the children. That's what you can do for them now."

Nodding, Jenny took a deep breath. "I will."

"Now, I think you'll feel better if you have something to eat then take a nap. *Ya?*"

"You're probably right."

Phoebe gave her a hug and stood. "Good. Come eat."

There had to be a way to do something, Jenny thought later as she stretched out on the bed.

Her eyes went to the journal she kept. Maybe when she wrote in it in the morning she'd find a solution. For now, she prayed. Then she slept.

■ ■ ■ ■

The next day, her grandmother asked Jenny if she wanted to go into town, but she didn't press when Jenny begged off. She left, promising to be back in a few hours.

Jenny was still really sore from the physical therapy. She knew to expect it, but that didn't make her feel any better. With a sigh, she took a few aspirin and rested on the sofa with a book.

The aspirin, the rest, and the warmth from the fire made her feel better. She read for a while and then put down the book.

She was strangely restless. Maybe it was because she'd been out yesterday, breaking the routine of being housebound. Maybe it was because she knew she had been hiding.

Or maybe it was because everyone else seemed to be out and about today. Going to the kitchen window, she watched cars and horse-drawn buggies travel up and down the road.

She realized she looked to see if Matthew was driving every time a buggy passed. *Now I'm behaving like a teenager,* she thought wryly.

How much did he remember about that last summer she'd visited? He'd pushed that jar of blueberry jam toward her and it seemed to her that he was trying to prod her memory. That his expression was . . . hopeful?

But maybe that was just wishful thinking. Just because she'd had a crush on him, had thought about him for years, didn't mean that he'd done the same. After all, not only had she never heard from him again, he'd gotten married.

That part hurt the most. From what she could figure out, he'd married about a year after she'd left.

So much for being unforgettable. Jenny sighed. That was the stuff of a young girl's daydreams. Something you only read about in a romance novel or watched in a movie. And being a practical person, she'd seldom indulged in romantic fantasies.

She picked up the book again but despite the fact that she'd wanted to read it for some time, she couldn't get interested. What else to do? There was no television, of course. Not that she watched much daytime TV at home. And there were no chores to do — the place was spotless. Phoebe had even prepared their evening meal, putting it in the oven before she'd left.

Jenny found herself longing to be outside. She'd been cooped up for months in the hospital and hadn't ventured outside here except for the therapy appointment.

She'd go crazy if she didn't get out. And walking was good for her, she told herself.

Before she could think better of it, Jenny put on her shoes, reached for her coat and cap, and wrapped a muffler around her neck.

The air was cold and crisp. She shut the door behind her and carefully navigated the steps. Her hip protested, but she told it to shut up and made her way down the walk gripping her detested cane.

She had no clear goal; she just wanted to get out of the house. But after a few steps Jenny realized she was walking toward Matthew's farm next door. She told herself it hadn't been intentional, just a desire to walk in the opposite direction of town. After a little while, she'd simply turn around and return home.

The landscape looked so different from her memories of summers years ago. Now it was white and barren, not green and lush. But the winter scene had its own beauty and appeal, especially after her stint in the grueling heat and devastation overseas. Fields slept under a blanket of snow, unmarked by human or animal feet.

Careful not to slip, she turned and saw

that hers were the only footprints leading from her grandmother's farm.

Her breath came out in little puffs in the cold air, but the exertion of walking caused beads of perspiration to pop out on her forehead. Though her hip had made a sharp complaint when she first stepped outside, it had faded to a stubborn ache, seeming to become a bit easier, so she walked a little further, careful with her cane.

Hearing the clip-clop of a horse-drawn buggy behind her, she moved closer to the side of the road. It stopped and the man inside touched the brim of his hat and smiled a welcome.

"May I offer a ride, Jenny?"

She stared at him, surprised not only by his use of her name but the informality of it. Then she remembered that here there were no formal titles; even children addressed their teachers by their first names.

Jenny shook her head. "*Nee, danki.* I'm getting a little exercise."

"I am Amos Yoder. Phoebe mentioned that her g*rossdochder* was making a visit. Well, gut day to you, then."

He nodded and with a quiet command to his horse moved on down the road.

Somehow, on a day like this, in such a serene spot in the world, the buggy didn't seem out of place. The car that followed it a few minutes later, one with out of state tags and tourists leaning out the windows to take photos, did. Jenny tried not to flinch when the cameras were aimed in her direction, bending her head and burrowing the lower part of her face into her muffler, turtle-like.

Then they were turning their attention to the buggy ahead, passing it and gawking, leaving too little distance between it and the edge of the road for her liking. The buggy driver veered to the right and made no protest. He was probably used to that sort of thing.

Jenny wondered if she'd be here in the spring. She hadn't really had a plan when she came, just a desperate desire to be out of the hospital and in the comfort of a safe place with someone she knew loved her. No one had been able to give her a really good timetable of when her body would be healed enough for her to go back to earning a living.

She saw Matthew going into the barn at his farm. As she walked closer and he exited the barn, he caught sight of her and waved. She waved back. He watched her progress for a long moment and then went back into the barn. *Probably working,* she thought. Work never stopped on a farm, especially an Amish farm.

Perhaps it was because she was looking in his direction and not concentrating on her steps that she hit a slippery patch of ice on the road. The world tilted as she fell. She cried out as she landed hard, jarring her sore hip.

The snow was cold and wet beneath her. The harder she tried to use her cane to get up, the more she failed. Tears of frustration sprang into her eyes and finally she gave up and just sat there.

Looking left and then right, she didn't see any vehicles of any kind. Several minutes before there had been traffic. Now there was nothing.

The day was so quiet. She couldn't remember ever being in a place that was so quiet. No birds singing. No airplanes overhead. No — anything.

She'd never felt so alone.

Anxiety came creeping in along with the cold and damp beneath her. She caught her breath and told herself to calm down. The road wasn't heavily traveled but someone would come along.

She'd be frozen by then.

Her heart was pounding, even though she hadn't moved. Pounding. She could hear it trying to beat its way out of her chest. Her head felt light. Maybe she was so cold the blood wasn't moving. No, now she was sweating, so hot she felt she'd melt the snow beneath her. Then cold again.

She'd felt like this before, when she'd woken up in the hospital and realized what had happened to her. When she'd tried to walk the first time during physical therapy but couldn't.

It was anxiety, pure and simple.

Breathe! she ordered herself. Everything's going to be all right. It was daytime. Someone would surely come this way soon. She might be getting really cold, but she doubted that she was in danger of hypothermia.

"Or frostbite where I sit down," she muttered and then she laughed. *Good,* she told herself, *facing anxiety with humor helps.*

She rolled over on her hands and knees and tried to push up to her feet using her cane. But she couldn't get any traction and came down hard.

This was what she got for feeling sorry for herself, for complaining about being shut up in her grandmother's nice, warm farmhouse down the road. Sitting before the fire, tucked under a quilt, sipping a cup of hot tea sounded pretty good right now.

No, she wouldn't berate herself for venturing out. She was proud of herself for doing it. If she got any colder, though, she'd be her own statue to courage, a frozen sculpture for all to see until the spring thaw.

She didn't know whether to laugh or cry.

Footsteps crunched on the snow. Jenny looked up to see Matthew walking rapidly toward her. His expression was concerned as he crouched down in front of her. "Did you fall?"

"Just thought I'd take a little rest," she told him tartly.

"Kind of a cold place to sit," he said, crossing his arms over his chest and regarding her gravely. But she saw the twinkle in his blue eyes.

"Okay, okay, help me up," she requested, holding out her hand.

"You sure? I wouldn't want to interrupt your rest."

"Now, before I turn into a Popsicle." Then, remembering her manners, she added, "Please."

He took her hand and pulled her up effortlessly, steadying her until she got her feet securely under her, then he reached down for her cane and handed it to her.

Jenny winced as her hip took her weight and she bit her lip to keep from crying out. Determined, she took a few steps.

"Did you injure yourself?" he asked her,

solicitous.

"Yes — no," she said. "I don't know. Everything hurts right now."

She tried to take another step and moaned.

"Let me carry you."

"Oh, I'll be okay."

He reached into a pocket of his coat, pulled out a snowy handkerchief, then touched it to her lips before she could react. When he showed it to her, she saw that it was stained with blood. She must have bitten her lip from the pain.

Taking it from him, she patted the handkerchief on her lip.

He held out his arms. "Come, you're cold."

She was shivering so hard he could probably hear her teeth chattering. "I'll be okay."

Ignoring her, he bent to lift her into his arms before she could stop him.

"Hey! Where are you taking me? Our house is the other way."

"To my place, of course," he told her, showing no signs of exertion at carrying her on the snowy road.

He looked down at her. "Don't worry. We'll have plenty of chaperones. The children are home."

"I'm an adult. I don't need a chaperone,"

73

she muttered.

But she was touched that his upbringing would make him think of such a thing. When was the last time she'd even heard the word *chaperone?*

"Get the doorknob," he instructed, and she leaned down to do so.

He carried her through the kitchen and into the living room. The room was comfortable, with a sofa and matching chairs arranged around a big brick fireplace. A fire burned merrily behind the grate. A tumble of books and toys showed children lived here.

He lowered her carefully to the sofa. Pulling a quilt from the back of a chair, he tucked it around her shoulders. "You can take your coat off when you've warmed up."

Taking off his own coat, hat, and gloves, he walked away, returning a few minutes later with a mug of hot chocolate for each of them.

"Getting warm?"

She nodded, taking a sip. "Mmm."

"The *kinner* like it in the winter."

Setting the cup on the scarred oak coffee table before her, she pulled off her coat and muffler.

"I'll hang your coat over a chair in the kitchen so it can dry," he told her, reaching for it. "If your clothes are wet from the snow I can find something of Hannah's for you to put on."

"I'm fine."

She took another sip of the chocolate. She'd forgotten how delicious the drink was. Or maybe it was just because she was so cold.

"I thought you said your children were home?"

"Hannah left me a note while I was working in the barn. She's taken them to a friend's for a visit."

"So no chaperones." She smiled into her cup.

"That's funny?"

She shook her head. "It was sweet of you to worry about my reputation."

"It's a cold day to come visiting, Jenny."

"I didn't intend to visit."

Matthew grinned "No? Town is the other way."

"I just wanted to get out of the house, take a little walk."

"I thought so."

"So you were teasing me." She looked around. "Nice room."

"It's the *kinner's* favorite."

She glanced at the clock hung on one wall. "I shouldn't keep you from your work."

"I have time for a visit with a friend."

They'd been more than friends that last summer, she thought, remembering. She'd realized she had a crush on him but she couldn't tell how he felt about her, he was so guarded with his feelings.

And then he'd kissed her that warm summer day. One kiss. Such an innocent kiss.

She wondered what would have happened if her father hadn't come early for her that summer. Would the crush have become more?

4

"What are you thinking, Jenny?"

She felt a warm blush creep up her neck. To hide it, Jenny leaned forward to put her cup on the coffee table. "Thanks for not saying 'old friend.' "

There was a commotion at the kitchen door.

"Your children?"

"Or an invasion," he told her, looking unfazed.

A few moments later, three children pounced upon him, their cheeks ruddy from cold. Jenny recognized Annie. With her was another girl and a boy. She guessed they were all younger than ten years old.

"This is Mary and Joshua. You've met Annie."

All the children were tow-headed with big, inquisitive blue eyes. *What beautiful children,* thought Jenny. They were obviously curious about her, but were very polite, looking to their father for direction.

"We don't often have *Englisch* visitors," Matthew told her.

He turned his attention to them. "Jenny is staying with Phoebe. I told you, remember?"

"Matthew?" a woman called from the kitchen.

"In here, Hannah!" he called out.

Glancing at Jenny, he rolled his eyes. "Now come the questions."

Hannah stopped dead in the doorway. "Why, Jenny! I didn't know you were here. *Willkumm.*"

She turned to her brother and frowned at him. "Why didn't you tell me she was going to visit today? I would have baked something special. And I wouldn't have left with the *kinner.*"

"It was unplanned," Jenny spoke up. "I was taking a walk and fell. Matthew brought me here to warm up."

Matthew watched as Hannah went into mother-mode, fussing over their guest. Was she warm enough? Had she hurt herself? Would she stay and share a meal with them?

He watched Jenny start to refuse and then Annie spoke up, asking her to stay. Jenny hesitated; her expression softened, and she smiled, clearly a victim of Annie's charms. She thought of how she'd let her grandmother know where she was and decided she'd be back home in no time.

Hannah left them and Mary and Joshua drew closer to Jenny, careful when they saw her cane. Matthew held his breath, fearing they'd ask about her injuries, concerned that they'd hurt her feelings.

But he needn't have worried. They were, after all, the children of his late wife, Amelia, who would shoo ants outside her house rather than kill them. She was the reason for their nature far more than he was.

"I'm the oldest," Joshua told her proudly. "I'm nine and a half."

Jenny thought he looked so much like his father with his quiet manner and his steady, intent blue eyes. His body was lanky; Jenny guessed he'd reach his father's height or more for he was already tall for his age.

Mary was a contrast to her younger sister, Annie. She hung back as Joshua and Annie sat near Jenny. She'd lost the baby fat that filled Annie's face, and though she was two years younger than Joshua, she was nearly as tall.

Like so many Amish children Jenny had met on her visits, they were blond, blue-eyed, healthy children. By the way they'd greeted their father, it was plain they were happy and well-adjusted, in spite of their mother's death.

It was hard not to compare them to the children she'd seen overseas. Deliberately she forced that memory away and tried to concentrate on the children before her.

She asked them about their favorite books, saying she'd noticed all the well-read books in their bookcase. They chattered about them, and Mary told a long story about visiting the bookmobile that made it easier to find new stories.

Once, while Mary was showing her a page in her favorite book, Jenny looked up and caught Matthew watching her. She smiled shyly and bent once again to be read to from the book.

Matthew watched Jenny's hand come up and stroke the child's hair and saw for himself the fondness for children that Phoebe said she had. He knew she'd paid dearly for it when she was the victim of a bombing overseas.

Hannah called out for the children to wash their hands and come set the table. They ran to do her bidding.

"How are you feeling?" he asked her when he saw her wince as she shifted to be more comfortable.

"Fine."

"I saw you walking this way," he told her as he stood before her. "I watched the way you pushed yourself, how you worked so hard not to be afraid of falling when the road was slick."

She stared at her hand on her cane, appearing embarrassed.

"I saw you fall and work so hard to get up," he went on. "And when you couldn't, you fought with yourself."

Her eyes cut up to his. "Wait a minute. I sat there for a *long* time! Why didn't you come sooner?"

He smiled at her. "I knew you wouldn't like it if I rushed to help you."

Jenny glowered at him, only partly mocking. "I was freezing!"

"Are you warm now?"

"Steaming," she told him sternly.

"Just as feisty as always," he laughed. "I've missed you, Jenny," he said before he could stop himself.

He held out his hand. After a moment, she took it, grimacing as she stood.

"Do you think you need to see the doctor?" he asked, looking worried now.

"No," she said. "I think I bruised my pride more than anything." She glanced at him. "Don't say it."

"Say what?"

"You know what you were going to do — the same thing David did the night he brought me — say, 'Pride goeth before a fall.' "

Chuckling, he shook his head. "No, I leave the sermons to others." He looked at her. "*David* said that?"

"I know. I was surprised, too. He was teasing me. I think all men have the same sense of humor. *Englisch* or Amish."

He held his arm out to her and tucked her free hand into the crook of it, escorting her into the kitchen as if they were going to dine in a grand ballroom.

Hannah zeroed in on the gesture as they entered the kitchen. She raised her brows in question at Matthew. Their eyes met. Then hers slid away before Jenny could see.

Joshua rushed to hold out a chair for Jenny, and she gave him her warmest smile.

Matthew sat and remembered the first time he'd seen her. She'd been walking along that same road, looking everywhere but where she should, and she'd fallen, just as she had today. It had been summer and there had been no ice, of course. But City Girl Jenny had obviously been so caught up in the sights and scents that she'd tripped over a rock.

He'd been passing in his buggy and

stopped to see if she needed assistance. They'd struck up a conversation. He'd never met an *Englisch* girl before and had to admit that he was intrigued. Jenny looked so different, seemed so different from the girls he knew. She wore her long hair in a ponytail. Instead of a prim dress she was clothed in a T-shirt and jeans.

But it was more than that. She didn't act the same way the young, unmarried Amish women did. There was no shy flirting or getting him to talk about himself as a way of easing him into a relationship. She treated him like a friend, said she had both male and female friends back home. Her gaze was always direct. When she asked him about himself, she listened, and then expected the same when she talked of what she wanted to do with her life.

"Matthew?"

"Hmm?" He looked up and realized Hannah was standing there, holding a serving dish. She gave him a knowing smile, as if she knew where his thoughts had wandered.

Matthew glanced over at Jenny, who was talking with Mary.

"There, everything's on the table," Hannah said, sitting down.

The prayer of thanks for the meal said, she began plying Jenny with what seemed a hundred questions, and she and the children listened, enthralled, as she brought a different world into their kitchen. Matthew already knew most of it. Phoebe liked to talk about her granddaughter when he visited. But if he said anything now it would look like he'd been asking about her.

"Matthew, you're being quiet."

He looked around the table. "Too hard to get in a word," he told them, but he tempered those words with a smile.

"Daedi!" Mary protested, giggling. She looked at Annie and Annie started giggling, too. Joshua didn't giggle like his sisters, but he wore a smile as he gazed at Jenny.

The thought came out of nowhere, not conscious, definitely not wanted. Matthew had loved his wife, had been devastated at her death, and still thought of her every day, especially when he looked at their children.

But as he looked at Jenny sitting at the table, so comfortable with his children in their space, it came to him in a flash that had things not turned out differently, these would have been their children.

She would have been his wife.

A knock at the door startled Matthew from his thoughts. He found Phoebe on the doorstep.

"*Gut-n-owed,* Matthew. Have you seen Jenny?"

Holding the door open wide, he gestured toward her sitting at the table. "She's right here. Come inside."

Jenny looked up. "Oh, I'm sorry; I didn't mean to worry you."

"I wasn't worried," Phoebe told her, patting Jenny's hand as she took a seat at the table.

"*Kaffi,* Phoebe?" Hannah asked.

"Ya, that would be *gut, danki.*"

Hannah pushed the cream and sugar closer. "Have you eaten?"

"*Ya.* Sit, sit. Finish your meal," she told Hannah with a smile as the woman hovered, ever the good hostess. She turned to Jenny. "So you got out of the house?"

"I decided to take a walk. I ended up here."

Phoebe nodded approvingly. "The exercise did you good. There's some pink in your cheeks."

"I didn't realize you'd be home so soon. Time flies when you're having fun," she said as she looked around the table.

Annie frowned. "Time fwies? Like a biwd?"

"It's something people say," Jenny responded.

85

"Jenny? More mashed potatoes?" Joshua asked politely, and when she nodded, he handed her the big bowl of potatoes drizzled with browned butter.

"No one makes them as good as these —" Jenny stopped, appalled at what she'd just said. "I mean, no one I know other than you, *Grossmudder,* and Hannah. They're richer than the way the *Englisch* make them."

"I knew what you meant," Phoebe told her, not offended.

"I add cream cheese to the potatoes," Hannah told Jenny. "I got the recipe from Phoebe."

Jenny poured rich brown gravy over the meatloaf on her plate and took a bite, smiling in pleasure.

"You should take a walk more often," Phoebe told Jenny as she sipped her coffee. "It's picked up your appetite."

Jenny nodded.

Matthew met Phoebe's eyes and nodded at the silent message. Phoebe had told him that Jenny was too thin and she cooked her favorite foods to tempt her appetite.

After they'd had dessert — pumpkin pie that Mary had helped Hannah bake — Phoebe looked toward the window. "We should help with the dishes and get going.

It's going to snow again."

The *kinner* protested their leaving. He'd been so fortunate to have Phoebe as a friend but the *kinner* regarded her as a *grossmudder* in heart as well.

"Jenny and Phoebe can come again," he reminded them.

"Soon?" Mary asked.

"Mariyefrieh," Annie said definitely.

Matthew loved the way Jenny's face lit up. "You can't tomorrow morning, sweetheart. You have *schul,* remember?"

"You remembered the language?"

"Just a little," she told Matthew. "But I remembered that word." She turned to Annie. "Maybe you can come over for some cookies afterward?"

Then she pressed her fingers against her mouth. "I should have asked your permission first," she told Matthew. "Sorry."

"It's *allrecht,*" he said. "But don't let them become too much for you."

"Daedi!" Mary protested as she got up to clear the table without being asked.

Jenny frowned at him. "Matthew, your children are always good!"

The children beamed at her. Matthew hid his grin. They were wonderful *kinner,* and there wasn't a day he didn't thank God for His precious gifts. But the three of them had certainly decided they liked Jenny a lot.

"The meal was wonderful, Hannah. Thank you all for inviting me."

Turning to Matthew, she offered him a smile. "And thank you for saving me from the elements."

"We loved having you," Hannah said.

The children chorused their agreement. Then Jenny felt a tug on her hand. She looked down to see Annie looking up at her.

Carefully, she bent as low as possible. "Yes?"

Annie stood on tiptoes and kissed Jenny's cheek — the one with the scar.

Jenny's eyes flew to Matthew. "Why, thank you, Annie. That was very sweet."

Matthew opened the door for the two women and followed them down the walk to Phoebe's buggy to help them in. Jenny murmured thanks but kept her face averted, hoping he wouldn't see the tears Annie's gesture had brought.

"Jenny? What's wrong?" her grandmother asked when they had started home.

"Annie's such a sweet child. They all are. I enjoyed the time I spent with them today."

"But it made you sad, too, didn't it?"

At a loss for words, Jenny lifted her hands, let them fall into her lap. "Yes."

"Try not to dwell on what you think you

might not have," Phoebe said quietly. "You don't know the future."

Taking a deep breath, Jenny nodded. She was quiet for a moment, then she turned to Phoebe. "I didn't mean to make you — wonder." She shook her head. "Worry. I didn't mean to make you worry."

"I try not to worry about someone," Phoebe said, signaling the horse to proceed home. "After all, it's arrogant to do so when God knows what He's doing. He has a plan for you."

"I sure wish He'd reveal it," Jenny said with a sigh. "And soon."

"You always did want to know something, do something, right away," Phoebe told her with a smile.

Jenny looked at her grandmother. Neither her words nor her tone held rebuke. Indeed, Phoebe was smiling indulgently.

"I wonder sometimes if I wasn't grateful enough for what I had before the accident," Jenny said as she stared out at the road. "I had this dream last night where I was running barefoot in the grass in the summertime here."

"You've never struck me as an ungrateful person, Jenny."

"But it was something I took for granted. Walking, running, being without pain." She sighed. "How did you know I was at Matthew's?" she asked, changing the subject.

"It seemed logical," Phoebe told her. "I knew you couldn't have gone far. But I noticed something as I drove this way."

With a jerk of the reins and a quiet word to the horse, she brought the buggy to a stop. "Look there, in the snow by the road."

Jenny saw the place where she'd fallen, the snow that had been disturbed as she'd tried to get to her feet. Just beyond it, for a few steps there were two sets of footprints, then one set leading to Matthew's farm.

"Does that remind you of anything?"

Yes, it does, thought Jenny. She remembered how she'd felt incredibly frustrated, incredibly cold . . . but her grandmother's intent stare seemed to require a better answer. She thought harder —

A single line of footsteps, deeply printed in the snow, because the walker was carrying her.

Jenny nodded slowly. "I know that God's been with me, lifting me, carrying me. He sent Matthew to help me this time, but there have been so many people who've done it in so many ways since I was hurt." Starting with the soldiers who'd stabilized her after the bombing, the medics on the trip to the field hospital. Those who'd kept her going on the long flight back home.

She smiled. "I remember how I felt when I woke up in the hospital stateside and realized I was wrapped in the quilt you sent. I've been like Linus with it ever since."

"Linus?"

"Little boy in a newspaper comic strip. Carries his blanket everywhere."

When they got home, her grandmother insisted that Jenny go inside while she took care of the horse and buggy. It didn't seem right to let the older woman do it, but Jenny knew she really wasn't physically up to it yet. Today had proven that.

So while Jenny moved about in the kitchen making tea for them she resolved that she would work harder to be of more help. Maybe she could cook their meal one night. Something easy. *Maybe I won't give my grandmother food poisoning,* she thought with a grin. *Could there be a takeout place anywhere close?* That might be better.

Later, when she'd retired for the night, Jenny found her body was tired from the day's exertion but her mind was still whirling. Being with the children and talking about books had made her think about her work and how much she missed it.

She reached for her journal and pen on

the nightstand and then sat up, propped against the headboard. But instead of words, she found herself exchanging the pen for a pencil and sketching the face of Annie, then Mary, then Joshua. She'd been told she had some talent for art as a child and particularly enjoyed catching the expression on faces. Now she became absorbed in doing so.

There, that was Annie, with the longing in her eyes for love, for a mother, and the soft, sweet nature of a wildflower — yes, a buttercup, she thought, and drew some in her hands.

Mary. Now there was a solemn quality about her, a quiet introspection. She had the same look in her eyes that Annie had, but she was more reserved about it, watching and waiting but not rushing to Jenny the way Annie did.

And Joshua. He was so curious; his eyes seemed to bore through her, they were so intense. Much like Matthew's. She remembered how proud Matthew appeared to be of his children earlier that day. How full of love his eyes had been. He was a good father, there was no question. But obviously the children missed their mother very much. In this they were no different from children Jenny had seen in the war-torn, poverty-stricken countries she'd visited.

Too often the *Englisch* world looked upon the Amish with a list of stereotypes and generalizations. But she knew from her summers here that beyond their unquestioning faith in God's will, the Amish loved their children with a deep and abiding belief that they were truly the most precious part of their lives, God's greatest gift to them.

The day had been a happy one — but very tiring. Jenny leaned over to put the journal and pencil on the bedside table. Yawning, she stretched out and savored the comfort of her bed. After she'd wondered earlier if she was going to freeze, it felt good to lie here all tucked up in a soft, warm bed.

She thought back to a conversation with her grandmother. She still wondered if she hadn't been grateful enough for what she had before the accident. Although she knew that the time she'd spent in impoverished locations overseas had helped her to realize just how much she had to be grateful for.

Tonight, she lay in a simple bed in a simple room and was grateful for the warmth, especially after her time sitting in the snow. She was also grateful for the warm welcome from Matthew, his children, and his sister.

And as she slipped into sleep, she sent up

a prayer that the dream of the night before would come again. She wanted to run barefoot through the summer grass on the farm, laughing, feeling so free and joyful, as she once had done.

She would be so grateful for that.

"It was nice to have Jenny for a meal."

Matthew sat at the kitchen table and sipped his coffee, enjoying a rest after a long day of chores, and waited. He was a patient man who knew his sister well. She never indulged in talk for talk's sake. No, this conversation would have a point, although she wouldn't always be quick about it.

Knowing her, he was pretty sure where the conversation was headed. So he nodded and waited. "Yes."

"She's changed a lot since she was here last."

"A lot of time has passed."

"It's more than just being older," Hannah said, putting a last dish in the cupboard and closing it.

She brought a mug of tea to the big wooden table and pulled out a chair to sit opposite him. "I hated to see how hard it was for her to move. She tried to hide how she was hurting from the *kinner,* but I could tell."

94

She stirred her tea and stared into it. "And her eyes."

Lifting her own, she looked at him. "Phoebe told me about the work Jenny's done, the places she's been. She said it's given her eyes age, Matthew. She's seen too much sadness, too much tragedy."

He had thought he knew where she was going with the conversation, but suddenly it seemed the direction had veered.

"What will she do now?"

"Now?"

"Will she be able to do her job again? I know the Englisch world values beauty so highly —"

"Jenny is still a beautiful woman," he interrupted her.

Hannah raised her brows. "But that world within a world that she worked in, *television.* It seems only perfect people are allowed on it."

Now it was Matthew's turn to raise his brows. "How do you know so much about it?"

"Mary Ellen spent some time away from home as a teenager during her *rumschpringe,* remember? She told me about many of the *Englisch* ways when she returned."

"I remember there was some doubt she would return."

"She said she liked many things. The clothes. Music. Being able to have alcohol if she wished. And television." She fell silent for a moment and stirred her tea.

"Mary Elizabeth chafed at the life here," Matthew pointed out.

"But she returned. Most do, after all."

He nodded.

"You never wanted to leave."

It was a statement, not a question. The land had always held Matthew. The hope, the continuity, the connection. The desire to make it more than what his father had given him and to pass it along to his son and daughters.

Well, on one occasion he thought about leaving, at the end of one summer when what he was had been more important than who he was. . . .

"Matthew?"

"Hmm?" He looked at her and saw that she was wearing the exasperated expression only a sister could wear no matter what her age.

"We were talking about Jenny before you wandered off on me there."

"Well, you wandered off in Mary Elizabeth's direction. . . ."

Hannah leaned forward, looking earnest. "I know when Jenny first came here I reminded you of how you felt about her all those years ago. I admit I wondered if she had come here to be part of your life again."

Ah, here she was. Destination, thought Matthew wryly.

"But I was wrong."

Matthew blinked. "Wrong?"

"I'm afraid she's just a shell of what she was before."

"A shell?"

"Her injuries are more severe than I had thought," Hannah said regretfully, shaking her head. "And she's so quiet."

"She was quiet because you and the children talked so much," he reminded her.

"It's as if her spirit has been broken," Hannah continued. "And when she speaks, she has difficulty —"

He frowned. "But aren't you judging her by the same standards as the *Englisch* world you mentioned?"

Hannah lifted her shoulders and let them fall. "Perhaps. But it's just that we work hard here, Matthew. How could she manage with her injuries?"

"Phoebe says Jenny is getting stronger every day, walking better, talking better. I saw that myself today when she visited."

"You said yourself she fell and you had to carry her."

She would bring that up, he thought without rancor.

Hannah studied him. "I know you always brought home wounded animals, *bruder.* But it is time for you to think about marrying again, and I don't think you should be looking in Jenny's direction."

"You were the one who was just trying to point me there a few weeks ago."

"Like I said, I was wrong. You deserve a healthy woman, especially since you lost Amelia. One who'll be your helpmate, the mother to these children and any you have together."

Matthew stood, nearly knocking over his chair. "I can't believe the way you're talking, Hannah! Aren't you the one who hates it when people judge? I see a different woman than you do, one who risked her life to make people care about children, who's trying hard to recover without whining about what she's lost."

He shoved a hand through his hair. "Jenny is not broken, she's just —" he stopped, trying to find the words. "She's had to walk through a valley few people have to in life. And from what I saw today, she is getting stronger from it." He stood and started out of the room.

"Where are you going?"

98

"To tuck the children in. They, at least, accepted Jenny the way they should."

Hannah watched him leave and smiled.

Matthew's children came to visit Jenny two days later, bearing an invitation, carefully lettered and colored, for Jenny and Phoebe to have dinner with them. Annie handed it to her with a big smile, while the other children waited expectantly.

"How sweet. Thank you."

"You'll come, *ya?*" asked Mary.

"I have to ask my grandmother if she has plans, but yes, I would love to."

"Papa will come for you in the buggy."

Jenny started to say she could walk, but after what had happened before, perhaps that wasn't a good idea just yet.

"Okay. I'll see him then."

The children fairly tumbled out the door, and she watched them run back to their house. Phoebe walked up behind her then, and Jenny showed her the invitation.

"How nice." Phoebe smiled. "They're such sweet children. You will go?"

"Yes. I told them I wasn't sure if you had plans."

"I'm having supper with a friend. I prepared a casserole for you to put in the oven but now we will just save it for tomorrow."

Her home had many modern conveniences, including a propane-powered refrigerator.

"Then we'll both have an evening out."

"*Ya.*"

Her grandmother hadn't gone out for the evening since she'd been there, but now perhaps she was feeling she could leave Jenny alone.

The day passed slowly, as days always do when you look forward to something so much. Jenny helped her grandmother bake bread, took a nap, read, did some more of the dreaded exercises, and was ready an hour before she was to be picked up.

She told herself she was worse than a teenage girl with her first date. Only this wasn't a date with Matthew, but one with his family.

Matthew brought the buggy, as promised. They passed Hannah on the way, going in the opposite direction. Hannah waved at them and while Matthew lifted his hand, Jenny saw him frown as his sister passed.

Then Jenny saw the children peering out the window, looking for them, and she smiled.

"They've been talking about you all day," he told her, helping her from the buggy. "They did some of the cooking, with Hannah's help. Don't worry — it's good."

"I'm sure it is," she assured him as they went inside.

Joshua took Jenny's coat and hung it on the peg by the door. Then he seated her the same way he had before — as an honored guest, with manners Jenny didn't think she'd ever seen a child exhibit out in the *Englisch* world.

"We made suppwer," Annie spoke up.

"*Aenti* Hannah helped us," Mary reminded her.

Matthew watched as Mary took a pan of biscuits from the oven and set it carefully on the stove. He smiled and nodded approvingly. Using a spatula, she transferred the biscuits to a woven basket lined with a cloth napkin and placed it on the table. Once his children were seated, Matthew brought the heavy cast-iron pot to the table.

"It's a simple meal," he said to Jenny as he took his seat.

"The best kind," she told him, smiling, and bent her head as he said grace.

Joshua ladled out the stew — big chunks of beef, potatoes, carrots, parsnips, and onions — into white crockery bowls as biscuits were passed around. The stew was the perfect meal on a cold winter day, warm and comforting.

Even better was the warmth of this family

meal, even if this was a borrowed family. Jenny looked around the table as the children ate hungrily. They hadn't spent the day inside zoned out on sugary snacks in front of the boob tube. Some *Englisch* children might complain about a day of chores, but these children just considered that a part of their day, their world. They enjoyed being useful doing things for their home.

Now came more questions about the places Jenny had visited. All this was more exotic to them than to *Englisch* children who could turn on the television and see the world. Mary spoke up, asking Jenny about books. Matthew said that of his three children, Mary loved books the most, although Annie had loved them since she was a toddler — even after they convinced her the pages weren't for eating.

Jenny's motor skills had steadily improved since her hospitalization but required complete attention. Concentrating on Joshua, telling her about his horse, Jenny felt her spoon slipping from her grasp. Grabbing it just made things worse — it hit the edge of the bowl, splattering gravy, then fell to the wooden floor with a clatter.

Little Annie is managing better than I am, thought Jenny, her face flaming. But Matthew simply picked up the spoon, set it in the sink, and brought another for her. Mary used her napkin to mop up the gravy. Joshua continued his story without missing a beat, while Annie sent her a sunny smile.

Dessert was a cobbler made with peaches canned last summer. Annie helped scoop ice cream on top. Jenny wasn't sure if the cobbler was still warm from the oven or if the amount of time Annie took making sure she did it just right caused the ice cream to melt so much. But they all laughed together.

After dinner, no one rushed from the table, leaving a parent with dirty dishes. Jenny was told she was a guest, and as such she was to sit and enjoy her tea. Each child had an assigned task, and before long the kitchen was sparkling clean again. She found herself drawing out the time drinking her tea, not wanting to leave.

Hannah returned and said hello, but hurried to her room, saying she was tired. Matthew paused in the act of hanging up a dishcloth and frowned after her, then turned to Jenny. "Can I get you more tea?"

"No, thanks."

He poured himself a cup of coffee, then, with a brief glance at the kitchen window, sat at the table again. "I should get you home soon."

"I could —"

"No."

"— walk home," she finished.

"No," he said more firmly. "Now you remind me of Annie," he laughed as she pretended to pout.

Jenny grinned. "All your children are precious, but there's something about Annie."

He nodded. "She's so much like Amelia, and yet she was just a baby when her mother died."

Jenny's smile faded. "She must have been wonderful. Not that you couldn't have raised such sweet children yourself."

"Her loving hand is surely on them," Matthew agreed.

"It must have been so hard to lose her," Jenny said quietly. She wished she knew what Amelia had looked like, but the Amish don't believe in having their pictures taken. "What did she look like?"

"You have only to look at Mary to know," he said simply.

"She must have been beautiful."

Annie ran back into the room. "*Daedi,* can I go wif you to take Jenny home?"

He hesitated. "Well, since you did all your chores, I suppose you may if you bundle up."

Shrieking with happiness, she ran to tell

Mary her good news.

"It's not that she wants you to leave now," Matthew assured Jenny. "She's just afraid she'll miss out if she doesn't ask now. I wouldn't let her come with me to get you because she didn't take her nap."

"Gee, I was a reward for taking a nap. Now I feel even more special than you all made me feel tonight," Jenny told him, feeling yet another tug on her heartstrings.

"Jenny? There's something I've been wanting to ask you —"

"Papa? I — I'm sorry to interrupt."

"Trouble with homework?" asked Jenny, seeing the paper clutched in her hands.

"I have to write an essay. I'm stuck. Can you help me?"

Jenny looked at Matthew as he nodded. "I'm going to look in on Joshua and Annie."

"Mmm," said Jenny, absorbed in what Mary had written.

When Matthew returned a few minutes later, Mary was bent over her essay, busily writing.

"I showed her a trick I use when I get stuck writing," Jenny told him with a smile. "She knew what she wanted to write after that."

Mary looked up. "I'm almost done." She

gave Jenny a shy smile. *"Danki."* She left them to return to her room.

"You're sure about the tea?" Matthew asked, pouring himself more coffee and taking his seat again at the table.

He'd said they should go, but here he was sitting again, drinking more coffee.

"I'd better not, or I won't sleep tonight."

"I never have that problem."

"You work harder than I do." She pushed the sugar toward him. "Matthew, you started to ask me a question before Mary came in. What was it?"

"Why did you never marry?"

5

Matthew wondered which of them was more surprised by his question.

Jenny stared at him. "Well, you don't say much, but when you do, you certainly don't hold back, do you?"

Feeling color creeping up his neck, Matthew ran a hand through his hair and swallowed. "I shouldn't ask such a personal question."

"It's okay," she told him. "I've been asked many more personal questions. Sometimes people stare, sometimes they ask about my scars, my difficulty walking. Talking."

She saw that even though he seemed embarrassed, his eyes were directly on her. All those summers ago she'd had a crush on him, and she'd thought he returned her feelings. But after her father had come for her, Matthew had never answered her letters.

Whatever his reason for asking, she didn't

think that he had any romantic interest in her anymore. She told herself that it was just that he had the same curiosity about her as an *Englischer* that his children did, that he was seeking to understand her since she was different from the Amish women he knew.

Fiddling with her empty teacup, she found herself thinking about his question. "I've had time to think about that," she said slowly. "During my stay in the hospital, you know? I had been too busy going to college, doing an internship at a TV station. Then, suddenly, I got the opportunity to go overseas, and time just slipped away."

She sighed. "It's hard to meet someone when you're on a plane going, coming, going, coming."

The only men she saw were soldiers who were concentrating on their job. Or they were men from foreign countries who considered American women to be too forward.

The years had slipped away. But it was more than being overseas or being so involved in her work. Because she'd found a way to go on camera, people thought she was outgoing, that she was career-driven. That she wanted to be "modern" and pursue a man or just be independent. But Jenny was pretty traditional — or, as a few people had teased her, "old-fashioned."

Feeling his gaze still on her, she looked at him. "Why are you asking, Matthew?"

"It is so obvious how much you love children. And you look like you enjoyed being at home with us."

"Oh, I have," she agreed with a smile. "Thank you for letting me be with you and your family, Matthew."

"We enjoyed having you," he said with that touch of gravity, of formality, in his tone and speech that was ever-present in the Amish world.

"You know, things are changing in the *Englisch* world," she said slowly. "Young men and women are waiting longer to get married. They feel they have to get a foothold in their career. And sometimes the —" she couldn't think of the word — "the broken marriages of their parents make them wary. When they marry, they want so much to make sure that the marriage will last."

Divorce — that was the word she hadn't been able to remember. Divorce was so unheard of in his world she wondered if she'd have to define it for him. But he nodded.

"My grandmother told me that many Amish marry young but all the marriages last a long time," she said.

"Our faith in God, our marriages, our families are not only important to us, they are everything to us," he said simply.

"But —" she stopped.

"But it does not mean we're guaranteed there will be no challenges," he said, as if he knew where her thoughts were going. "And it does not mean we're guaranteed our spouse will be with us for fifty years."

He glanced at the window and stood. "It's getting late. I should take you home."

Nodding, she pushed her chair back and used the table and her cane to lever herself up. She'd sat too long and was stiff. The first few steps were always tricky.

Moving carefully, she reached for her coat and was relieved to find that she didn't waver on her feet.

"Let me help you." Matthew took the coat and held it so that she could slip one arm in, then the other.

He called his *kinner* and they came running to say goodbye.

Annie jumped up and down, excited that she was going with her father to drive Jenny home.

"Maybe you can come again?" Mary asked shyly.

Matthew laid a hand on Mary's shoulder as he looked at Jenny. "We hope that she'll visit us often."

Jenny nodded. "I would love to. Thank you all again for the wonderful meal and company."

Her grandmother was in the kitchen, stirring something in a pot, when Jenny got home.

"Mmm." Jenny sniffed the air. "Is that hot chocolate?"

"I knew you would be home soon. I made enough for both of us."

"Great." She hung her coat on the peg.

"Did you have a good time?" Phoebe served the chocolate in thick white pottery mugs.

"I had a wonderful time."

Taking a seat, she took a sip of the chocolate. "This is so good on a cold night."

A memory came to her of Matthew fixing her hot chocolate after he'd carried her to his home to warm up. She'd felt so taken care of that day.

She came back to the present, conscious that her grandmother was looking at her, waiting for her to continue.

"Matthew's children are so sweet. They cooked the supper with Hannah's help, before she left."

"I am sure their mother looks down on

them with pride."

Chin in hand, elbow propped on the table, she studied her grandmother. "Funny, I thought that too. Now I know where I must have gotten it. I remember one summer, when I was visiting, you found me crying about my mom being gone. I was so sad, and you said something like that. It made me feel better, made me feel she was still close by."

Now wasn't the time to tell her grandmother that she'd felt her mother very, very close when she was injured. But maybe one day —

"I'm glad you remembered. You understand how hard it is for them to be without their mother."

"Yes. Maybe that's why we have sort of a bond."

"It was very hard for Matthew to lose his wife, too."

Jenny nodded.

"But it's been almost three years," Phoebe said. "Time for Matthew to think about marrying again. He's a good man who deserves to be happy. And his children deserve a mother."

"Has he been seeing anyone?" Jenny asked, hoping she sounded casual.

"Courting, you mean?"

"That sounds so charming," mused Jenny, taking another sip of her chocolate.

"Some of our customs must seem old-fashioned to you."

"Well, my coworkers sometimes teased me that I was old-fashioned," she confessed. "I happen to think I just prefer tradition, you know?"

Phoebe reached across the table to take Jenny's hand. "Sometimes it's hard to remember you're not Amish."

"Well, I'm sort of half, if you think about it. Even though Daddy left, I think he still considered himself one of the Plain People." She sighed as she glanced around the kitchen, always her favorite room of her grandmother's house. "I always loved it here. It felt like my second home."

Her grandmother nodded. "It's good to hear you say so."

Smothering a yawn, Jenny rose. "I'll wash up, and then it's bed for me."

Her grandmother patted her hand. "See you in the morning."

Jenny washed the mugs, dried them, and put them away. It had been a very long time since she'd done any housekeeping. She realized she liked the feel of doing such a chore instead of letting the dishwasher do the job.

Standing here in her grandmother's kitchen felt very homey to her in a way that her own never did. And it wasn't just that a modern kitchen made it feel sterile. Working so much, she'd seldom been home enough to really enjoy any part of her apartment, she realized. And the kitchen had been merely a place to nuke a frozen dinner or eat takeout.

Maybe while she was here she could try cooking some of her grandmother's recipes. After all, she had the time to stop and enjoy the simple pleasures of home-cooked food.

Now she'd had time to smell — the hot chocolate!

"Jenny!" Annie cried as she ran up the walkway a few days later.

"Annie, be careful!" Matthew called after her.

The child stopped a few feet before Jenny. "Rweady to go?" she asked with a big smile.

"Yes, I was just waiting for you." Jenny maneuvered the steps carefully.

Matthew waited beside the buggy. He helped Annie up, then held out a hand to Jenny.

"It's very nice of you to give me a ride to the speech pathologist."

Annie bounced on the seat. "I like it!"

"You're sure it isn't too much trouble?"

Matthew climbed in and started the buggy moving. "None at all. You're seeing a different speech therapist than Annie's, so we don't even have to wait for each other."

The receptionist appeared surprised when Jenny walked in. She looked from Matthew to Annie and then back at Jenny. She handed over a clipboard with a new patient form for Jenny to fill out but didn't say anything.

Naturally speech therapy was less physically taxing than physical therapy, but Jenny was disconcerted when Carol, her therapist, told her she needed intensive speech therapy several times a week.

"It's going to take that much to get you where you want to be. But we can get you there." She paused. "What is it? What's wrong?"

Jenny sighed and shook her head. "I wanted to be away from the hospital, but at least it was easy to do the therapy there. Here, it means asking someone to drive me in each time — and in bad weather, too."

Carol tapped her pen on the desk. "You told me you're living with your grandmother. Do you think she would be willing to do some of the verbal exercises with you?"

Jenny nodded.

"What if I stop by her house and work with the two of you once or twice — show you what you can do at home? If you follow my plan faithfully, I think we could have you come into the office less often and see how you do."

"You'd do that?"

"Sure."

"I would appreciate it so much. I mean, I feel terrible having you take the time —"

"It's no problem." Carol checked her calendar. "I'll do it on my way home from work. How about 5:30 tomorrow?"

"That would be great." Jenny breathed a sigh of relief and felt a weight lifting from her shoulders. "It would help so much. Thank you!"

When Jenny emerged from her session, Annie was just coming out of hers.

"See?" said Matthew.

"Okay, I see," said Jenny, smiling.

"See what?" Annie wanted to know.

Matthew and Jenny laughed. Annie tugged at his coat, and he bent down to let her whisper in his ear.

"Annie wants me to ask you to eat with us in town."

"Annie?"

"I would like it, too," Matthew admitted with a smile.

Jenny looked at the little girl, then her father. "That would be very nice."

They went to a restaurant that Jenny remembered from her previous visits, one the tourists didn't seem to know about.

Annie didn't need to look at the menu. "Grwwied cheese and Fwench fwies, pwease," she told the waitress who called her by name.

"We eat here sometimes after her appointment," Matthew explained. He ordered the buffet.

Jenny hesitated. The buffet was loaded with so many foods, and while her appetite had improved, she didn't think she needed more than a sandwich.

"Try it," Matthew urged, seeing her glance at the buffet.

She nodded. "Okay. But just to balance out how much you eat. They can't be making much money off you if you still eat as much as you did years ago."

Although his manner was more formal than other men in her world, she saw the twinkle in his eyes.

He stood and helped her to her feet. They made their selections, and then, when it came time to take their plates back to the table, he took hers for her.

Annie was absorbed in coloring on the

paper placemat used for the kiddie menu. She smiled as her father and Jenny sat down but returned to her coloring, content to wait for her sandwich.

As they ate, Matthew asked Jenny how her session had gone.

"I'll take a hundred of those sessions compared to physical therapy," she told him as she buttered a biscuit hot from the oven. "Sometimes I wonder when I'll see the end of this."

She sighed and set the biscuit back on the plate. "Sometimes I wonder when I'll feel normal again. . . . I'm sorry. I'm complaining."

"It's understandable. You've come so far," he told her seriously. "Phoebe told me what you've gone through since you were injured. You're a brave woman, Jenny Miller."

"It doesn't take bravery to be in the path of a bomb."

"It takes bravery to go where you went, to tell people who don't always want to hear. To get up and start again when you're hurt so badly."

Jenny stared at him, not knowing what to say. "Thank you," she finally managed. "But really, what else can you do?"

"Some would sit and feel sorry for themselves."

She smiled wryly. "Been there. Done that."

"Not for very long." He might have said more but a middle-aged Amish couple approached their table.

"Hello, Matthew, Annie."

"Amos, Esther, good to see you."

Matthew introduced Jenny. "We heard you were visiting your grandmother," said Esther.

The woman's eyes were bright with curiosity as she scanned Jenny, her gaze going to her cane. "The women in the quilting circle hope you'll join your grandmother this week."

"Thank you for the invitation," Jenny said politely.

Amos chatted with Matthew for a moment about the weather and the farm. Esther patted Annie's head and smiled as she bent to see what the child was coloring.

They'd barely left when another couple stopped by, then two women the age of Jenny's grandmother. While she sensed their curiosity, their innate reserve and courtesy prevented them from prying.

"People want to meet you, but they won't intrude," Matthew told her.

She'd been reluctant to "go out in the world" and asked herself if she had come here to her grandmother's home to hide.

This morning, she'd ventured out and the experience hadn't been painful at all.

The midday rush at the restaurant eased. They were left alone to finish their meal.

Pushing back her plate, Jenny sighed. "I ate so much."

"*Daedi,* wook! I ate it awl!"

"Why, sure and you did," he said, nodding approvingly. "I guess you don't have room for ice cream now, do you?"

"Silwy *Daedi!*" she told him, giggling.

Matthew turned to Jenny. "And you? Are you too full for dessert?"

"Silly *Daedi!*" she laughed, struggling to get up with them to get soft-serve ice cream from the dessert buffet.

They fell into an easy routine. Matthew came for Jenny for the occasional speech-therapy appointments, for dinner with him and his children, for errands in town. They talked as they had so many years ago, about so many things.

With the maturity of years, Jenny could see past the attraction she'd once had to the man Matthew had become. He worked hard, but loved the work he did, loved his children and enjoyed this time of year when he had a little more time for them.

Her visit was an eye opener. She'd had no

idea how much he did for her grandmother. It went beyond stopping to see if she needed something from town. After her grandfather had died, Phoebe had written Jenny that she thought she might sell the farm and get a smaller place. But a few months later, she wrote that Matthew wanted to lease some of the land to raise more crops.

Jenny knew where the division of the land had once been, and although it was winter and there were no crops planted, it appeared to her that the section from her grandparents' farm hadn't been planted in a long time.

One day, when they were driving past it, she asked him what was planted there during the growing season. He shrugged and said he hadn't had time to do much with it the last few years and changed the subject.

Jenny knew the Amish took care of their own, but she hadn't realized it hit so close to home.

Watching as benches were unloaded and carried into her grandmother's home, Jenny was reminded of the saying, "If Mohammed will not go to the mountain, then the mountain must come to Mohammed."

In the time she'd been here she'd avoided attending religious services. She'd hidden out at first, not comfortable being around anyone the way she looked. But she'd been doing physical and speech therapy, gotten out into town with Matthew and Annie and her grandmother, and felt more at ease.

Now all that was being tested, right here on what she'd started thinking of as her "home turf."

The Amish didn't have a formal church building. Instead, they met every other Sunday in a member's home. Since most people didn't have seating for dozens, sometimes a hundred or so parishioners, a carriage full of benches made the rounds for services.

Her grandmother came to stand next to Jenny as she watched the unloading.

"How often does everyone come to your house?"

"Usually once a year." Phoebe put her arm around Jenny's waist and squeezed her. "You don't have to attend if you don't wish. Everyone knows you're visiting and you're not a member. Besides, you're recovering."

"But I really liked attending when I visited years ago." Jenny chewed on her fingernail.

"Ya, I know." Phoebe held the door so another bench could be carried inside. "Whatever you decide will be fine. There's certainly no reason you can't stay in your room if you wish. Everyone will understand."

"As I remember, the services are pretty long."

Phoebe nodded. "Sometimes three hours. Sitting so long might aggravate your back and hip. If you attend, I'm sure no one will mind if you get up and move about as you need to. After all, children attend, and while they're usually well-behaved, they are, after all, children."

"Is there anything I can do?"

Phoebe shook her head. "There will be plenty of help." She glanced around her kitchen. "And plenty of food for the light meal afterward."

"Meal? You have to feed all those people?" She hadn't remembered the meal.

"Some of the women are bringing bread, but yes, we'll be feeding everyone a light meal. What do you do after church?"

"Sometimes my church would have potluck suppers," Jenny said absently. "Everyone brings something."

"It's a big expense, but it's just once a year or so," Phoebe said.

Jenny looked down at her simple dove-gray turtleneck sweater and matching calf-length skirt. "Am I dressed all right?"

Phoebe patted her cheek. "You look very

nice. No one will expect to see you in Amish dress. Everyone knows you're my granddaughter who's visiting. You've already met some of them."

So many buggies began arriving. Just as her grandmother had told her, there was help. Lots of help.

Several men and boys helped put horses in the barn. Extra food was carried into the house. Chairs were brought for older members who needed more support than the backless wooden benches. Matthew came with his children and Hannah. Men sat in one room, the women and children in another.

The service started just after 8 a.m. with a sermon. Religion was such a part of everyday life, it was no surprise to Jenny that services would be in the home. Or that the ministers weren't formally trained but were, instead, average men like John from the community. To her surprise, the German she'd studied in college came back in bits and pieces as she listened to the service conducted in the Pennsylvania Deitsch dialect and the Scriptures read in High German.

In his simple sermon John talked about David and Goliath and how David never called Goliath a giant, he simply went after his adversary and won. Jenny thought about how her own problems seemed so big, so overwhelming. She wondered what would happen if she thought of them as just a challenge, as David had.

The songs were Jenny's favorite. Her hip ached, but just as she was about to go into her bedroom where she could ease it with some movement, the singing began.

There was no musical accompaniment and only the words were printed in the hymnal. Jenny listened but didn't participate as the attendees sang from memory. Generations had passed the songs down, one to the next.

Something was so simple, so pure, about hearing songs of praise to God. Afterward the down-to-earth message from Scripture resonated in her heart. *Faith here is so basic,* she thought, a little awed as she surreptitiously looked around at the congregation. For them, home was not only where you were supposed to practice what you believed — you had church there as well.

Her father had searched for a place to call his spiritual home after he left the Amish, Jenny knew, and so she'd attended many churches with her parents. None had affected her as much as this.

Peace fell over her like a gentle snowfall.

Afterward, the benches were turned into tables and a light lunch was served. Women gathered in the kitchen to organize the food. Children played games but kept an eye open for when goodies would be put out. The men stood outside in the mild winter air talking about farming and business.

Matthew found Jenny standing outside, wrapped in her coat.

"Hello, neighbor."

She turned. "Hello."

"Why are you standing out here?"

Hugging herself for warmth, Jenny smiled. "It feels good after being inside with so many people all morning."

Matthew watched her glance wistfully over her shoulder. "Now you're acting as if you wish you were inside."

"I felt in the way in the kitchen." She glared at the cane in her hand.

"It is just a tool to help you," he said. "Don't be angry at the help it gives. Be grateful for it now and be grateful when you can give it up."

"Soon," she told him fervently. "I want it to be soon."

"I know."

Two words from a Plain man spoken with such understanding, she thought, feeling

126

touched.

"What did you think of the service?" he asked as he leaned on the railing, watching the children play in the snow.

"Very spiritual," she said. "But this wasn't my first, remember?"

He turned to look at her. "*Ya,* I do remember. You seemed very interested in the Plain life when you were here those summers."

"I was."

"But you flew away."

"That's — an unusual way to look at it. I had to leave. Summer was over."

"Spring is not so far away now." He scanned the sky, the nearby trees.

She shivered. "I hope so."

"Will you fly away again soon, Jenny? Is your time here nearly over?"

"Time has been on my mind," she said slowly. As he'd said, winter was nearly over. "To every thing there is a season," she whispered, remembering Ecclesiastes as she stared out at the snow. "And a time to every purpose under the heaven."

Her fingers tightened on her cane. "It's been my time to heal here in this place." She fell silent.

"Jenny?"

When she wouldn't meet his eyes, he lifted

her chin with his hand. "Why do you grow sad?"

She bit her lip and fought tears. "Long — story."

Just then a man left the house. He frowned when he saw Matthew's hand on Jenny's face. They moved apart so that the man, a church elder, could proceed down the steps.

When Jenny shivered again Matthew opened the door. "Inside, before you freeze into — it was a Popsicle, was it not?" He was reminding her of the day he'd found her sitting on the road, unable to get up.

Nodding, she walked inside. He didn't follow her, going instead to the barn. She looked out the window after him and found the church elder, looking at her.

Matthew hoped it wasn't obvious that he found every excuse to be around Jenny.

It was logical, after all, that he picked her up for speech-therapy appointments when Annie had hers. There was no point in their going separately.

So they usually had a meal afterward before heading home. He told Jenny that he and Annie did this often as a treat for her doing well with her therapy. But now he and Jenny talked while Annie busied herself with coloring or chatted with her favorite waitress.

He was careful not to make any overtures to Jenny. After all, he had no idea if Jenny had any feelings for him anymore. She'd come here to heal, but who knew if she would stay?

But he watched her, and as she grew stronger and more confident, she went to the quilting circle with her grandmother and moved about the community with her and by herself. Time passed without her talking about returning to her world.

When the Sunday services were to be held at Phoebe's home, Matthew found himself looking forward to seeing what Jenny thought of it.

Joshua came to tell him he was worried about Daisy, Phoebe's horse, and as he passed through the kitchen, Matthew was concerned that he didn't see Jenny helping with the food. *Was sitting through the service too much for her?* He knew inactivity still caused her so much pain. Or had one of the women said something to hurt her feelings? He'd noticed most people responded to her well, but you never knew.

He found her shivering as she stood on the front porch.

Something was bothering her, but she

wouldn't tell him. She brushed off his concern, flippantly telling him it was a long story.

The morning after the service, he found a way to hear her story. Phoebe called, needing him to drive Jenny to physical therapy.

Jenny was obviously waiting at the door for she came outside as he pulled up.

"I'm so sorry, Matthew. I had no idea my grandmother called you," she said as he helped her into the buggy. "I could have called a taxi."

"I am happy to take you," he told her as he joined her, then, with a jerk of the reins, got the buggy moving.

She settled in for the ride.

"Now," he said, turning to her. "We have time for that long story."

6

Jenny looked at Matthew, then out the window of the buggy. "It's nothing."

"I think it *is* something, Jenny. You seemed not yourself yesterday."

She shifted in her seat.

"Are you in pain?"

"I'm okay."

"Did sitting for so long yesterday trouble your hip?"

Grimacing with the memory, she nodded. "I knew I should have gotten up a couple of times, but I didn't."

"Why not? Didn't Phoebe tell you no one would mind?"

"She did." Jenny stared at her hands folded on her lap. "I didn't want to call attraction —" she stopped — "attention to myself."

"Call attention?"

Jenny touched her cheek. "It's still hard to be around people, looking like this."

He frowned at her, clearly not understanding. "Like what?"

"My scars, Matthew. You can't say you don't see them."

He touched her cheek. "I don't expect you to be perfect, Jenny. That's your world, not mine. I see a woman with a beautiful heart who loves children so much she risked her life for them, who had something terrible happen to her but is trying to find her way, who respects the customs and traditions of people who are not her own."

Her eyes filled with tears. "I'm bumbled —" her eyes widened — "humbled." She shook her head. "Just when I think speech therapy is doing some good."

"It is. You're just impatient."

Jenny smiled. "Grandmother says that, too."

She shifted again to ease her hip. "That's another reason I didn't want to leave the room. I'm used to going to church, a formal church," she told him. "Many of them, in fact, because my father looked for a spiritual home after he left the Amish.

"At all of them, I listened to someone trained in a seminary talk about God, about the Bible, about faith. Sometimes the service seemed a little distant. That wasn't true here when I visited during the summers. Or yesterday."

She paused, studying the passing landscape. "What I see here, what I feel here is that people in your world believe spirituality isn't distant. It's close and real. Religion seems born in the home, stays in the home. I mean, the services are even held in the home. And there's not one person in charge, one speaker set above others. It's farmers and carpenters, and well, just average folk speaking spontaneously about the message they find in the Bible."

She looked at him. "A message from the heart, to the heart."

"And what did you hear for your heart, Jenny?"

"I've heard a lot about God's will, about God's purpose for us since I've been here. When I was younger, I decided what I wanted for my wife — my life," she corrected herself, wishing her tongue would catch up with her thoughts. "I believed I knew what I was supposed to do with it. But after the accident, I started wondering if I'd been trying to tell God His job."

Matthew pulled the buggy into a parking spot near the therapist's office building. But instead of getting out, he turned to her.

"And what did God say when you told

him His job?"

Jenny couldn't help smiling wryly at Matthew. "Well, I haven't heard directly. But I'll be working on listening better. I mean, I'm God's creation, so He's created me for something. Does that make any sense?"

Matthew nodded. "It makes a lot of sense."

She checked her watch and sighed. "I should go in."

"You make it sound like you're going to your doom, Jenny."

"I had this idea that physical therapy meant lovely massages and heating pads and gentle, caring manipulation of your hurting body." She laughed. "Well, they're caring, but as for the rest? Sometimes, after the therapy's over, I feel like I've been put on a medieval torture rack."

Ever the gentleman, Matthew walked up to the office with her. "But they're helping you. It seems that you move with less pain than when you first came."

She nodded. "You're right."

"I'll be back for you in an hour."

Nodding, she watched him return to the buggy.

"Hi, Jenny," the receptionist said with a smile when she signed in. "Listen, I'm sorry, but we're running about ten minutes late today."

"No problem." Jenny sat down and flipped through a magazine.

A woman pushed a wheelchair out a few minutes later. The little boy in it looked to be about five years old. He wore braces on both legs.

"Great session," the therapist said as she walked out with them. "Good job, Jason." They exchanged a high five, and Jason gave her a gap-toothed grin.

The mother pulled out her checkbook to pay. "We'll see you Friday."

The therapist turned to Jenny. "Ready?"

She nodded and followed the woman.

"We'll be using Room 4 today."

As she stood, Jenny couldn't help looking back. The boy looked so familiar. And yet, how could he? He wasn't Amish, and she hadn't been out much since she'd been here.

"What is it?" the therapist asked, noticing Jenny's attention.

"I — I don't know. He looks like someone I know."

And then she realized that if his hair was slightly darker, he might have been the twin of a little boy she'd met in Romania. She closed her eyes, remembering.

"Jenny?"

She opened her eyes and shook her head. "I'm all right."

Walking into the room, she took off her coat and laid it in a chair. Propping her cane there, she moved carefully over to the treatment table.

"You turned awfully pale. Did you move wrong?"

Climbing up on the treatment table, she tried to smile at the therapist. "No, I'm fine."

The receptionist knocked and poked her head in. "I'm sorry to interrupt, Sue, but Jason's mother has a quick question about his exercises. Could you answer it before you start your session with Jenny?"

Sue looked at Jenny.

"It's fine, go ahead." Jenny was grateful for the moment alone to think.

She first met Andrei when she went to Romania. He lived in an orphanage there with too many children cared for by too few adults, who were losing hope of keeping the orphanage open. Every day there were more orphans and less money.

Andrei was three and had big brown eyes that followed her around the room as she met the children and interviewed the staff. When she approached his crib at last, he held up his arms and grinned at her. There was no way she couldn't pick up the little charmer.

"Andrei is one of the lucky ones," her translator told her, tickling the child under the chin. "They have finally located his grandmother. She will travel here to take him home next month."

"But the others," she said, her voice growing sad as she looked around the nursery. "You will show the people back in your country what is happening here, please? Help us help the children."

The door opened, and Sue walked in. "There now. Sorry that I kept you waiting."

"No problem." Jenny was grateful to the woman for interrupting her thoughts.

"You're looking sad. Did Jason remind you of someone?"

"How did you know?"

"It's not hard to make the connection," Sue said. "I remember this commercial I saw once. You know, where they show children from those terribly poor countries and ask you to send in money to help feed them? Well, there was a little boy, maybe four or five, in the commercial, and he looked so much like my little nephew."

She started flexing Jenny's right leg. "Here, give me some resistance."

Jenny did as she asked, and they worked through the set, then turned their attention to the left leg.

"When are you scheduled to go back to work?"

"I'm on indefinite leave."

Matthew asked me when I would fly away, thought Jenny.

"I still have trouble with my speech," Jenny told her slowly and carefully. "If I can't get my body and my speech better I may not be able to do the work I did."

Sue patted her on the shoulder. "I'm sure it will work out. If it's meant to be."

Sort of like saying, *If it's God's will,* thought Jenny, sitting up with Sue's help.

"Now, let's go work with the machines," Sue said briskly.

So much for the warm and fuzzy, thought Jenny, smiling wryly. *Back to the torture.*

"I'm here to pick up Jenny Miller," Matthew told the receptionist.

"Oh, sorry, we're running a little late," she told him. "She'll be out in a few minutes."

"Thank you. Please tell her I'll wait outside."

A car full of tourists had parked near his buggy. Two children sat in the car playing with some sort of little box. A man and a woman stood beside his buggy, taking photos.

"Oh, look, there's the man who owns the buggy!" the woman said loudly. She started toward Matthew, snapping pictures.

Matthew held up his hand.

"Tiffany, maybe you should stop," the man called to her.

"Oh, I just want a few photos," she told him, continuing to take pictures. "You don't mind, do you?"

"Yes, ma'am, I *do* mind," he told her. "I would prefer that you not take pictures."

She gaped at him. "I thought that was just something they said. You know, to make you more mysterious, live up to the whole image."

"Image?" Matthew stared at her, confused.

"What, is it like the Indians? You know, how they used to think if someone took a picture that the camera would steal their soul?" The woman snapped her gum as she let her camera drop on a strap around her neck.

"Matthew?"

Glancing back, he saw Jenny walking toward him. "There you are."

Instinctively, he turned his body to shield her from the woman with the camera as he did when he was out with Hannah and the children. Then he remembered that she was used to being photographed. Phoebe had told him it was her job.

He held out his hand to Jenny to help her down the walk.

The woman raised her camera and then paused and stared at Jenny. "Gee, how come you're not wearing your costume?"

"Costume?"

"You know, the Amish dress and hat thing."

Jenny was too polite to roll her eyes. But she wanted to. "I'm not Amish."

"Oh." But the woman aimed the camera at her anyway.

"Ma'am, please don't do that," Jenny said firmly. "You're invading our privacy."

The woman bristled. "Well, you don't have to get snippy about it."

"I'm not," Jenny told her evenly. "I'm simply making a request." She climbed into the buggy.

"Say, you look familiar." The woman peered at Jenny.

"Yes, I'm told that a lot."

Matthew tipped the brim of his hat at the visitors and joined Jenny. As they pulled away, he couldn't help looking back. "She listened to you."

"You just have to use the right tone."

He sighed. "It happens a lot during tourist season. I don't know why they want to take so many pictures. What is it the *Englisch* find so fascinating about us?"

"I vant to be alone," she said loftily in a bad German accent.

"I apologize, I —"

She laughed and shook her head. "No, it's a quote, something Greta Garbo said."

"I don't know Greta Garbo."

"She was a famous movie star many years ago. She retired at the peak of her career, but people pestered her. So that's what she said. The trouble is, I think the more she wanted to be left alone the more people wanted to approach her."

She tilted her head and studied him. "You know, the fact that Plain People want to be left alone has made others even more curious."

Matthew nodded. "Now we're a tourist attraction."

His tone was so dry she didn't know whether he was being serious or joking. Then he glanced at her and she saw the twinkle in his eyes.

"You know, when I first visited my grandmother it seemed strange to me that she had no photos."

"And what did she say?"

"That not all Amish dislike having their photos taken, but many feel that posing for a picture is an act of pride and it's considered unacceptable."

"Amelia let me take a picture of her," Matthew told her quietly.

"She did?"

"I told her I would never forget her face. But Annie was so small and would never have a memory of her mother. It seemed right to do it. I'll show it to Annie when she's older — the other children, too, if they wish."

Jenny reached over spontaneously to touch his hand, and he turned it over to clasp hers.

"You know how hard it is to lose a mother," he said quietly.

She nodded. "It helped to come here to visit my grandmother after Mom died."

"Perhaps losing your mother and then your father made you more sensitive to the children you film. Many of them are orphans, are they not?" He withdrew his hand and signaled Pilot, his horse, to pull out onto the road.

He's so perceptive, she thought. *So thoughtful.* And never tries to get something from her, the way *Englisch* men might.

142

Funny, she thought. She hadn't been here very long, but already she was thinking of men from her world as *Englisch.*

"Are you hungry?"

"Are you sure you have time? I don't want to take you away from your work."

He spared her a glance. "I would like to share a meal with you, Jenny."

They went to the same restaurant they'd visited with Annie. Although it had been fun to eat with Annie, it was nicer still to sit with Matthew and talk, just the two of them.

"You're awfully quiet," Matthew said as they drove home.

"Just enjoying the ride. You're so lucky to live here. I loved it from the minute I saw it." She watched the passing countryside, wrapped in a mantle of snow. "I don't know which I like better, summer or winter." She sighed. "And I love being with Grandmother again."

The clip-clop of the horse's hooves was hypnotic. Tired from therapy, she found her eyelids drooping.

"Jenny? Jenny, we're home."

She smiled. What a lovely word, said by the man she loved.

"Jenny? You need to wake up. I think you have company."

143

Groaning, unwilling to let go of the pleasant feeling of resting her head against his shoulder, she opened her eyes. What she saw had her straightening so quickly her back protested the movement.

A car bearing a New York tag was parked in front of her grandmother's house.

The driver's side door opened and David stepped out.

"Hey, stranger," he said.

Matthew watched as Jenny dropped her cane and threw her arms around the man. It seemed they held each other for a very long time.

He heard Jenny tell David how she'd missed him and felt a moment of envy. She hadn't been able to remember him when she'd come here.

"Matthew!" David held out his hand. "Good to see you. So were the two of you out for a drive?"

"He took me to a therapy appointment." Jenny shivered. "It's cold out here. Let's get inside and have some coffee."

"And maybe your grandmother baked a pie?" asked David as he reached inside his car for a package.

"Did you come to see me or to have a piece of her pie?" Jenny demanded, hands on her hips.

David grinned. "You know I love you. But that pie I had last time —"

Love. The Englisch *toss that word around so casually,* thought Matthew.

Laughing, Jenny elbowed him and turned to Matthew. "You're coming in, aren't you?"

He hesitated. Surely the two wanted to talk privately.

"Matthew?" Jenny gestured at him. "Come in and have some pie and coffee. We didn't have dessert, remember?"

He heard a buggy approach and lifted his hand in greeting as he saw Josiah passing. But Josiah was staring at David's car, then at him standing with Jenny in the doorway of Phoebe's house. Matthew watched as the older man frowned and then stared directly ahead at the road, ignoring him.

That was the second time in as many days that the man had seemed so dour, so disapproving, thought Matthew. Not that anyone would accuse him of having a sunny personality. But it did seem that Josiah didn't like the presence of Jenny here. Josiah was one of the older, stricter Old Amish members who often complained about the influences of the outside world on their community.

Feeling a little uneasy, Matthew went inside.

"So this time we don't have to carry Ms. Lazy inside, eh?" David asked Matthew.

"Hey, Matthew carried me in last time," she told him tartly.

"She did fall asleep on the way home," Matthew acknowledged. "But I think she can manage to walk this time."

Jenny glanced over her shoulder as she stood at the stove. "You'd be tired if you'd had a session with the therapy tyrant, too!"

She poured coffee for the three of them and then lifted the checkered cloth from a plate on the table. "Dessert, gentlemen?"

"Looks like it has my name on it," David said with satisfaction as he took a seat. "Apple pie is my favorite. I don't suppose there's ice cream?"

Jenny drew a carton from the propane-powered refrigerator-freezer and put scoops of vanilla ice cream on each of the plates. "Of course. It's as though my grandmother knew you were coming."

She stopped and frowned at him. "She didn't, did she?"

"Nope. I was sort of in the neighborhood and thought I'd stop in." David took a bite of the pie and closed his eyes. "Fabulous. Where is your grandmother, by the way?"

"Visiting friends. What does 'sort of in the neighborhood' mean, exactly?" Jenny returned the ice cream to the freezer.

Matthew stood and held out Jenny's chair. As he did, he saw that David was staring at him oddly.

"We're getting a lot of mail about you," David said, taking a sip of coffee. "People want to know how you're doing."

"That's nice." Jenny stirred her coffee.

"How *are* you doing?"

"Much better," she said slowly. "I wrote you that, remember?"

David met her eyes directly. "Yes, but I wasn't sure if you were telling the truth."

"Jenny is a truthful woman," Matthew told him staunchly.

David lifted his eyebrows and looked at him for a long moment. "Yes, well, she also has a tendency to hold things in, to not want to worry people. She kept telling me she would be okay, but when I visited the hospital the first time after she was returned to the States, I was — well, let's just say I was shocked."

Her appearance had shocked Matthew, too, when she first came here and that had been months after she'd been recovering in the hospital, he knew.

"The boss wanted me to stop by, talk with you."

"Really?" Jenny frowned. "I just wrote him

that I wasn't sure when I can come back."

David waved his hand. "Not about that. He wants me to do a story on you. Update the viewers on how you're doing."

Matthew watched her hand come up to touch her cheek, watched her smile fade.

"I can't do that, David."

"Why not? You're looking better. Your speech has really improved, too."

"Would you want to go on —" Emotion made the search for the word harder. "Would you want to go on camera like this?" she asked him as her tears welled up. "*Would* you?"

"A little makeup and a hairstylist and you'd be fine. And your speech is truly better when you speak slowly and don't get upset." He pushed the package he'd brought toward her. "Open it, Jenny."

Jenny did as he asked, drawing out printed e-mail messages and handwritten notes, cards, and letters. She looked at one, then another, and then her lips began trembling.

She stood and grabbed her cane. "I — excuse me." With a jerky gait, she walked out of the room.

Matthew watched her leave, then glanced at David. The man shoved his hands in his hair, disordering the careful style. He had to admit he was a little curious about David's fancy appearance.

"Well, that didn't go well." He looked at Matthew. "I didn't mean to upset her."

"May I?" Matthew asked him, gesturing at the letters.

"Sure."

Matthew read several of the messages. "People really care about her."

David nodded. "Because she cares so much about the children." He sighed. "And because of the way she was hurt. Be glad you didn't see the film of the bomb going off. I've had a few nightmares since I saw it."

"I don't need to see it to know how Jenny has been hurt." Matthew stared down into his coffee, then up at David. "It's hard to understand such hatred."

Just then, Phoebe walked in the door. She brightened when she saw them sitting at the table. "David! How nice to see you. You, too, Matthew."

She hung her outerwear on the peg, then walked to David and gave him a hug.

"Good to see you, too, ma'am. You're looking well."

"Thank you. You look well, too." She moved to pour a cup of coffee, then joined them at the table.

"We were just having a piece of your

wonderful pie."

Phoebe beamed. "Next time let me know you're coming, and I'll bake you one to take home." She glanced around. "Where is Jenny?"

David exchanged a look with Matthew. "I'm afraid I upset her. Our boss wants us to do an interview, let the viewers know how she's doing."

"I see." Phoebe took a sip of her coffee.

"I think she's looking great. But I guess I didn't think about how she'd feel about being on camera."

"Jenny is not a vain young woman," Phoebe said slowly. "But it has been hard for her to reconcile the way she looked and talked before the accident and now."

Sighing, David nodded. "But people are worried about her. They've sent e-mails and letters."

Phoebe's expression softened. "When she thinks about it, I'm sure that Jenny will be grateful for their concern, their caring."

David looked hopeful. "You think she'll change her mind?"

"I —"

Jenny walked in just then. "*Grossmudder,* I didn't hear you come in." She bent to kiss her cheek.

Straightening, she looked at David. Matthew could tell she'd been crying, but now she looked more composed. "I'm sorry for getting upset with you. I — tell Nate I'll think about it, okay?"

"Sure. You just let me know, and we'll bring a crew here —"

"No!" she said quickly. "It wouldn't be right to bring a TV crew here into the community."

"Oh." David glanced at Phoebe. "Sorry, ma'am, didn't mean to offend."

Phoebe patted his hand. "I'm not offended."

"I'll let you know," Jenny told him.

"Great." David glanced at his watch. "Well, I should be going."

"You are not having another piece of pie?" Phoebe asked.

Hesitating, David looked toward the kitchen window. "Looks like it's going to start snowing again."

"I'll wrap it up for you to have later," Phoebe said as she got up.

"One for the road. Works for me," David said with a chuckle. He stood, pulled his coat from a peg, and put it on.

Jenny got to her feet and hugged him for a long moment with her cheek against his shoulder. "I'm so glad you came."

He kissed the top of her head. "Me too,"

he said, and his voice shook.

Then he was hurrying out the door, holding his precious package of pie.

"I should be going, too," Matthew said. "Thank you again for taking me to therapy. And to eat afterward."

Matthew nodded. "I enjoyed it. I enjoyed the pie, too, Phoebe."

"Do you want to take some home?" she asked him.

"No, thank you. That might not please Hannah. You know how hard she works on her baking."

Phoebe watched him fondly as he left. Then she turned to Jenny and her eyes were troubled. "Jenny, there is something we must discuss."

7

Stricken, Jenny stared at her grandmother. "Oh no, shouldn't I have had Matthew and David here without you?"

Phoebe patted her hand. "That is not what I need to tell you." She frowned. "I was driving home and passed Josiah. He is an elder in the church. You may have met him on Sunday?"

Something about the name was familiar. Jenny wondered if he was the man who had frowned at her as she stood on the porch with Matthew.

"I'm not sure. There was this one man who looked disapproving as I stood talking with Matthew after the service. What is it? Does he have a problem with me being here?"

"You are my *grossdochder,*" Phoebe said firmly. "No one in this community would have a problem with me taking care of you in my home. Family is so important, second to our relationship to God."

Confused, Jenny stared at her. "Then what is it?"

"Josiah had two concerns. The first was that you are here to bring the attention of the press to the community."

"But that's the very opposite of what I'd want!" Jenny got up and walked to the window with some difficulty so soon after her therapy, returned and sat again. "I've been here for weeks. If that was what I intended —" then she stopped and stared at her grandmother. "Wait, did you say he stopped you on the road just now?"

Phoebe nodded.

"He went past the house when David was here. But how would he know David works for the media? He doesn't watch television."

"I think you were so happy to see David you didn't notice the sign on his automobile with the network's name," Phoebe told her. "But you have only to look at David to know he is an important man in the *Englisch* world."

Jenny laughed. "Oh, David would love to hear that. But don't tell him. His ego is already so big."

"It's obvious he cares very much about you."

"He treats me like a little sister. And since

I don't have any brothers or sisters, I kind of like that. He and his wife, Joy, are my best friends."

Actually, almost my only friends, since I was out of the country so much, she thought. That was one of the things she liked about being here — she'd begun to make really nice friends.

"He brought you to me so I'll always be grateful to him." Phoebe reached over to squeeze her hand.

Jenny looked at her grandmother's hand, slim and strong and work-worn. "So what should I do to allay Josiah's fear?"

"I think since he's the only one I've heard of who has such a concern that it's enough for me to tell you."

"You're sure?"

"Yes."

"You said Josiah has two concerns. What's the other one?"

"Josiah is concerned that Matthew is spending so much time with you. He worries that Matthew is courting you."

I wish, Jenny thought.

"I can see that you've thought of this yourself."

She sighed. "Yes, but I know it is just a fantasy. Matthew considers me to be a

155

friend and that's what he must be for me, too."

"Why is that?"

"He needs someone who's whole. Someone who can be his partner and help him with the farm. Who can have his — his children."

She rose to put her mug in the sink and turned to face her grandmother.

"I know that you have the *Ordnung,* that there are different rules here, that there is respect for those rules. But Matthew is a grown man. Doesn't he have the right to see who he wants as long as he doesn't violate any rules of propriety?"

"I think some of the older generation worries that we will lose young people like Matthew. His family has been here for generations, and he is well-loved. I might not agree with Josiah, but I understand his concern."

Jenny covered her hand with hers. "Oh, you're thinking of Daddy, aren't you? You can understand because it happened to you."

Phoebe raised her eyes to Jenny's and she saw the emotion in them.

Jenny bent to hug her grandmother. "I'm sorry that this has made you remember."

"I never forget." Phoebe's voice trembled. "But it was not God's will for him to live here. He wasn't happy here as he grew older. I think he needed to see more of the world, to do other things."

"I have been happy here," Jenny whispered. "Very happy."

Phoebe smiled. "I am glad, then, that you've come home to heal."

Her grandmother had said that Jenny didn't need to worry about Josiah, that he was the only one who had approached her with the concern that Jenny would draw media attention.

But it still bothered Jenny; she found herself thinking about it all the next day. If anything, she had come here to heal and had practically been a hermit while she did. She would never have accepted her grandmother's invitation if she'd thought she would cause any kind of problem for her.

Thank goodness I told David I couldn't do an interview here, Jenny thought.

So far as Josiah's concern about Matthew . . . well, maybe she needed to think about that. This was the second time she'd begun to entertain a fantasy about having a relationship with him. Hadn't she learned anything?

Their friendship had deepened since she'd been here — there was no question about that. He understood her in a way no one else ever had at a time when she didn't fully understand herself.

She wasn't going to give up riding with him and Annie to the speech-therapy appointments. After all, no one could say a man was courting when his little daughter was along with them, could they?

And she wasn't going to give up her friendship with him.

Josiah had seen Matthew touching her face. It had been harmless by any standards in her world or Matthew's. But she'd make sure no one saw anything like that again.

Perhaps she should reconsider letting him drive her to physical therapy. Without Annie along, perhaps those who saw them could assume their relationship was more than friendship.

She had to find another ride, and she didn't want to impose on her grandmother. It was time for her to be more independent.

But she was still in too much pain and moved too awkwardly to feel safe driving a car. Even if she could, renting a car was expensive. And it was a long distance for a taxi to come to the farm.

Her grandmother had the perfect solution. "There are a number of *Englisch* who can be hired to drive you. If you're determined to do this," she added. When Jenny nodded, she got up, drew a small address book from a kitchen drawer, and gave it to her.

Jenny called the driver her grandmother had used several times and made her next physical therapy appointment. When she finished, she hung up the phone, turned, walked back into the house, and found her grandmother watching her as she stood at the sink.

"You don't have to do this," she told Jenny. "As you said, it is not the business of others."

"I don't want to make things difficult for you or for Matthew."

"You are not making things difficult for us, child." Phoebe patted her hand. "Don't worry, Jenny. Worry about tomorrow steals the joy from today."

Jenny sighed and nodded. "I know."

She'd already made plans to have dinner with Matthew and his family that evening, so she went. Whether she'd tell him about Josiah would depend on opportunity and need. It wasn't a topic she intended to discuss in front of the children.

Her grandmother gave her a ride, since she was to pick Hannah up so they could visit at a friend's.

When they pulled up, the children were

outside, playing in newly fallen snow.

"It is good to see them like this," Phoebe said to Jenny as they watched. "There was so much sadness here after Amelia died."

Jenny knew, too, that the children led more serious lives than *Englisch* children; there were chores before and after school, and those and homework were never brushed aside in favor of playing on a computer or talking on a phone.

Joshua and Mary were tossing snowballs at each other. Mary had the better aim, and Joshua was running for cover.

Annie was lying in the snow, moving her arms and legs.

"That one is a little angel, is she not?"

The child popped up just then and ran over. "Come see my snow angewl?"

Jenny greeted Hannah as they traded places and exchanged a hug. Phoebe and Hannah waved as the buggy started down the road.

Annie took Jenny's hand and led her over to the snow.

"Very pretty," she told Annie.

"You make one."

Jenny laughed. "I haven't done that in years."

Standing there, she remembered what her grandmother had said about not letting worry about tomorrow steal the joy from today. It was such a beautiful day, clear and crisp and cold. There was a patch of undisturbed snow right beside Annie's snow angel.

Annie looked up at her with big, bright-blue eyes. "You make one," she repeated.

And so, Jenny found herself throwing down the hated cane, lying down in the snow, and moving her arms and legs.

Annie and Jenny giggled together. *It feels so free, so fun, to be like a child,* thought Jenny.

A shadow fell over her, and she looked up to see Matthew smiling.

"Well, well, what is this?"

"Jenny's making a snow angewl, *Daedi.*"

"And a very beautiful one, indeed."

"You haven't seen it yet," Jenny pointed out, feeling her cheeks warm.

"Yes, I have."

Was she blushing? She never blushed. But his eyes were so warm on her.

He held out his hand and helped Jenny to her feet. Then he brushed the snow from her hair.

"Cold?"

She shook her head. No, she didn't feel cold at all anymore, warmed by what she saw in his eyes.

Annie tugged on her coat, and Jenny looked down to see that she held her cane.

"Thank you."

A snowball hit Matthew from behind. Joshua was running away. Since Mary was nowhere in sight, it was obvious who the culprit was.

Matthew scooped up a handful of snow, quickly packed it into ball, and hit him in the legs as he ran.

Joshua collapsed into the snow and lay still.

"Joshua?"

Matthew ran to his son and knelt by his side. Joshua's hand came up with a mound of snow, and he laughed as he scrubbed it over his father's face.

"Why you —" Matthew grabbed him up, turned him upside down, and carried him back to where Jenny and Annie stood.

"Hey, I —" Joshua spluttered as his father casually dragged him through a drift and he got a face full of snow. "I —" he gulped as he hit another drift.

"Daedi!" Annie giggled. "You awe howding Joshua upswide down and his face — his face!"

"Something wrong with his face?"

"He's getting awfully red in the face," Jenny said sternly. But she had to cover her

162

mouth to keep the giggles from escaping.

Matthew turned him right-side-up. "Oh, sorry, Joshua. I didn't realize." But his grin said otherwise.

Out of the corner of her eye, Jenny saw something move. *Splat!* A snowball hit Matthew in the back of the head. He dropped Joshua lightly into a pile of snow and growling, went after Mary.

Joshua sprang up and ran after his father, pelting him with snowballs. Annie joined in the chase, but with every step, she kept sinking in the snow. Matthew tripped — or pretended to trip — and fell. The children tackled him, Joshua first, then Mary, and then Annie.

"Let me up!" Matthew cried out. "You're crushing me!"

But the children just giggled and held on.

"Jenny! Save me!"

"I'll be right there!" she called. Whistling, she tucked her scarf around her neck and adjusted her hat.

"Jenny!"

"Coming!"

Matthew got to his feet like a big lumbering bear covered with snow. Annie wrapped her arms around his neck and hung on. Looping Joshua under one arm and Mary under the other, he staggered toward Jenny who stood laughing near the road.

"You didn't help."

"You look like the abominable snowman!" she gasped. Her sides hurt from laughing so much.

Throwing back his head, he roared and shook himself. "I am eating all of you for dinner!"

Mary shrieked. "Let go of me! I need to check dinner in the oven."

Matthew considered that. "Well, maybe I won't eat the skinny one."

He set her on her feet, and she scampered into the house, laughing.

"If you eat me there will be no one to help you with the farm work," Joshua told him.

"Well, there is that." Matthew dropped him into the snow.

Laughing, Joshua got up, shook himself like a dog, and ran into the house.

Matthew turned his head to look at Annie who was still hanging on around his neck. "Then I must have you for my dinner," he said, and he growled again and nipped at her hand. "Mmm, very sweet. Like one of your *Aenti* Hannah's doughnuts."

"Jenny, save me!" Annie cried, giggling.

"Even monsters must eat their dinner before they have dessert," Jenny said sternly. "Mr. Abominable, behave yourself."

164

"But I want to eat dessert now!"

Jenny shook her finger at him. "You must obey the rules!"

He set Annie down but shook the snow from his hair and his coat onto her. "Run inside and get ready for dinner." He put his hands on his hips and growled down at her. "I cannot wait for dessert!"

Giggling, Annie stumbled twice, then ran into the house and slammed the door.

"It was three to one," Matthew told Jenny as he walked toward her. "You couldn't help me?"

Jenny shrugged and gestured toward her cane. "Well, you know I'm a bit incognito —" she stopped. That wasn't the word. "Incapacitated right now."

"Then maybe I should take a few bites of you to tide me over until dinner." He stood close, so close, then he bent down and their breaths, puffy warm clouds in the cold air, mingled.

"I —" Jenny saw the three faces pressed against the windowpane. She drew back. "We should get inside. The children."

Matthew glanced toward the house, then back at her. "Jenny —"

"I'm cold, can we go inside?" she asked quickly, and before he could answer, she moved toward the door.

"Jenny!"

She thought she could avoid him in the house where children surrounded them, but Matthew simply bided his time.

Halfway through dinner, they heard a ringing coming from Jenny's purse hanging from the peg by the door.

"I'll get that for you," Mary said, jumping up and bringing Jenny's purse to her.

"Is it your cell phone?" Joshua wanted to know.

"Yes, Joshua." Reaching inside her purse, Jenny checked the display, then set the ringer on vibrate. She looked at Matthew. "I'm sorry. I forgot it was in my purse."

"Do you need to speak to the person calling?"

She shook her head. "It's just David. He was to call me about arrangements for New York City. To do the interview next week. I'll call him later."

"You're going so soon?"

"Is it one of the iPhones?" Joshua asked. "Can we see it?"

"No, Joshua, eat your supper," his father responded firmly.

"I'm sorry," Jenny said again.

Matthew looked at her. "It's all right, Jenny."

He turned to Joshua. "How is it you know about this *Englisch* device?"

"Everyone does," he said, his eyes on his plate.

There was silence at the table. Matthew frowned. Although Jenny said she was just going back for the interview, he feared she would stay there. He watched her push food around on her plate with her fork. Once or twice she looked guiltily at Joshua, as if she felt she had gotten him into trouble.

"Mary, tell Jenny how you did on the essay she helped you with."

"I got an A."

"That's wonderful!"

Conversation started again. The children were full of questions about New York City. They were curious about the world Jenny had lived in before she came to stay with her grandmother.

Tonight, though, Jenny seemed to give them quick answers and then change the subject. Sometimes it even seemed that she looked to Matthew first, before she answered.

"Now you get to eat dessert, monstewr," Annie told him as she helped clear the dishes.

Matthew bent to loop his arm around her waist and pull her toward him. He nibbled at her neck. "Mmm, very good dessert."

Annie giggled and tried to pull away. "Monstewr is not going to eat Annie."

He pretended to look disappointed.

"But we made pie. You wike pie," she added.

"What kind?"

"Pumpkin."

"With ice cream?"

Smiling, Mary went to get it. "Of course."

Matthew let go of Annie. "I'll have the pie."

Annie just giggled and went to hand the dishes to Joshua to put into the sink.

The children ate their dessert, then excused themselves to finish their chores.

Matthew poured coffee for himself and Jenny, and they sat at the kitchen table just as they'd done so many other nights.

"How long will you be gone?"

"A few days."

Matthew felt relief course through him.

Jenny covered a yawn with her hand. "I'm sorry. I'm a little tired."

"What did you do today?"

She shrugged. "Not much."

"When is your next physical therapy appointment?"

"Next week."

"You don't have one this week?"

Jenny nodded. "I went today."

"I would have driven you."

"I know. But I feel like I'm taking you away from your work."

"Jenny. You know I don't mind. In fact, I enjoy the time talking with you and sharing a meal. But maybe you don't feel the same?"

She met his eyes. "You know I enjoy being with you."

He reached to touch her hand but withdrew when Joshua came in to get a glass of water.

"Being in a car was good for one thing today," Jenny said when Joshua left the kitchen. She told him what had happened when David drove her here that first night, how the time overseas in the war-torn country had made her fear if the car stopped, they could be victims of a bomb.

"Maybe I had enough distance from the wars overseas, or the landscape was different enough," she said. "I was awake, not half-asleep from painkillers as I was that day when David was driving. Whatever the reason, I was all right riding in a car."

She looked at Matthew. "It's important because one day I'll be going driving or riding in cars, not riding in buggies."

"You were in a war?"

Startled, Jenny saw that Joshua and Mary

were standing in the doorway, listening. Biting her lip, Jenny looked to Matthew and he nodded, giving her permission to answer Joshua.

"Yes, I was. But I wasn't fighting or hurting people."

She thought for a moment, trying to figure out how to explain what she did to them. This was such a different place, without much knowledge of the bad things in the world. And the children were so innocent.

"I was there to send film — pictures — back to people here so they could see what was happening to children where there is war."

"Is that where you got hurt?"

"Yes." Again, she looked to Matthew. She wasn't sure how much he wanted them to know.

"A bad person hurt Jenny," Matthew said quietly. "He thought if he did, she wouldn't be able to tell people."

Matthew immediately was sorry for what he had said when he saw the stricken look cross her face.

"He won," she whispered so softly he almost didn't hear her.

"What did you tell people about the children?" Mary wanted to know as she and Joshua came to stand near them.

"Matthew?" Now she looked even more upset than she had before. "I know that you try to stay separate from my world. I would not bring it here to your children."

From the time he had invited Jenny into his home, Matthew knew that the time might come when his children would learn more of the ways of her world than he wished. He could have avoided her to keep it from happening. But he had been drawn to her again, just as he had years before, and his feelings for Jenny had made him want to be close to her, to be with her. She was a good person, a loving person. He could tell that she was in distress that she might say the wrong thing to them.

"Tell them, Jenny," he said finally. "They know that the *Englisch* world has war and many bad things."

"There are many good things, too, but yes, there is war and it's horrible." She stared down into her coffee. "Children sometimes lose a parent, even both of them. Sometimes their grandparents and aunts and uncles. Even their sisters and brothers. They don't have their homes when they're destroyed."

She lifted her eyes. "But the hardest thing was seeing they didn't have enough to eat."

"We could send them some food," Mary said. "We have lots of food."

171

Jenny smiled and hugged her. "That's very sweet. There are people who are doing that, sweetheart, helping the children."

"Are they going to stop the wars?" Joshua wanted to know.

"They're trying."

Mary stood closer to Matthew. "Why does God let these things happen, *Daedi?*"

Jenny stared at the girl. It had been her question, too, one she had asked so often.

Matthew put his arm around her and hugged her close. "I know that it's hard to understand why God would allow bad things to happen, especially to children. But the Bible tells us that God allows free will. He allows people to do as they wish even if it is not what He would have them do."

The children seemed satisfied with his explanation.

Annie stumbled in, rubbing her eyes. "Mary? Read me a stowy?"

Hannah walked in the door. "Jenny, your grandmother is here to take you home."

Matthew rose to help Jenny with her coat. "I'd like to speak with you," he said in a low tone. "Can I come by tomorrow?"

"I —" Jenny looked past him and saw Hannah and the children watching them. How could she refuse? "Yes, sure."

172

■ ■ ■ ■

Jenny wasn't surprised when Matthew came the next day just as he'd said he would. Her grandmother's friends were visiting in the living room so when he suggested they go for a drive so they could talk. Jenny agreed.

"Just say it," she told him, staring straight ahead.

Matthew stared at her. "What is it that you expect me to say?"

"I'm an outsider here, Matthew. I know that. I've tried not to offend. I didn't come to expose your children to everything you've worked to protect them from."

"Jenny! What are you talking about?"

She turned and looked at him. "Be honest, Matthew. You didn't have reservations about them being around me?"

"We're careful with our children," he said slowly. "We want to hold them safe. But even if I had reservations, they were gone after the first time I saw you again. I saw then that you hadn't changed from the person I knew."

"But you were different last night. You were upset with Joshua for being curious about my cell phone and you were sharp with him. Then you looked unhappy when

173

the children asked me so many questions about New York City."

"Jenny —"

"And then —" she stopped, touching her fingertips to her lips to make them stop trembling. She looked back at the road ahead. "And then to have them ask about things like war and children being hungry . . . I didn't want to tell them about all that."

He frowned. "I'd prefer to protect them from all that. It's what any parent wishes, isn't it? Plain or *Englisch?*"

"Of course. I understand."

"I'm not upset with Joshua or you, Jenny. Believe me. I'm sorry if you sensed my disapproval last night. I was . . . well, I have a lot on my mind right now, some things to work out for myself."

"It's okay. Listen, I need to get back home. Can you take me back home, please?"

"You were quilting?" he asked, surprised.

"Yes — no. I — I just need to do some things."

Matthew reached over to touch her hand and she stared at him, surprised.

"Jenny, it's such a wonderful day. Come, let's enjoy it. There aren't many days before you leave for New York City."

Is it an attempt at a truce? she wondered,

174

gazing at him. She told herself she shouldn't go. But as she saw the sincerity in his eyes, felt the pressure on her hand, she found herself saying yes.

When she'd first come here, Jenny had felt that buggies were quaint and she'd chafed a little at how hard getting around was without the mass transportation she'd grown accustomed to in New York City.

Yet buggies had helped to protect the Amish community, she'd come to realize. You could only go so far and then you needed to let your horse rest, eat, and get some water. There was no jumping into a car when you were mad and driving for miles and miles away from your family, friends, and problems. Like the prohibition of electricity that kept out television, the buggy helped keep the community inclusive, safe from negative outside influence from the *Englisch* world.

But now as they drove along back roads, the slow pace, the repetitive clip-clop of the horse's hooves was soothing. Jenny felt her tension melt away like the snow melting beside the road. Matthew talked about the homes and farms and sights they passed, waved to people he knew, some Jenny had met. Talk became easier between them, and by the time they turned toward her grand-mother's home, she began to feel that things were back to normal.

When they pulled up in front of the house, though, Jenny saw several men getting into buggies.

"I wonder why those church elders were here?" Matthew mused.

Jenny closed her eyes, then opened them. "I think I know. I'll talk to you later, okay?"

He hesitated.

"Please, can we talk later?"

He nodded and let her go.

Phoebe looked up from washing coffee cups at the sink. "Did you have a nice drive?"

"Josiah talked to the elders, didn't he? I saw them leaving."

Phoebe wiped her hands on a towel and turned to face Jenny. "Yes. I didn't think he would take it this far, but I was wrong."

8

Jenny sat down. "Why am I afraid to hear why they were here?"

Phoebe brought them mugs of tea and pushed a plate of freshly baked cookies toward her. Jenny took the tea but had no appetite for cookies.

"They're concerned that you're here to do a story for your network."

Jenny laughed and then she just couldn't seem to stop. She covered her face with her hands, then dropped them and stared at her grandmother. "How can they think that? Look at me."

"Jenny, Jenny, Jenny," Phoebe said, shaking her head. "You are a beautiful young woman who has so much heart and so much intelligence. But you are so much more aware of your scars than anyone else. And your speech is improving by the day."

Her eyes filling with tears, Jenny shook her head. "And I have you to thank for helping me with the speech therapy." She sighed. "Oh, you are such a wonderful grandmother. But you see me differently than others do."

Phoebe shook her head. "You worry too much. But as to the elders, you need to remember that they don't know you as I do. They see people of the media as a threat to the Plain People, to our community."

"I understand that. I really do. A tourist was obnoxious with Matthew and me after a therapy appointment once," Jenny said. She told her grandmother what had happened.

"Josiah saw David here, and as you said, he represents something that Josiah fears — the *Englisch* bringing their curiosity, their technology, their money, which seems to enthrall our young," Phoebe said.

"And yet there are so many *Englisch* who are enthralled by the simplicity and spirituality of your life," Jenny pointed out. She stirred her tea but didn't drink it. "I told David that he can do a story about how I'm recovering. Thank goodness I made it really clear that he can't bring a crew here."

"Where will it be then?"

"I'm going to New York City next week. I'll be gone a few days."

She finally took a sip of her tea and found

it cold. Getting up, she dumped the contents of her mug in the sink, then went to the stove for hot water.

"David knew what to do to make me — say yes — agree," she corrected herself. "He brought mail the network had received that showed me viewers were concerned about me." She laughed and shook her head. "David is so smart. He knew showing me was better than telling me."

"That's it, Jenny!" Phoebe cried. "You have your answer of how you can reassure the elders!"

Jenny blinked. "I do?"

Her grandmother went into her bedroom and returned with a big notebook. Sitting at the table again, she opened the book. "I told you when you first came here that I enjoyed the letters you sent me from overseas."

"How can my letters reassure the elders?"

Phoebe drew out a big manila envelope. "Our talk of the letters reminded me of something else."

She pulled several printed sheets from the envelope. "Although I had no television, I found a way to know what you did. I liked the letters you wrote from overseas about the children the best, but I found the ones where you talked about your friends at work to be so entertaining. You wrote such funny things about David."

She handed Jenny the printed sheets with the air of bearing a great gift.

"These are transcripts of my segments on the network."

"Yes, when I wrote David that I didn't have a television but wished to know what you did, he sent them."

"How will these convince them?"

"It's said that a man is known by his deeds," Phoebe told her. "They can see from these the type of work you do — these show you do stories about children. They speak loudly, don't you think?"

"You think that this will help?"

Phoebe nodded.

"Then I'll do it."

Hannah came to get Phoebe the next day. Since she was early and Phoebe was still dressing, Jenny invited her inside.

Acting as hostess for her grandmother, Jenny offered Hannah a seat and tea or coffee. But after taking a seat, Hannah shook her head, refusing the refreshment, and regarded Jenny with a frown. *Brother and sister look so much alike,* she thought. Especially when they frowned.

"Matthew says that you are going to New York City in a few days."

180

"Yes."

"But I thought you liked it here."

"I do. I just have to take care of some business."

"So you're going back to work then?"

Jenny shook her head as she sat at the table. "No, I'm not ready for that yet."

"But you will one day?"

Shifting in her chair, Jenny glanced in the direction of her grandmother's room, willing her to appear quickly. Matthew had said he often teased his sister for her direct way with conversation. She always had a point, he told Jenny, and he had to just wait to find out what it was.

"I'm not sure what the future holds," Jenny said quietly.

"There's been talk about your work. Some say you've been an important *Englisch* woman, that you've been on television."

Jenny wasn't surprised at the interest. She often experienced it in her world. "I just do my job."

"And it's an important one."

"No more than anyone else's."

"You are being humble, Jenny. Phoebe has shown me the papers about what you do."

"The children are the important ones," Jenny said quietly.

"I have seen for myself how you love

them." Hannah said. "And Matthew's *children* love you. Perhaps one day God will bless you with some of your own."

Jenny bit her lip. "Perhaps." The doctors hadn't held out much hope, but that was personal. She didn't want to share such information with Hannah.

When she saw the other woman hesitating, Jenny sighed. Was there yet another person who was upset with her?

"Hannah, do you have something you want to say to me?"

The woman nodded. "I was concerned that Matthew seemed unhappy when I came home last night."

"I know." It had hurt when she felt Matthew was upset with her. "We talked today," she said finally.

Hannah brightened. "Then you have fixed what is between you."

Before Jenny could respond, her grandmother entered the room. "Hannah, you're here early."

"Yes, I wanted to talk to Jenny. Are you ready to go?"

Phoebe pulled on her coat. "Jenny, are you sure you wouldn't like to go with us?"

"No, but thank you. I have some things to do." She sighed inwardly. It was the same excuse she'd given Matthew so that she could be alone.

But as the two women walked out, she thought how that hadn't worked then and it hadn't worked now. Picking up her mug of tea, she went to her room. If anyone else came to the house, she would pretend she wasn't home.

Of course she got over her mood.

And since she was leaving in a couple of days, Jenny knew she had to talk to the elders before she left. She didn't want them to be any more concerned than they were. If they heard that she had gone to New York City, they might worry that she would return with a film crew. So she took the list of names and addresses and mailed notes asking the elders to visit to talk.

The morning of the visit, she and her grandmother frosted a freshly baked cake — something to offer the men with their coffee. Well, her grandmother baked the cake. Jenny had little experience in the kitchen and figured that it would be very bad if her baking accidentally made the elders sick.

"I wish I knew how to cook," she told her grandmother.

"You don't know?"

Jenny shook her head, watching as Phoebe

creamed butter and sugar. "Mom didn't want anyone in her kitchen. And she felt I should be studying." She shrugged. "It's not as important these days with people eating out so much. There's a *lot* of eating out. Microwaving. That sort of thing."

"Eating out is not cheap."

"I agree."

Phoebe sifted flour in a bowl. "And this *microwaving.* What is it?"

"I don't understand how it works, but it's the closest thing to putting food in a magic box where it cooks quickly. Very quickly."

Phoebe shook her head in wonder. "Imagine."

"But nothing it makes has ever tasted like your cooking. I think it's because the microwave doesn't use love when it cooks as you do." She hugged her. "Thank you for helping me today."

Phoebe patted Jenny's cheek. "You'll be fine. I'm sure you've had similar situations, have you not?"

"Well, yes," Jenny admitted. "I have had to use some persuasion to be allowed to go into places to see the children, to have a crew film them."

She looked down at her outfit, the slim tunic sweater and long wool skirt she'd worn that first Sunday. "And I don't dress

'American' when I go to countries where women are more covered."

She looked at the table set with coffee cups and plates and silverware. Smoothed napkins and took a last look at the cake. Not a bad frosting job she'd done, if she did say so herself.

"I think everything's ready," she told her grandmother.

"Well, there's one more thing we can do. We can pray."

Jenny took a deep breath and nodded. "Wonderful idea."

The men came after the noon meal, filing in silently and purposefully.

They took off their coats and wide-brimmed felt hats. Everyone sat at the table in the homey kitchen, where Jenny served them coffee and cake.

Two men Jenny hadn't met accompanied Josiah. To her relief, they didn't seem stern or judgmental as Josiah did.

"I wanted to talk to all of you about Josiah's concerns," Jenny said, looking at each of them in turn. "I came here because when I woke up injured in the hospital, I was covered with a quilt that my grandmother had sent for me."

She pressed her lips together, trying not

185

to become too emotional; it was important to stay calm, to stay focused. "I felt I was wrapped in home. All I wanted to do was come here and heal in a place where I had been so happy many years ago."

"You were involved in a war," Josiah said with a frown.

"I didn't fight in a war," she told him. "I went there so that I could show people what war was doing to the children, the —" she paused, struggling for the right word — "innocent children."

"Do the people who watch television care about such things?"

Jenny nodded. "There are many things on television that not only the Plain People think are inappropriate, but also the *Englisch.* But sometimes, one of the good things on television can be a news program. I know that the media has at times been intrusive here, just as the tourists have been. But some of the networks, like the one I work, for show problems around the world that need to be addressed."

"If the *Englisch* took care of themselves and didn't interfere elsewhere, things might be better," Josiah stated emphatically.

"Perhaps. But there are those who would do bad things and hide what they are doing to the innocent — especially to the children.

They're being maimed, killed, starved. Often orphaned."

She paused. "It's difficult to show you what I do since there's no television here. All I have are written accounts from several of the shows I did. And some articles I wrote for a newspaper. I hope that you'll read them and know better what I do."

"Even if we concede that the work you do is worthy, that is not to say that you won't feel a need to show your world something you think needs to be improved in ours," a man named Benjamin said, sitting back in his chair and stroking his bristly beard.

"I'm here to heal from my injuries," she said quietly. "When I first came, I had trouble walking and talking."

Her hand went to the scar on her face. "I know that the Plain People think the *Englisch* are fancy and too concerned with appearances, with the shallow and not the spiritual. And maybe you're right. But even if I wanted to go on the air, I feel that many people would be paying so much attention to how I still look and sound that they would miss any message I might have."

Phoebe made a sound and Jenny turned to her with a smile. "I'm sorry that I upset you when I say that. But it's true."

She got up to serve more coffee and felt

their eyes on her moving slowly with the use of her cane. For once she didn't mind because it just emphasized her words. She hadn't done it deliberately, she had just felt the tension and needed to move.

"But let me tell you why David, the man who works at the network, came to see me the other day," she said as she sat down again. "Months ago, the network reported on how a car bomber came after me and they showed the film that was being shot at the time. People have been writing to say they're worried about how I'm recovering. David wants to interview me and show them that I'm doing well." She laughed, but it wasn't a sound of humor. "Or let's say as well as can be expected. Anyway, I told him that he couldn't do this here, that I didn't want the community upset in any way with such an intrusion."

Her hip was really hurting, not just from sitting but maybe also from the tension she was feeling. There was no way, though, that she would show any discomfort to the men; she didn't want them to think she was manipulating their sympathy. "What I'm going to do is return to New York City so that David can film the interview there."

She looked at each of the men to try to judge whether she was reaching them. "I felt very peaceful returning here. Like I was coming home. Some of you may remember me spending summers here as a teenager with my grandmother."

"I remember your father," Josiah said, frowning. "He rejected life here."

Jenny nodded. "I know it can seem that way. Although he didn't choose to be baptized and stay here he didn't forget God. Daddy made sure that we went to church, and I grew to love God the way he did."

She looked at her grandmother. "My father let me come here for two summers to be with my grandmother, to know the life here. He even encouraged my studying German in school. I grew up to respect your way of life from him, not to show it —" she stopped, fighting for the word — "disrespect." She paused.

"You know, some people see only the difference in clothing, in the way you live without what they see as conveniences. I know that it's about wanting to stay separate, for your desire to live your lives according to your religious principles. To do the best for your family."

She drew a breath. "I've done a lot of talking today," she said. "Do you have any questions?"

"What about you and Matthew?" Josiah

wanted to know.

Jenny straightened. "Whether Matthew is a friend or if he is something more is between us," she said quietly but with dignity.

"Not when you behave as you did Sunday."

Stunned, Jenny stared at him. "I don't know what you mean."

"The two of you were standing outside, standing close. And he had his hand on your face."

Now she remembered. How could he twist something so innocent? "He merely touched my face to get me to look at him, to talk about why I was standing outside when it was so cold. He thought someone might have hurt my feelings at the service. It was a gesture of concern, not inappropriate flirting."

"Did you not feel welcome with the women?" asked Isaac, his eyes intent on her.

Gesturing at her cane, Jenny shook her head. "It wasn't that. I felt in the way because I can't move as well as I should."

"All in God's time, child," said Phoebe. "There is a time and a season and a reason."

"Wise words," Benjamin agreed, nodding. "When are you going back to your home?"

Josiah asked abruptly, not sounding friendly at all.

Sighing inwardly, Jenny tried to smile. "I'm not sure. I'm still healing, and I'm on a leave of absence from work."

Isaac shuffled together the papers she'd given him. "I will read these tonight. I'm glad we had this talk," he said as he stood. "Benjamin?"

The other man nodded. "I'll do so as well." He turned to smile at Phoebe. "Thank you for your hospitality, Phoebe. No one bakes a cake like you."

"Jenny helped," she said, smiling at her.

Not much, thought Jenny.

They left and when Jenny turned to clear the table she saw that Josiah had left his papers. She sighed.

Phoebe patted her back. "You cannot please everyone, Jenny. You know that."

Jenny nodded. "I did the best I could." She reached for her grandmother's hand and squeezed it. "Thank you for helping me."

"You're *willkumm,* dear one."

Jenny thought later about the conversation in the kitchen.

Not the conversation with the elders — the one with her grandmother about cooking. It seemed every woman here was a good cook. Even Matthew's daughters knew how to cook with their aunt's help.

She thought about how things had gotten awkward the other night when her cell phone had rung during dinner and Matthew had been stern with Joshua about his interest. How things had become strained that night between her and Matthew.

"Could I cook supper and invite Matthew and his children to eat with us here?" she asked her grandmother as they spent a quiet afternoon reading before a crackling fire.

"That would be wonderful," Phoebe said, beaming.

"I don't cook much, but I know how to follow a recipe." She bit her lip. "But I would like to make the meal myself, if you don't mind?"

"Whatever you wish. There's a ham I was going to bake tonight, but we can save it for tomorrow if you'd like to make something else."

"No, that sounds good. And it's not hard to do, is it?"

"It's very easy."

Jenny went to look at supplies. Her grandmother kept an extensive pantry and the refrigerator and freezer were filled as well, unlike those in her kitchen back home in

New York City. She found paper and a pencil and began making a menu.

Baked ham and a pan of scalloped potatoes, she decided. It was a good, hearty winter meal, one that could go into the oven while you did other things. And baking them would heat the kitchen and make it smell wonderful, which was a big plus. There was plenty of cake left. But that would be coasting on her grandmother's work. So what, then, for dessert?

She'd noticed Matthew liked apples and the children loved oatmeal cookies. What was that dish that used apples and cinnamon and oatmeal?

"Apple crisp," Phoebe told her when she asked.

The only thing left was a vegetable. Maybe some canned vegetables which would require just a quick warm-up. She wrote that down.

"Looks like a tasty *nachtesse*," her grandmother said when Jenny showed her the list. "Have you made all of these things before?"

Jenny chewed on the pencil. "Well, no, but I think I can do it. I saw your recipe box. Could I look in it?"

Phoebe smiled and fetched it, placing it in front of her.

"I guess I just need to invite my guests to

dinner, then." Jenny set down the pencil and wondered if she should use the telephone in the shanty to call them. The call was for a purpose, not idle chatter, so she could use it. But she still felt she wanted to make the invitation in person.

She pulled on her coat, muffler, hat, and gloves. "I'm going to walk over and invite them."

Then, just as she started to open the door, she glanced back. "I don't suppose you'd take my suggestion to put your feet up and be a lady of leisure for an afternoon, would you?"

Phoebe tilted her head and considered that. "No," she decided with a smile. "But perhaps I will cut some more pieces for my quilt."

"I guess that's as close as *you* get to not doing anything," Jenny said with a chuckle.

Moving carefully, she walked to Matthew's house. Her knock was immediately answered by Hannah.

"Is Matthew home?"

"He's in the barn. Shall I get him for you?"

"No, I'll go out there, if you don't mind."

Hannah nodded. "Of course."

Jenny opened the door to the barn. The air inside smelled of hay and horses. Matthew looked up in surprise as she stepped inside. "Hi."

He walked toward her, the bridle he'd been repairing forgotten in his hand.

"Hello. What brings you here today?"

"I want to invite you and the children and Hannah to supper. Will you come?"

"I heard *Englisch* women don't cook much."

"I take . . . offense at that," she said, grinning. "Okay, many of us don't cook as much as Amish women. But most of us work outside the home these days, remember?" Actually, many Amish women these days did so as well, but Matthew didn't correct her on that. And she almost added that she often worked out of the country, in remote locations. But that would sound too defensive and besides, she seldom cooked even with her state-of-the-art kitchen.

"Yes, we would love to come."

Letting out a sigh of relief, she smiled. "Good. I'll go ask Hannah."

"I could tell her."

"No, she should get her own invitation. Can you come at six?"

"We'll be there."

Jenny stopped back by the house and invited Hannah, who couldn't have looked more surprised. "You haven't started supper yet, have you?" When Hannah shook her head, Jenny grinned. "Great. See you at six."

Cooking in her grandmother's kitchen was an adventure. The oven was nothing like the one at home. Well, she'd only used the appliances that were the latest stainless-steel design a couple of times; mostly she used the microwave. But it seemed like this older model white stove that ran on gas wasn't heating well. Each time she checked inside it, it didn't seem warm. Getting out the ham, she put it in a pan, scored the fat on top the way she'd seen her grandmother do, and set it into the oven.

Next came the scalloped potatoes. Jenny considered it a success when she only nicked herself twice peeling them. *Battle* scars, she told herself determinedly and worked more carefully as she sliced the potatoes. Once she was past peeling and slicing, the process was simple. She buttered the baking dish, layering the potatoes and dotting them with butter. Then she poured in the milk and carefully set the pan in the oven next to the ham.

That done, she glanced at the time to figure out when to check them. The vegetable was easy — there were rows upon rows of glass jars filled with brightly colored vegetables that had been canned during the height of their summer goodness. The canned tomatoes looked really good.

Jenny eyed the basket of apples. More peeling. Maybe it was time to think of another dessert. She flipped through her grandmother's recipe file but decided that other than the peeling, this was a simple dessert. So she sat down and peeled and peeled, then mixed the cinnamon and sugar and oatmeal and nuts for the crunchy topping.

"Mmm, it's smelling good in here," Phoebe said as she walked in.

Jenny checked the time. "I think I'll stop for a cup of tea. Will you join me?"

"Sounds good."

They sat in the comfortable kitchen, surrounded by more mess than her grandmother usually made when preparing a meal, and drank their tea.

"You seem to be enjoying yourself."

"I am," Jenny said, a little surprised at her own admission. "I don't usually have the time to do this. And honestly, it's just easier to pop something in the microwave."

"We need to feed ourselves first," Phoebe said. "And not just with food. Women are the nurturers, the caregivers. We need to have time to go to God in prayer, to find a quiet moment for ourselves, to take good care of ourselves, or we can't be there for others. Cooking is nurturing."

"True." Jenny got up to check on the ham and potatoes. "I thought I would put the apple crisp in when I take the other things out of the oven."

Phoebe nodded. "Would you like me to set the table?"

"Absolutely not. You go back to your quilting and let me take care of things. Tonight, you're a guest in your own home."

Jenny set the table and then checked on the ham and potatoes again. Funny, they weren't getting done as fast as they should. She turned the temperature up and went to change.

When she returned to the kitchen a little later, she took another look in the oven. Things were progressing better, she saw. Then she realized she hadn't thought about bread or rolls. She didn't want to use the loaf her grandmother had made that day, just as she hadn't wanted to use the cake because someone else had made it. But there wasn't time for bread to rise.

Once again she consulted the recipe box. Biscuits. They were simple and quick. She never helped her grandmother make them as she had bread, but the recipe didn't seem much different. In fact, it looked easy.

Getting out a big bowl, she sifted flour and baking powder, then cut in the shortening. The recipe said to stir in just enough milk to wet the ingredients, form a ball, knead the dough, then roll it out. Jenny kneaded the dough vigorously for a few minutes before rolling it out. She cut the dough in rounds and placed them on the tray. The whole process took longer than she thought it would. When she opened the oven, she was horrified. The ham was burned in places on top, and the potatoes looked awfully dry. She pulled them both out and put them on top of the stove.

She wanted to cry.

"I smell something burning —" Phoebe stopped in the doorway. "Oh." She walked in and hugged Jenny. "Now don't be upset. Everybody has a time like this. Sometimes lots of times like this. It's how you learn. We can fix it."

They cut off the burned places on the ham, coated it with a honey glaze, then used toothpicks to stick store-bought canned pineapple all over it. The dry potatoes got some cream and extra dots of butter.

"Just turn down the oven and put them back in for a little while longer."

"Oh." Jenny pressed her fingers to her lips.

"I turned the oven up when things weren't getting done."

"Then you didn't check to see how things were going?"

"I got busy making the biscuits." She eyed her grandmother who was pressing her lips together, trying not to laugh.

Phoebe brushed the flour from Jenny's cheek as she chuckled. "You always were impatient."

"I know." Jenny put the biscuit bowl in the sink and looked again at the time. "Everyone will be here in a few minutes. I can't wait."

9

As Jenny welcomed them into the kitchen, Matthew couldn't help noticing the faint burnt odor on the air. He glanced at Hannah, who, he saw, had noticed the same thing. She shot him a warning look. He knew he'd teased her a lot about her cooking when she first started. Her look told him not to do that with Jenny.

Fortunately, Jenny didn't see their exchange. She was too busy receiving exuberant hugs from the children, especially Annie.

"It smells good," said Mary, the family diplomat, as she took off her coat.

"I'm *hungerich*," Joshua told her. "I can't wait to eat what you've made, Jenny."

Annie tugged on Jenny's skirt. "Did you make Thrwee Beawr Soup?"

"Oh, no, I don't know how to make that. Maybe you can tell me how to make it sometime?"

Sometime. Matthew wondered when that would be. He still believed that when she went to New York City she would not return.

After all, it had happened before, hadn't it?

"Jenny, it was so nice of you to invite us to supper," Hannah said as she and the family took their seats.

"It was about time," said Jenny. "I've lost count of how many times you've had me to supper at your home."

Hannah smiled. "The children loved helping with the cooking on the nights you came." She gazed at them fondly. "They are always good helpers, but those nights they wanted things to be special."

"That's so sweet," Jenny said.

Matthew could see that Jenny was affected by his sister's words. Her eyes grew bright with tears as she turned back to the oven. When he saw her set her cane aside so that she could lift the ham's platter, he jumped up and tried to take it from her.

"She wouldn't let me help her," Phoebe warned Matthew.

"Jenny, please," he said quietly.

Their eyes met. After a long moment, Jenny nodded and relinquished the platter. As she did, she caught Phoebe and Hannah exchanging a glance. Before she could wonder about it, Matthew held out his hands for the big casserole of scalloped potatoes.

When all of the food was on the table, Jenny smiled at her guests. "I hope you like it. I don't cook much." She laughed self-deprecatingly. "Mary probably knows more about cooking than I do."

Mary straightened and sent Jenny a smile. "I like to cook."

"She makes good Thrwee Beawr Soup," Annie volunteered.

"It's vegetable soup," Joshua leaned over and whispered to Jenny. "Annie was sick one day and wouldn't eat so *Daedi* called it that."

Jenny looked at Matthew and her heart warmed. He really loved his children. And it was so obvious they loved him.

"Matthew, would you say the blessing?"

They bent their heads and as he spoke, his voice was rich and warm with praise for God's abundance. Then everyone was piling food on plates.

"Oh, I almost forgot the biscuits," she said, getting up. She wished she'd had time to sample one. They didn't seem light and fluffy like her grandmother's, though she had used her recipe. She brought the basket lined with a checkered napkin and filled with biscuits to the table. "Joshua, why don't you take one and pass the basket?"

He did as she asked but the biscuit he lifted from the basket slipped from his fingers and landed with a big *Clunk!* on his plate. Picking it up, he tried to pull it apart.

Matthew didn't need to look in Hannah's direction to see that she was watching. He took a biscuit when the basket was passed to him and used a knife to split it open so he could butter it. Then he handed half to Joshua and took a bite from the half he kept. The biscuit was hard as a rock. He prayed that his teeth wouldn't crack.

"Delicious," he said, crunching away.

Jenny served Annie a small slice of the ham and cut it up for her. Then she put a spoonful of potatoes on the child's plate. Looking around, she made sure her guests filled their plates and had begun eating before she put food on hers. She tried to open her biscuit, then did as Matthew had and cut it open. It should have easily separated in the middle like Phoebe's. Instead, it was a hard lump. Her heart sank.

She buttered it and took a bite. It was hard as a rock. Looking around the table, she saw the family gamely eating theirs. A lot of loud crunching was going on.

Picking up the basket, she passed it to Joshua sitting on one side of her.

"Oh, no, thank you," Joshua said. "I haven't finished my first one yet. But it's very *gut*."

"It's very awful," she disagreed, smiling wryly. "Put it back in the basket, please, then pass it along so everyone else can do the same."

Joshua looked to his father, and only when he got his nod did he put his biscuit back into the basket. Then he passed it along as Jenny had requested. When the basket was handed to her, she went to the door, opened it, and threw the biscuits out.

"Maybe there's some wild animal desperate enough to eat them," she told them as she shut the door.

"With strong teeth," Joshua said.

"Joshua!" Matthew admonished.

Laughing, Jenny patted Matthew's shoulder as she walked past him. "It's okay; it's true."

"It's not easy to learn to cook," Hannah put in.

"She'd know, she's still learning," Matthew told Jenny. "Ouch! You kicked me!"

Hannah looked at him with an innocent expression. "I don't know what you're talking about."

"*Aenti* Hannah kicked *Daedi* under the table!" Mary said with a giggle.

Jenny grinned as she got out the loaf of bread her grandmother had baked that morning. Knowing how well prepared the older woman was, another loaf was undoubtedly tucked away in the freezer for when they needed it. She sliced the bread and brought it to the table.

"This is safe. *Grossmudder* baked it, not me."

"Jenny, the ham is delicious," Hannah told her. "I love the glaze on top."

"You've probably eaten it many times like this," Jenny said. "It's Grandmother's recipe."

Phoebe smiled and took another bite. "You did a good job with it, Jenny."

Annie speared a piece of potato with her fork and the fork stuck straight up in it. She jiggled the utensil and laughed when it bobbed but didn't fall over.

Jenny took a bite of the potatoes and had to take a drink of water to get the gooey lump down. She looked over and saw Matthew eating it heartily. Well, perhaps if you were really hungry from a day's hard chores it wasn't so bad.

The canned tomatoes and the bread went fast. Both were her grandmother's contributions. But the ham was delicious, even if it had a slight smoky taste and was a bit dry.

Time for dessert. As Jenny pulled it out of the oven, she saw that the top was golden brown. She prayed that it would be good. Then she thought: Ice cream. Put some ice cream on top. Nearly everything was better with ice cream.

The apples could have benefited from being baked just a little bit more, she thought, tasting the crisp. They were . . . what was that phrase people used to describe pasta that was still just a little firm to the bite? *Al dente.* That was it. The apples were *al dente.* Well, that might have been a good term with pasta, but it wasn't exactly what apples should be. Still, they weren't bad. To her relief, everyone was scraping their bowls.

Matthew wiped his mouth with his napkin and set it down beside his plate. "It was very *gut,* Jenny."

Relieved, she beamed. "Coffee?"

Without being asked, the children began clearing the table.

"I have some games set out for you to play in the other room," Phoebe told the children.

"Shouldn't we do the dishes first?" Mary asked.

Jenny shook her head and smiled. "You go

have fun. We'll do them later."

The adults enjoyed coffee while the children laughed and bickered good-naturedly over the games in the living room.

"When are you leaving for New York City?" asked Hannah.

Jenny saw Matthew's frown. "Day after tomorrow," she said, pushing the cream and sugar toward him.

"I'll drive you to the train station if you like," he told her.

"Thanks, but David said they're sending a car."

Disappointed, Matthew nodded and stared into his coffee for a long moment.

When he glanced up, it was to look at Phoebe with a worried expression. "Phoebe, I noticed that some of the church elders were here. I've been worried about you ever since."

Phoebe looked at Jenny, then Matthew. "You need to talk to Jenny about that."

She stood and spoke to Hannah. "Come look at the quilt I'm making for Fannie Mae's new baby. You can bring your coffee."

As they left, Hannah glanced over her shoulder at her brother and her expression matched his.

Jenny sighed. "Josiah saw David here last

week and was concerned that I came here to call media attention to your community."

"That's ridiculous." He thought about it for a moment. "And I'm surprised that he got Isaac and Benjamin to agree with him."

"I don't think he did," Jenny said, remembering the way they had asked her questions and seemed more open-minded. She told him what Phoebe had suggested she do to allay their fears, described the meeting, and finished by telling him that while Josiah had left his, the other two men had taken the materials she'd given them.

"Let's hope that's the end of that."

Jenny bit her lip. "There was something else that Josiah was concerned about, Matthew. He asked me about our relationship. You remember he frowned at us when he saw us on the porch that Sunday. He thought you shouldn't have been touching my face — he felt it was inappropriate."

"What did you say?"

"That you're my friend. That it was a gesture of concern, not flirting. And that whether you are a friend or something more is between us."

"He should have come to me," Matthew said, frowning. "I can understand he might have concerns —"

"Matthew!" she cried, shocked.

"I'm not saying he *should* have concerns, just that I understand he might be concerned," he said firmly. "I know you so I know that you are not a woman who would ever do anything to hurt the community. Josiah does not know this."

Leaning back in his chair, he sighed. "Josiah is elderly. He has talked about how our children are being seduced by the *Englisch* way of life."

"He doesn't need to look to me as a corrupter of your youth. . . . Or of you."

Annie came in just then and tugged on Jenny's hand. "Can I go with you?"

"With me?" Jenny stared at the child. "Where?"

"Wherwe you awre going. To the New City."

Helplessly, Jenny looked at Matthew, then back at Annie. "No, sweetie, I can't take you. But I'll only be gone a few days."

Tears welled up in the little girl's eyes.

"Annie?" Matthew held out his arms. "Come, child, what's wrong?"

"Mommy gone. Jenny gone." Annie pressed her cheek against her father's chest and wept.

Seeing the little girl in such distress had Jenny fighting tears herself. She pressed her fingers against her trembling lips.

"Annie, calm down. Jenny is just going to go do some work. She'll return." He drew her back so that she would look at him. "But Jenny doesn't live here, Annie. She's been visiting Phoebe. One day she will have to go back home for good."

"No, *Daedi*."

"Yes, Annie."

"But I wove Jenny."

Matthew looked at Jenny, and she saw such emotion in his eyes. "I know. I know." He swallowed and broke the eye contact. "Annie, it's time for us to go home. You're tired, and it's bedtime."

When she started to protest, he shook his head. "Annie, if Jenny has time tomorrow, I will let you and Mary and Joshua come over to see her so you can say good-bye. But there is to be no making Jenny feel bad about leaving, do you understand?"

Annie wiped her eyes with her hands. When she went to swipe her runny nose with one, Matthew quickly drew his pocket handkerchief and took care of that.

"Now, we must do the dishes and then we have to go, all right?"

Jenny shook her head. "No, I'll do them. You get the children home to bed."

He regarded her gravely. "Are you sure?"

When she nodded, he set Annie down and

211

told her to go get her brother and sister.

She scampered off.

"And get *Aenti* Hannah," Matthew called after her.

Matthew picked up the coffee cups and carried them to the sink as the children returned with Hannah.

"*Daedi,* we must wash the dishes," Mary said.

Jenny touched her head. "I can do them. Annie is tired, and you children need to get to bed. Thank you for coming."

"Thank you for having us," Hannah said. "We had a wonderful time."

Without being prompted, the children nodded and thanked Jenny politely.

Jenny stood at the door, watching them leave. When she turned, she saw her grandmother watching her. Was it her imagination, or did Phoebe wear an expression of sadness?

"What is it?"

"They love you."

"I love the children, too."

"They are not the only ones who love you," she said obliquely.

Jenny stared at her grandmother. "What?"

"I'm feeling tired," Phoebe said. "Would you mind if I didn't help you with the dishes?"

"Of course not. Are you all right?"

"Yes. Just tired." She hugged Jenny and left the room.

Jenny stared after her.

Phoebe didn't mean that Matthew loved her, did she?

Jenny went directly to the television studio when she got to New York City.

Sometimes she felt a little disoriented, a little disconnected, entering such a high-tech environment in a high-tech city after she'd been away overseas where life in a war zone was so basic.

This time she didn't feel the same kind of disconnect — she hadn't physically been that far away, and even though so many people had misconceptions about the lifestyle of Plain People, she hadn't felt like she'd visited some strange and alien country.

But she'd been away from the hustle of New York, the frantic pace of the studio; she found herself standing in the middle of the lobby unable to move. This had become the alien place somehow. She'd been away healing so long that it felt like someone else's place, not hers.

"Oh, my, look, it's Jenny!" someone cried.

Coworkers who'd become friends

swarmed her, chattering, until David arrived to rescue her. "Jenny, there you are!" He hugged her and began leading her toward the elevator to a chorus of disappointment from the others. "I'll bring her back, I promise!" he assured them.

The doors shut, and she breathed a sigh of relief.

"I'm sorry, I should have come down to the lobby a few minutes early," he told her. "You can't blame them. They've been worried about you."

Jenny remembered what her grandmother had said once about not worrying because that was arrogant; it was acting like God didn't know His job.

"You're looking better," David said, giving her a critical look up and down.

She shook her head, smiling wryly. "Better than what? I felt positively dowdy next to everyone down in the lobby. You better have that hair and makeup person you promised."

"I do. She's waiting for you. The stylist, too." He brushed at a speck of imaginary lint on his expensive suit.

"You told her about —"

"Jenny, everyone knows what you've been through," David said quietly. "Now, do you trust me?"

214

"I wouldn't be here if I didn't."

"Okay, let's take you in to hair and makeup."

When he opened the door, his wife, Joy, and their four-year-old son, Sam, yelled, "Surprise!"

Jenny couldn't help it. She started crying as Joy and Sam hugged her. "Oh, I missed you guys."

"I know you and David have business," Joy told her. "But we wanted to stop by and say hi and make sure you'll have dinner with us later." She looked at her son. "Right, Sam?"

"Right," he said, grinning.

Joy was a tiny, red-haired dynamo who was a perfect match for David. She knew how to keep him from taking himself too seriously.

"I may need to take a rain check if I'm too tired."

"Of course." Joy shot David a look. "Don't let him railroad you into anything you're not comfortable with."

"Too late," Jenny muttered.

"Yeah, I figured." Joy gave her another hug. "You're looking just wonderful. Getting away to the country was good for you."

Jenny sat down so she could put Sam on her lap. He gave her a card he'd colored as she reached into her tote bag and pulled out a wooden train she'd bought for him at a store in Lancaster. She'd brought it to the studio to give to David for him if she didn't get to see them.

A few minutes later they left, Sam blowing her a kiss, Joy reminding David again not to overtire Jenny.

Charmaine, the hairdresser, was happy to see her but unhappy to find so many split ends.

"We need to do some major conditioning," she tsk-tsked, examining them. "I'll have to take an inch or two off. And since you're looking kind of washed-out, how about we put in some streaks to give you a little color?"

When she saw Jenny's look of horror in the mirror, she rolled her eyes. "Okay, maybe not. But definitely we're getting rid of the split ends."

David abandoned her, claiming he had to go over his notes.

"Chicken," said Charmaine as he left.

Next was Mandy, who studied Jenny's skin with an intensity that unnerved her. She was new and young, and Jenny feared she'd slap a bunch of heavy makeup and color on her face. But Mandy got out some special foundation and explained that she'd

216

done some volunteer work with an organization that did makeovers for women who had suffered burns or scars.

"Your scar is barely visible to the eye, but the foundation makes it disappear for the camera." She added some subtle eye makeup and lipstick and stood back to admire her work. "What do you think?"

"I look like I did before — before." Her skin looked flawless, her hair shiny and bouncy. The dove-gray pantsuit that Joan, the stylist, brought in could have been made for her it fit so perfectly. She looked polished and professional and still herself. If her cane hadn't been at the ready, no one would have thought anything was different from the Jenny of the past.

David stuck his head in. "Is it safe?" Then he got a good look at Jenny. "Wow."

They went to one of the small studios to do the interview.

"We're going to start the segment with scenes of your visits with children in several countries overseas," he explained. "I'll do a voiceover about what the children are experiencing because of war. Then we'll shift to the footage of the explosion."

"Can I see it?"

David hesitated. "Are you sure?"

She nodded. "My life changed forever that

day. I'd like to see it."

He spoke with one of the crew and they set up the tape so she could watch it on a nearby monitor. It felt surreal to watch the explosion, to see herself tossed into the air, then fall twisted and motionless on the ground. She forced herself to watch, unflinching. Then the scene shifted to her being airlifted, first to a military hospital nearby, then being flown back to a stateside hospital where she was shown learning to walk again.

"Jenny? You okay?"

She felt him take her hand. Her throat clogged with tears, she nodded. "I'm okay. I needed to see it."

"Let me get you some water —"

She smiled and squeezed his hand. "Thanks, but I'm fine."

Taking a deep breath, she looked around. "Where did the crew go?"

"They're giving you some time —"

Glancing at the clock, she shook her head. "Boss'll kill you if you go into overtime."

"Boss is fine about it," said a deep voice. "Take as long as you need."

Nate stepped in front of her, looking just as tall and imposing as always. But he wore a smile as he reached for her hand and held it. "Good to see you, Jenny." With a nod to

218

David, he left them.

"Okay, let's roll," David called out to the crew.

To start the interview, he asked how she was doing. She spoke simply but honestly about the challenge of physical and speech therapy. "I have a lot of work to do," she said slowly. "But I'm feeling better."

The questions were low-key, not challenging, and shied away from when she'd be returning from work. David was usually fast-talking, almost hyper, but today he was going at a slower pace, giving her time, and it helped. She found herself relaxing so that her speech flowed almost normally. It felt strange to be on the other side of an interview, but David made it easy. He stuck by his promise that he wouldn't reveal she'd been staying in the Lancaster County area with her grandmother and exercised more patience than she'd ever seen because she needed so much time to answer.

"And now, is there anything you'd like to say?" David asked, leaning back in his chair.

"You gave me a stack of letters and e-mails from viewers who were concerned about me and they meant so much to me," she told him honestly, tearing up. "I appreciated having people want to know I am all right. But I'd like them to think of someone more important. If you can just spare a few dollars and send it to one of the organizations that feeds children and gets them medical care, it would mean so much to me. Just a few dollars can make an enormous difference to a child's life."

"We can do that," he told her, his voice husky with emotion.

They closed with a montage of scenes from Jenny's visits with children. There were smiles and tears and haunted eyes.

Tears ran down Jenny's face as she watched the monitor. She hadn't shed a tear when she watched what had happened to her, but when she saw the children again, she cried.

The interview wasn't the only reason Jenny had returned to New York City. She didn't tell anyone, not her grandmother, Matthew, or David.

Her doctor had agreed she could go to her grandmother's house as long as she did her therapy and returned for a checkup. When Jenny called, the nurse told her to come over the next day.

A new series of x-rays were taken and duly frowned over. Jenny sat in suspense, waiting for the doctor to speak. When he turned from them to look at her, her heart sank.

"You're going to need another operation," he told her. "We did the best we could with the two operations before, but I told you that we might need to go in again. There's still some shrapnel, some bone chips, some tendon repair. That's why you continue to have so much pain in your hip." He paused when he saw tears in her eyes. "Jenny, you knew you might need another, maybe two."

"I know. But I was hoping . . ." she trailed off.

"Let's schedule it for next week."

She wasn't looking forward to it, but she wanted to get it over with, especially if it would help relieve the pain and the difficulty of walking. But there was a little girl back in Lancaster who already thought she wasn't coming back.

"I need a little more time," she told the doctor. "I'll call you next week."

He nodded. "Just don't put it off too long, okay?"

"Okay."

"And Jenny, there's one more thing. We'll be testing the shrapnel and the other metal we take out this time. There's been some concern that metal in bombing victims where you were is showing some contamination."

She sighed. "Just something else to be

worried about, huh?"

He patted her shoulder. "So far the doctors there haven't found any problems. But we figure it's time to start being proactive about this just in case."

She dressed and took a cab over to her next appointment. There, it wasn't x-rays but a sonogram. The ob/gyn specialist asked Jenny to dress and then, when she sat down in front of her desk, came around to sit in the chair beside her.

It can't be good when the doctor sits beside you, thought Jenny.

"There was a lot of internal damage," the woman said, looking at her kindly. "We both know you're lucky to be alive. You're a young woman. I know that you want to hear that you'll still have a baby one day. I wish I could give you a guarantee, but I can't even do that with healthy young women who've never been injured."

"So we wait and see?"

The doctor nodded.

"What do I tell him?" Jenny asked her. "The man who might be in my future?" She shook her head. "I mean, presuming someone would want to take me on with all my other problems. What if he wants a child?"

"Then, if you can't have one, you adopt. You of all people would adopt, wouldn't

222

you? I've seen you on television. I'm surprised you didn't bring a couple of those children home with you."

Jenny smiled slightly. "I wanted to, but then who would have taken care of them when I had to go back overseas?"

The doctor patted her hand. "The human body is a miraculous thing, Jenny. There's no telling what's in your future."

She stood and went to sit behind her desk so she could make notes in Jenny's file. "I want you to come back in six months and just keep doing what you've been doing. The therapy is obviously doing great things for you."

Jenny found herself out on the sidewalk a short time later, hailing a cab back to her condo.

She'd called her landlord before she arrived and told him to let her friend Joy inside. Joy had had some cleaning done and even placed a bunch of flowers in a vase.

Jenny wandered into the kitchen and looked in the refrigerator. Joy had stocked it, even filled the freezer with microwavable entrees that Jenny always used to have for dinner. As she stood there, Jenny gazed around at the custom-made cabinets, the stainless-steel appliances, the granite countertops, and longed for a homey kitchen back in Lancaster. And not necessarily her grandmother's.

Back in Lancaster, everyone would be getting ready for supper. Hannah and Mary would have prepared the meal, and Matthew and Joshua would be coming in from doing farm chores and washing up. Even little Annie would have a task like helping to set the table. The food would be simple, the atmosphere warm and loving. Heads would be bent over the meal, thanking God for His abundance.

Closing the refrigerator, she went to lie on her bed, still in her clothes, and pulled the silk comforter over her.

She lay there as the light that came in through the drapes faded and darkness fell. Finally, she slept.

10

Jenny woke suddenly, feeling disoriented. Then she realized she was in her apartment, not her grandmother's home, and the door-bell was ringing.

She slid from the bed and made her way to the front door. Apparently the person ringing the doorbell didn't intend to give up and go away.

When she looked out the peephole, she saw why. Joy was holding Sam up so he could press the doorbell, and he was gig-gling with delight.

"You're home!" Joy said with a grin when Jenny opened the door. "We thought you might be. Were you sleeping?"

Sam grinned. "Hi, Jenny Banana."

She smiled. "Hi, Sam the Ham. Yeah, I fell asleep. I had a long day."

"Yeah? Doing what?"

Jenny shrugged. "Stuff."

Joy let Sam down, and he scampered

inside. "I brought dinner. I thought we could watch the interview together."

"I'm not sure I want to see it."

"Why? You don't think it went well?"

"Of course it did. David did it."

"Then what is it?"

In the kitchen Joy unloaded a bag from a local Chinese restaurant. Jenny got out Sam's special Superman plate and scooped lo mein onto it. He climbed up into a chair and started munching.

"Jenny?"

"I'm not sure I want to see myself."

Joy rubbed her hand on Jenny's arm. "You look wonderful. Relax."

Glancing at the clock, Jenny turned on the TV set on the counter.

"I haven't had Chinese food for ages," she said, sampling the cashew chicken.

"You look so healthy," Joy told her, opening a container of fried rice and serving them. "Must be all those fruits and vegetables on the farm, huh?"

"You're being polite about the weight I've gained," Jenny said ruefully.

"You're still too thin. But I don't know how. I convinced David he had to share that pie your grandmother gave him. It was fantastic."

Music signaled the start of the six o'clock news.

"Daddy!" Sam cried as his father's face showed onscreen.

David was only in his late thirties, but network executives had recognized he had the knowledge and authority to move into the anchor seat after Edmund Mallory retired. Ratings had immediately soared.

"In the headlines tonight . . ."

"Sam, want an egg roll?"

". . . and a special visit with a friend of ours you've been writing us about."

"Jenny!" Sam cried as her picture flashed on.

She smiled at Sam. "Yes, it's me. Your daddy and I talked earlier because he wanted me on his show."

"Jenny? You okay?" Joy wanted to know.

"Butterflies," she muttered.

Sam looked over at her plate. "You got butterflies in your dinner?"

Jenny and Joy laughed. "No, it's something silly that people say," his mother told him.

Sam grinned. "Funny Jenny!"

Oh, I've missed him, and my friendship with David and Joy, thought Jenny. She leaned over to kiss his cheek.

The broadcast went quickly. Nothing was left but the fortune cookies when the interview came on. Sam immediately became riveted to the screen.

Jenny had seen part of what they would broadcast — the film clips of children overseas and the bomb blast.

"Joy!" she whispered urgently. "Sam shouldn't see this part."

"Sam, you want to get the ice cream?"

He jumped up and pulled out the bottom drawer of the freezer. Joy watched the broadcast as she got bowls and Sam helped her scoop out the ice cream.

By the time they returned to the table, things Sam shouldn't see were over.

Jenny felt a lump in her throat as she watched how she struggled when David asked if she wanted to add anything. But it had been good to tell the viewing audience how she wanted them to focus on the children. She knew the truth that even a few dollars apiece would help. The screen was filled with a montage of scenes from Jenny's visits with children who smiled or cried and looked into the camera with haunting eyes. Then the camera cut back to Jenny watching the studio monitor, tears running down her face.

Jenny bit her lip as she watched now. "I didn't realize I was being filmed then," Jenny whispered, and Joy reached out to take her hand.

Over that image of her face, the names and 800 numbers of organizations that helped children were shown.

David came back on. "I hope you'll join me in donating," he said quietly. "It'd mean a lot to the children. And to Jenny."

Jenny burst into tears.

"Mama?"

"It's okay, Sam," his mother said quickly. "Jenny's doing happy crying. You remember happy crying?" She wrapped her arms tightly around Jenny.

"I didn't know he was going to do that," she sobbed.

"Me neither," Joy said, and her voice was thick with tears, too. "He's one special guy, isn't he?"

"Told you — told you so."

Joy grinned at her. "Yeah. You did. I owe you for introducing us."

Jenny handed Joy a paper napkin and used one to wipe away her own tears.

Sam got out the fortune cookies and passed them around.

Joy paused as she read her message. "Hmm, it sounds mysterious. 'You will help a friend to see what she has not seen.' " She tried to see Jenny's. "What does yours say?"

"Not as mysterious as yours — kind of

stereo— stereotypical," Jenny said, shrugging.

"Jenny!"

"You will have a long and happy life." She picked up her green tea.

Joy propped her elbow on the table, her chin in her hand, and regarded Jenny. "I like that one. So, tell me about this Matthew."

She nearly did a spit-take. "Matthew?"

Nodding, Joy stared at her intently. "Yeah. Matthew. David told me there was this guy who seemed to be crazy about you. So spill it. I want all the details."

"He's just a friend," Jenny tried to say.

"Jenny!"

"Joy!" she returned.

But Joy was as relentless as her husband.

"Well, I was a teenager when I met Matthew," she began.

Jenny went home the next day.

That was the way she had come to think about her grandmother's house, she realized. The trip to New York City had been emotional for her, seeing the places she'd lived and worked, the coworkers and friends, the doctors who had cared for her and helped put her back together.

As the limo pulled up to the old farmhouse, she saw the door open. Children tumbled out and ran to meet her.

"You came back!" Annie cried as Jenny stepped out of the car.

"I promised, didn't I?"

Annie wrapped her arms around Jenny's legs. "Yes."

Joshua and Mary had come out, too, but they hung back, letting Annie go first.

Jenny held out her arms and they ran into them.

Her throat tight, she looked up. Matthew stood in the doorway, watching her. "Hello, Jenny. Welcome back."

"Thank you."

He walked down the steps and enveloped her in a warm hug, then smiled down at her. "Let's get you in from the cold." He took her arm and led her into the warmth of her grandmother's home.

Joshua took the suitcase from the driver and waited for his sisters to walk ahead of him.

Phoebe was pulling a big roasting pan from the oven. She set it down and held out her arms to Jenny. "Welcome home!"

Jenny rushed into them and hugged her. "Oh, it's good to be back."

"Things went well?"

How to answer that? thought Jenny. "Yes,"

she said. "Yes, they did." She patted her purse. "I can show you David's interview."

"It's in your purse?"

"Something to look at it is, yes," said Jenny.

She glanced back at the children, who were taking off their coats. "We'll look at it later."

"Perhaps we could see it, too?" Matthew asked quietly.

Jenny searched his face. "Are you sure?"

"Yes."

She drew him aside as Phoebe was getting the children to help her finish supper preparations.

"Matthew, there are scenes on it of children who are suffering," she said quietly. "And the scene — the scene where the bomb hit me. I don't think they should see it until they're older. Especially Annie."

"We talked, the children and I, after that night we talked about war," he said, looking at her. "There are things you protect your children from, and things that they should know so that they can understand, so that they can make better choices, like whether this is the life for them. They need to know that being *Englisch* is not bad, right?

"And as much as we would like to protect them, we can't — maybe shouldn't —

protect them from knowing that bad things happen?"

Nodding, she kept looking at him. *There is something different about him tonight,* she thought. "Is this . . . a truce?"

"There was never any need for that with us, was there? We talked about things before you left, remember?"

She glanced at the children, then back at him. "I don't know. Sometimes it seemed as if you didn't trust me. It hurt."

"I was afraid, Jenny."

She stared at him. "You — afraid?"

"I don't want those I love to be hurt — especially my *kinner.* Do you understand?"

She didn't answer for a moment. "Yes, I do. Especially after you went through the long illness with your wife."

She looked into the kitchen where the children were talking with her grandmother, then back at him. "It's hard, Matthew. I can't help remembering how you frowned at me so many times that last night I was here."

"You said you were going home."

"I said I was going to New York City."

"Isn't that where you live?"

"It's where I live. But I don't think of it as home."

"Matthew? Jenny? Dinner is ready,"

233

Phoebe called.

Jenny started to turn, but Matthew put his hand on her arm so that she would look at him.

"Where do you consider home, Jenny?" he asked with an urgency about his question, a tension that radiated from him.

"Here in Lancaster County, Matthew," she said simply. "Here."

He let out his breath and nodded. Taking her hand, he walked with her into the kitchen and helped her with her chair. She looked up at him and smiled, and when she looked away, she caught the children watching.

It felt good to be back here in the kitchen, listening to the happy chatter of the children. They told her all about what had happened while she was gone: the taffy pull, the ice-skating, the silly things a friend had done or said. Just happy chatter.

They wanted Jenny to tell them what she'd done every minute while she was gone. She talked about David and Joy and especially about Sam. They laughed when they heard that Sam called Jenny silly names like Jenny Banana. They'd never had Chinese food so she promised to try to make some one night.

"Do you cook this Chinese better than

biscuits?" Joshua teased, and she laughed and reached over to tousle his hair.

After dinner, they washed the dishes. They didn't ask, as *Englisch* children might have done, if she'd brought them something back. So she really enjoyed opening her suitcase and surprising them with the small presents she'd bought. For Annie she'd found an animal alphabet book with buttons to press to hear their names. The book wasn't just beautifully illustrated — the sounds would also help Annie with pronunciation. There was a book on horses for Joshua, who loved them. And shy Mary got a journal to write in, one that had a key to keep nosy siblings out of, Jenny whispered to her.

Jenny saw Phoebe frown as she watched Mary look at the journal. She wondered if there was a reason she shouldn't have bought it, but when Phoebe looked up and saw Jenny standing before her, she smiled.

"You didn't need to get me anything," she protested as Jenny handed her a package of fabrics for quilting.

Then Jenny turned to Matthew and gave him his present. "It was hard to find something for you," she told him as he ripped away the wrapping paper.

"Why? I'm easy to please."

"He loves everything we give him," Mary agreed. "He keeps everything, all the things we make him for Christmas and birthdays."

Matthew discovered it was a book about farming.

"You probably know everything in it," she said, watching him.

"There's always something new to learn," he said. "Thank you, Jenny."

He and the children lingered, not looking like they wanted to go home though the hour grew late. Annie climbed up into Jenny's lap and rubbed her eyes. But she protested when her father said it was time to leave. Jenny looked at Matthew and mouthed to stay a little longer. So even after Annie stopped rubbing her eyes and simply fell fast asleep in Jenny's arms, they stayed.

A different woman came home this time, thought Matthew as he gazed at her across the big kitchen table in Phoebe's home.

Jenny's skin glowed, and her hair seemed shinier. From some *Englisch* beauty treatment, no doubt. She wore a new outfit, a navy sweater and long wool skirt — at least, he hadn't seen her wear it before. Perhaps she'd brought it from her apartment.

Gone was the wan, too-thin woman who avoided his eyes and touched her hand to her face to hide a scar.

But was it just beauty treatments and new clothes? he wondered. He was glad she'd said she felt she'd come home. Otherwise, he would have thought she was just looking happy because she'd visited her familiar *Englisch* world and her friends.

She told the children she'd been busy while she was gone and that time had flown. Matthew had never found time to pass so slowly as the last few days. He'd stopped by Phoebe's twice with trumped up excuses just so he could find out if she'd heard from Jenny. And if he was honest, he needed to make sure that she was coming back. Both he and Phoebe knew she hadn't returned for years and years after that last summer. And then she was a pale shadow of herself, a broken shell of a woman.

Now, as he took his youngest from her arms, he smiled at her and silently thanked God for returning her to him.

"It is good to have you back, Jenny."

"It's good to be back."

"I know it isn't New York City, but would you like to drive into town and have a meal tomorrow?"

"I would like to because town is *not* New York City," she said, smiling.

"How about eleven?"

Jenny nodded and then she turned and saw that Joshua and Mary were watching them instead of putting their coats on.

Matthew saw, too, and his eyebrows rose. They quickly donned their coats, but Jenny saw them exchange secret grins when they thought no one was looking.

Phoebe brought a quilt for Annie so that they didn't have to wake her to put her coat on.

"Oh, I nearly forgot," Jenny said, pointing at the package that lay on the table before them. "Here, Mary, would you make sure your Aunt Hannah gets the present I brought for her? Tell her I missed seeing her tonight and I hope she's feeling better."

Matthew settled his children in the buggy, and as he got in, he glanced over and saw that Jenny stood in the doorway. He lifted his hand in farewell, and she waved in return.

When he glanced back as the buggy moved forward, she stood at the window.

Jenny turned back and sank down into a chair.

"Tired?"

She nodded. "It's been a long couple of days."

"Do you want some tea before you turn in?"

"Yes, thank you. That would be so nice."

"Let me turn the kettle up."

Jenny had been tired from the hectic days in New York City when she arrived, but then the children had swarmed out and their welcome had energized her. Dinner with them, with Matthew and her grandmother, had been just what she needed, too.

But she felt she'd been on a roller coaster of emotion. Jenny swallowed and looked at her hands folded on the table.

"And some talk?"

Jenny looked up. "If it isn't too late for you?"

"It's never too late for a talk about a troubled heart."

"Things just seem so complicated sometimes," Jenny said with a sigh.

"Only if you're trying to figure them out for yourself."

"True." She was silent for a moment as she watched her grandmother fix the tea. "Have there been any more visits from Josiah?"

"No. I doubt there will be. Isaac and Benjamin didn't seem to have a mind about things the way he wished they would. I suspect Josiah will just settle down and keep his unhappiness to himself."

Sighing, Jenny shook her head. "Actually, Josiah won't have to worry about me being around for a while."

"But you said you were happy here!"

"I have to go back for a visit in a week or two."

"For another interview?" Phoebe brought the tea to the table and sat down.

Jenny shook her head. "We haven't talked about it, because I was in such pain and maybe a little depressed. I just wanted to avoid it."

She lapsed into silence as Phoebe poured the tea. Accepting her cup, she added a teaspoon of sugar and a drop of cream and stirred it around and around, studying the pattern the cream made before it was incorporated.

"You wanted to avoid what, child?"

"The doctors operated on me twice before I came, but they warned me that they needed to do it at least once, maybe twice more."

Phoebe sat down heavily. "I had no idea."

"I wanted to believe that I was healing, that the pain would go away with therapy and time." Jenny stirred her tea. "But I saw the x-rays myself. The doctor wanted me to stay for the surgery."

"You should have called me. I would have come to take care of you after you got out of the hospital."

"I couldn't. I mean, I had to get back here. I'd promised Annie I would return. I didn't want to break that promise. Not with her mother gone. I couldn't do that to her." She pressed her fingers to her mouth to stop it from trembling.

"So you'll stay for a little while and then go back?"

"Yes." Jenny took a sip of her tea.

"Then I'll go with you."

Jenny reached over and grasped her grandmother's hand. "Thank you." She glanced around the kitchen. "Maybe I can cook you something in my microwave while you're there."

"Will it be better than your biscuits?" Phoebe asked with a wry smile, echoing Joshua's words.

Jenny couldn't help it. She laughed until the tears came.

"I thought I heard voices."

Jenny looked up and saw her grandmother standing in the doorway of her bedroom. "Oh, I'm sorry, I thought I had the volume low." She tapped a key on her laptop and shut it down.

"It wasn't loud," Phoebe told her as she sat at the end of the bed. She gathered her shawl around her thin shoulders. "So I am not the only one having trouble sleeping?"

Jenny sat up in her bed. "Aren't you feeling well?"

"I'm fine. As I get older, sleep becomes a little elusive at times."

"Maybe I shouldn't have told you about the surgery. It worried you."

Phoebe shook her head. "No. I told you, I try not to worry —"

"Because that means you don't think God's doing His job," Jenny finished for her, remembering her grandmother's words. "But this is the first night I can remember you having trouble sleeping."

"Most of the time I don't get out of bed, but I went to the kitchen for a glass of water and heard voices."

She looked curiously at the flat silver-colored box that lay on the bed between them. "You were talking to it?"

Jenny opened the laptop, displaying the interior. "I had to buy another one since the laptop I took overseas vanished from my hotel after the bombing. The battery's going to go out soon since there's no electricity here so I won't be able to use it much longer. But it should last for you to see the DVD."

She popped the disk out of the laptop and showed her grandmother. "It can be a movie or just about anything recorded on one of these. This one has the interview David and I did. The staff made this copy for me."

She hesitated. "I wanted to show you what David did but I'm not sure if now is a good time to watch it. Or if it's not too upsetting for you."

"Show it to me. It is important. Besides, it seems both of us are having trouble sleeping."

"Okay." Jenny started the DVD. She found herself watching the play of emotions on her grandmother's face rather than the interview.

"There," Phoebe murmured. "See how lovely you look? Can you see it for yourself now?"

Jenny smiled. "They did a good job with makeup, but yes, I can see that I worried far more than I needed to about the scar."

"David looks so handsome," Phoebe said, seeming as proud of him as she was of Jenny. "He asks good questions."

Then she grew quiet as the clip was shown of Jenny overseas, talking on-camera, surrounded by children and some parents.

"They look so frightened. So hungry," she whispered. "Now I understand why you were so troubled when we talked about them."

Jenny stopped the DVD. "The next part shows the bombing," she told her grandmother. "I don't know if you should see it. I just saw it for the first time, and it was hard to watch."

Phoebe put her hand over Jenny's. "If you could watch it, I can watch it. Remember, David told me enough to know how badly you were hurt."

So Jenny started the DVD again, and together they watched Jenny talking to the children and their parents with the help of the interpreter. Then the cameraman was pulling his camera away from her and focusing on a car that was speeding toward her. She glanced behind her as she saw this, then turned back with an expression of horror. Everything happened so fast, the screaming and the people running and the car exploding and Jenny being tossed into the air and landing like a broken doll.

Phoebe's hand tightened on Jenny's until she thought the bones would break. Tears streaked down her wrinkled cheeks, and she was whispering the Lord's Prayer under her breath.

"I'm sorry, I'm sorry, I shouldn't have let you see it," Jenny whispered, tears running down her cheeks, too.

Phoebe gathered her into her arms. "Truly God was with you," she said.

"Let's not watch any more."

"No, I want to see it all," her grandmother said firmly.

Jenny started the DVD again. Jenny was shown being flown home and in the hospital.

"Look," Phoebe interrupted. "That's my quilt."

Sliding her arm around her grandmother's waist, Jenny smiled. "It meant so much to me. Somehow I knew I would be okay, that I'd be coming here to get better."

The program drew to a close. Phoebe watched intently as the camera focused on Jenny watching the final scenes of the children with tears in her eyes and then letters and phone numbers played across the screen as David spoke.

"It would mean a lot to the children and to Jenny," Phoebe said, repeating David's words. She looked at Jenny. "I knew that David was a good man," she said with satisfaction. "I'm so glad that he talked you into the interview.

"And you — if you hadn't started the

work and then done the interview when you were afraid to do it, it wouldn't have happened. Aren't you glad you did it?"

Jenny nodded. "It's all made me feel like I'm on a roller coaster again. My emotions are all over the place. But I think it was good that we did it."

Phoebe seemed lost in thought for a long moment. "When we talked about the children not long after you came here, do you remember what you told me the therapist said?"

Jenny thought back. "She said she'd watched me on television and I — I cared so much about the children. And she said no one else had done what I did. No one had rushed in to do it since I'd been hurt."

"You said that you knew someone would step in, that you were not the first and would not be the last."

"I remember."

"Look what happened today. God is looking out for all His children, even when it seems He is not."

"I remember that you said to pray for the children," Jenny said. "I did."

Phoebe's smile was radiant. "And look what He has already done through you and David."

Jenny felt a weight lifting from her shoulders. "Yes. And now I'm glad it's done. I just want to get my surgery done and get better . . ." she trailed off.

"And see what God has in mind for you for the rest of your life," Phoebe finished for her.

Jenny thought about Matthew and how she felt about him, his children, and the life she hoped to make here.

"I think we should say a prayer to thank Him," her grandmother put in quietly.

Holding out her hands to her grandmother, Jenny nodded. "Yes, please."

They bent their heads and gave thanks, and when they had finished, Phoebe leaned over to hug Jenny. "I think we can both sleep now."

Jenny nodded and smiled. "I think so, too. *Gut nacht.* I love you."

"I love you, too."

As she lay in bed, staring at the ceiling and waiting for sleep to come, Jenny thought about the events of the evening.

She'd thought she would return home and have a quiet dinner with her grandmother, talk a while, and go to bed early. She'd told Matthew before she left that she didn't know how late she'd arrive and planned to see him and the children the following day.

But plans had changed.

Matthew, the children, and her grandmother had made her arrival an occasion with a family dinner, and there had been happy chatter and good food and a loving atmosphere.

The way that the children had shown how fond they were of her warmed her heart. She knew how much they had come to mean to her but she'd had no idea how much she meant to them. *Could they need me as much as I need them?* She'd fantasized about what it would be like to be married to Matthew, to love him and his children, to be a family.

Jenny knew that these children had not lost as much as some of the children overseas. But they had lost their mother and needed one again. And she wanted so much to be that mother to them.

She drew in a deep breath and let it out. She could relax more now that David had interviewed her and he'd invited other people to continue her work. She could have her surgery and get better.

It was very, very clear that she'd had an answer to prayer about the situation. With Him in charge, she knew she could relax and let go.

Sighing, she fell asleep.

11

Matthew pulled up at Phoebe's, but before he could get out, Jenny emerged and came down the walk.

"Phoebe's taking a nap," she told him as she got into the buggy. "I thought I'd wait by the door so we didn't wake her."

"Is she ill?"

"She's fine. We both stayed up a little late last night."

Matthew signaled the horse to enter the road and then turned to nod at Jenny. "You had much to catch up on, eh?"

"I — yes, I guess you could say so." She sighed as she looked out at the passing scenery. "The snow's melting. It isn't ugly and messy the way it was back in the city."

"But you seem glad you went there."

"It was good to see David and his family. I saw some of my friends at work. Saw my boss." She sighed. "Busy."

"And you still found time to buy presents

for everyone." He glanced at her and grinned.

"I liked that part of the visit." She smiled at him. "It's nice to be going into town just for fun, not for some kind of therapy."

"When do you go there again for therapy?" When her smile faded and she didn't answer, he glanced over. "Jenny?"

"I won't be going again."

"You're through?"

"Not exactly. Listen, could we talk about something else?"

He turned to frown at her. "Jenny, are you certain that it's a good idea to stop the therapy?"

"Matthew, please?"

Their eyes met. He hesitated and then nodded. "We'll discuss it later."

He thought about how different this ride was than those than had come before — not just the ones where he'd driven her with Annie to speech therapy or to the physical therapist. No, he was thinking about the rides they had taken in his buggy when they were teenagers years ago.

He glanced at her, wondering if she ever thought about those times. Sometimes he saw something in her eyes when she looked at him, something that made him wonder if they would stay friends or become more.

Then, last night, he'd felt that things had changed. That was why he'd asked her out today. They needed to talk. He was no longer that young man who felt so elated that he'd found a woman he wanted to love for the rest of his life.

After she'd left that summer, reality had hit him hard and disillusioned him for a time. He'd thought they could surmount the distance between their worlds, and it had been a bitter pill to swallow to find out that he was wrong.

And then Jenny had returned, and though many years had passed and many joys and pains, it seemed that their paths had converged for a reason. He'd been afraid to think that it was a second chance.

She'd said she felt this was home. When her being in the community had been questioned, she had reacted with dignity and respect, but a stubborn belief that she and Matthew were entitled to have a relationship without others' scrutiny.

And she had returned even after she had visited her *Englisch* world, this time when he'd feared that she would not.

He'd watched her and seen that she loved his children. That was so very clear. But did she love their father as much?

"Matthew?"

He turned. "Yes?"

"You're being awfully quiet. I'm sorry if —"

"I am not angry with you," he assured her. "I was thinking."

She tilted her head, studying him. "About what?"

"I have something to show you."

"Okay."

The next road seemed familiar, then they stopped near a huge tree. Snow covered the ground beneath its bare branches. They walked over to the tree, hand in hand.

This tree looks vaguely familiar. Then she remembered. "We picnicked here that last summer."

Something was carved on it, just a little above her head — a heart with their initials.

"When did you do this?" she asked, touching her fingers to it.

"The last day you were here. I was going to show it to you, but Phoebe said that your father had come to get you and I didn't see you again."

Her eyes flew to his. "Oh, Matthew, I'm so sorry."

"I was angry," he admitted. "But later, I understood why you had to leave."

She found that she was holding her breath.

"Matthew, why did you bring me here to-day?"

"I've watched you with my *kinner*, Jenny, and I know that you've come to love them."

"Who could not love them?" she asked, smiling.

"Is it possible that you could love me, too?" he asked quietly.

Before she could answer, he grasped her hands tightly. "I loved you as a pretty, young girl, and I love you even more now as the beautiful woman you have become."

He stole her breath. He made her speechless.

Jenny threw her arms around him. "Oh, I don't think I ever stopped loving you," she cried against his shoulder.

Pulling her back so that he could look at her, his eyebrows rose as he saw the tears. "You're crying?"

"Happy tears," she said, sniffing. "Don't you know about happy tears?" She laughed. "Joy had to explain them to Sam, but you're a man, you should know."

He pulled out his handkerchief and wiped them away. And then he bent his head and kissed her.

Jenny closed her eyes and savored the kiss. This wasn't the kiss of a tentative young man who had kissed her when they were out picking blueberries. This was the kiss of a man who was not moved by youthful impulse and passion. It was the deliberate, intense kiss of a man who loved.

He held her then, grateful that he had spoken his heart. Grateful to God for bringing her back to him.

When at last they separated, he smiled. "Will you marry me, Jenny, and be my love?"

She stared at him as the words sank in. And then she cried, "Yes!"

"You said I was quiet a while ago," he said as they drove to the restaurant in town. "I was thinking about the past. Have you ever wondered what might have happened if your father had not come early for you that summer?"

"I'd still have gone away," she said slowly. "College was so important to me. I guess I thought you'd be here when I finished. You know, that I'd come back summers and see you. I know that sometimes you marry young here, but I still felt college was something to be done first."

She frowned as she remembered. "But you didn't answer my letters, and so I thought you weren't interested in me, that my feelings weren't returned."

"It was never that," he said quietly. "But I felt we would not be able to have a future together and I had to move on."

She put her hand on his. "Tell me about Amelia."

"I knew her all my life," he said. "We were friends, and she comforted me after you left. Friendship turned into a quiet kind of love."

He turned to look at her. "It wasn't the kind of intense feeling that I'd had for you, but I think I was afraid that kind didn't last. Instead, I had only to see you again and there it was, strong and true."

They had arrived at the restaurant. He guided the buggy into a parking place and when he turned to her, he saw that there were tears in her eyes again.

"Those don't look like happy tears, Jenny."

Pressing her fingers to her trembling lips, she shook her head. "I need to tell you something. Something serious. What I have to tell you may affect how you feel about me, Matthew, and I'll understand if it does."

Taking a deep breath, she turned to face him. "While I was in New York City, I went to see the doctors."

His heart constricted. "Jenny, please don't tell me there's bad news. God wouldn't bring you back to me just to take you to be with Him so quickly."

"Well, that puts things into perspective," she said, staring out pensively. Then she turned to him again. "I'm sorry; I didn't mean to worry you. I'm not ill, not the way you mean. I had injuries, scarring —"

"I've told you that you shouldn't worry, that you're beautiful —"

She smiled at him. "And I love you for that." Her smile faded. "But I'm not talking about scarring on the outside. Matthew, there is a real question about whether I will be able to have children."

He laced her fingers with his. "I would be sorry if that didn't happen since you so obviously love them and want them, Jenny. Children are such a joy and a blessing from God. But I'd like to share my children with you and hope that they would be enough?"

"Would they be enough for you, Matthew?"

"Whatever is God's will is enough for me, Jenny. If we're to have more, we will. But in the meantime, we're blessed."

Hope blossomed in her heart, swelling outward. She squeezed his hand. "Yes, we're blessed. Imagine, in a short time I've gone from thinking I would have no children to suddenly having three."

They went inside then, to eat and to get warm.

They served themselves from the buffet, sat down, and thanked God for the meal. Matthew picked up his fork and began eating.

Then he looked up at her. "Jenny? Aren't you hungry?"

"I'll eat in a minute. There's one more thing I need to talk about," she said. "You asked about physical therapy earlier and I didn't want to talk about it."

She bit her lip, upset to have to even say this, then plunged in and told him about the surgery. He put down his fork and listened, looking more and more concerned as she went on.

"The doctor wanted me to stay and do it right then," she finished.

"I don't understand why you didn't stay. If it was needed, you shouldn't have come back home." Then he shook his head as she hesitated. "Ah, I know why. You made a promise to Annie."

"I couldn't break my promise. She wouldn't understand. Now she'll trust that I'll come back next time."

"And I'll trust, too," he said slowly. "I worried that you wouldn't return this time. Now I'll know, too."

The Amish were careful about public displays of affection, but Matthew reached across the table and squeezed her hand.

"It just feels like I'm going backward," she confessed. "I got my hopes up that I wouldn't need more surgery."

"If there's a problem still, it needs to be fixed."

"I know."

"And you're getting better."

"I'm just going to backslide a little," she mused, tracing the design on the tablecloth with her finger. "It'll be a time of recuperation again, a walker for a while, intense physical therapy."

"But you're stronger this time, and you said the surgery is to get out more of the metal. It won't be as bad as last time, right?"

Taking a deep breath, she nodded. "You're right. And hopefully this will be the last surgery."

He withdrew his hand. "I know you're upset, but you need to eat," he told her.

Picking up her fork, she forced herself to take a bite and slowly her appetite returned. Before she knew it she'd finished most of what was on her plate. Matthew had her laughing over a story Mary had told about a boy at school.

On their way home a thought came to Jenny. She turned to Matthew. "Well, I'm disappointed. You never asked me on a date

— I don't even know if you call it that?"

He grinned. "The younger generation calls it dating. The older ones in the community often call it courting." His grin faded. "I didn't know if you'd welcome it."

"I'm teasing you. What would we have done on a date?"

Now it was Matthew's turn to smile. "Many of the courting activities are for the younger couples. Singings, buggy rides, that sort of thing."

"Then I guess we could pretend we're doing it now."

"You know that you don't take on just the children and me?" he asked her earnestly. "You must be baptized into the Amish church. That is, if we stay here."

"Stay here?" Then she realized what he was saying. "Matthew, I would never ask you to leave here!"

"And I would never ask you to stay if you couldn't embrace the religion, the life here," he told her firmly. "I've done a lot of thinking about that."

"I was attracted to your life when I was a teenager, remember?" She paused, then grinned at him. "As well as to you."

He grinned back, and his relief was palpable. "Marriages take place in November, after the harvest. Well, sometimes we have a

259

few at the beginning of December, but the weather can make travel to a wedding difficult."

"November? That's so far away!"

He took her hand. "You'll need the time to have the operation and recover. And you'll need to study to join the church."

Lifting her chin with his free hand, he studied her. His eyes were warm. "The time will go quickly, Jenny."

"I guess." Then she realized that she was being impatient again. She barely envisioned a future with him, and now that one lay on the horizon, she couldn't wait. But it wasn't as if she wouldn't see him every day.

"Who shall we tell first, my grandmother or the children? Or shall we tell them at the same time?"

"Let's tell them at the same time."

Jenny leaned her head on Matthew's shoulder and savored the closeness. She was disappointed when they arrived at her grandmother's home. But he kissed her and promised to return to pick them up for supper at his home.

Dinner was fun and noisy, as it had become since the children had grown more relaxed and comfortable around her. Every night had become special but tonight . . . Jenny knew she would remember this night forever.

"Jenny and I have an announcement to make," Matthew said after supper and dessert were eaten.

Immediately Jenny noticed that Phoebe and Hannah exchanged a look. Jenny glanced at Matthew and saw that he'd noticed, too. Then she jerked her head in the direction of Joshua and Mary for him to see that the two of them were grinning at each other.

Only Annie was looking expectantly at her father, her big blue eyes wide. "What's your 'nouncement, *Daedi?*"

"I've asked Jenny to marry me and she said yes."

Hannah closed her eyes. When she opened them, Jenny was touched to see that they were wet with tears. She jumped to her feet, rushed to Matthew, and threw her arms around him.

"I'm so happy!" Then she turned to Jenny and embraced her, too, more carefully but with just as much heartfelt emotion.

Joshua got up to give Jenny a hug, and when he returned to his seat, Jenny saw that Mary was standing there, looking uncertainly at her. "You will really be our mamm?"

Jenny took her hand. "You'll always have your true mother looking down from heaven on you. I don't ever want you to forget her. But I would love to call you Daughter and be your mother here, if you'll let me."

Mary nodded, and they hugged. And then Jenny felt a tug on her arm. Annie stood beside her.

"Me too," she said, raising her arms. "I want hug, too."

Jenny lifted the child onto her lap and squeezed her. It was so moving that the older children loved and accepted her, and yet it was almost unbearably poignant that the youngest she held now would always know her as her mother since she had no memories of her mother.

Looking up, Jenny found Matthew watching her and saw tears in his eyes. She nodded and something passed between them that didn't need words.

Phoebe dabbed at her eyes with one of her ever-present handkerchiefs.

"Come, let's clear the table," Matthew said when he saw Jenny looking at her grandmother.

Jenny got up and walked over to sit next to her. "I hope that you're not hurt that I didn't come to you first. But I didn't know until today how Matthew felt about me."

Phoebe shook her head and smiled wryly. "I don't know how you could have missed it. Hannah and I knew. Even Joshua and Mary noticed." She took Jenny's hands in hers. "I am happy for you, so very happy, child. You will be good for each other."

Glancing over at the man she loved, Jenny nodded. "I think so, too." She held out her hand to him and he came to take it.

"So you approve, Phoebe?"

"You don't need to ask for my approval or my permission," she told him. "You're old enough to make your decisions. But if you ask if I think it is a good thing, I think it is a very good thing. From the time Jenny came back, I wondered if God was giving you both a second chance."

Hannah glanced over from helping the children with the dishes and Jenny was warmed by the smile she sent.

The Plain People were seldom seen in New York City so Jenny supposed that the stares she and her grandmother received were only natural.

"The buildings look like huge mountains," Phoebe marveled as they rode in the cab. "But there's no grass anywhere."

"I'll take you to Central Park one day," Jenny promised.

"So where'll it be, ladies?" asked the cab driver. "You going to Broadway?"

Jenny shook her head and gave him the address of her apartment.

"Huh. I thought maybe there was a revival of *The Crucible,* you know?" he said, pulling out into traffic.

Phoebe grabbed the handle of the door as the vehicle took off and looked at Jenny with raised eyebrows.

"So what's the getup for?" the cabbie asked.

Jenny met the cabbie's eyes in his rearview mirror. "Getup? Oh, you mean her dress?"

"Yeah, getup, costume, whatever it's called."

"I'm from Lancaster County, young man," Phoebe told him politely, showing no sign of displeasure at being spoken about as if she weren't there.

"Ah, I see. Amish. So, you planning to move here?"

Jenny and Phoebe exchanged looks. "No," said Phoebe, her eyes twinkling. She gazed out the window. "I've never seen so many people. And they're rushing everywhere."

So many people, thought Jenny. *And yet sometimes it's an easy city to feel lonely in.*

The doorman welcomed them with a

touch to his hat and held open the door. If José was curious, he was too polite to say anything.

"Good to see you back, Ms. Miller, ma'am," he added for Phoebe. "Leave that luggage there by the door, and I'll see that it's taken up to your place."

"Thanks, José, that would be great." Jenny turned to her grandmother as they approached the elevator. She eyed the closed doors . . How to explain? "It's like a box that we get inside —"

"I thought the box cooked food."

"This is different than the microwave," Jenny told her. "It takes us up to my apartment."

The doors slid open, and they walked inside. Then Jenny noticed that her grandmother was trying to hide her smile.

"You've been in one!"

Nodding, Phoebe chuckled. "They have them in the hospital in Lancaster."

"I feel so foolish." She punched the button for her floor.

Phoebe hugged her. "I couldn't resist teasing you. It's *allrecht.* You don't know what I know about your world."

"Hold the elevator, please!" someone called.

The Donaldsons and their little boy

265

stepped in after them. All three stared, but Billy was the most obvious. He tugged at his mother's dress. "Is it Thanksgiving?"

Jenny bit back a smile.

"It's good to see you doing well," Mrs. Donaldson rushed to say. "Are you back for good?"

Jenny shook her head. "Just for a little while."

"You're always rushing off to some exotic place," said Mrs. Donaldson, trying not to look at Phoebe. If the woman had known she was going to Lancaster, she'd probably still think so. After all, so many people were intrigued by where her grandmother lived, thought it was an anomaly, a place out of time and culture in the United States. She introduced her grandmother to them and saw the couple exchange a look of surprise.

She settled her grandmother in the guest bedroom and went into her own room to rest from the trip. When she got up an hour later, she found her grandmother sitting in her room reading her Bible.

"Are you feeling better?" Phoebe asked her. "You looked tired."

"I was tired," she admitted. "I feel better now. I thought I'd see what we have to eat. Joy stocked up some things last time I was here."

"Show me how to use the microwave and I'll prepare supper."

Jenny put her arm around her grandmother's shoulders. "I hope we can do better than that tonight. Matter of fact, we could even go out if you want. To a restaurant, I mean."

Phoebe glanced down at her clothes. "If we go out, I wonder how many other people here will think I am a Pilgrim?" she asked, smiling.

A packing company brought boxes to the apartment the next day.

Jenny labeled several of them with her grandmother's address, and the rest of them she marked DONATE. She filled a box with books she couldn't do without, and packed some of her writing supplies. Into another box she put clothes. A small portion of her wardrobe would be enough to get by with until she was told she could join the church. She didn't want to offend anyone by automatically adopting Plain clothing until then.

A few things that she'd worn to parties — fancy dresses and pantsuits and shoes to match — went into a box for a consignment shop.

Phoebe held up an emerald silk blouse Jenny had worn to a Christmas party.

"Jenny, are you sure that you won't miss clothing such as this?"

"I wore that just once, to a party," she said, taking the blouse and folding it neatly into the box to donate. "I'm not much of a party person. I had more fun sharing a family dinner with Joy and David and Sam than going out."

"They'll miss you."

"I know. But they'll visit. They promised, and they keep their promises."

Jenny looked around the room. What did she need to take that she felt she just couldn't live without?

She found another box and placed in it her treasures: the album her mother had made for her of childhood photos, several framed photos of her parents and one of her with Joy and David at their wedding and another with them holding Sam.

Journals took up another box. She'd been writing in them since she turned twelve and the pile had grown. But sometimes she found solace rereading them, seeing how she'd worked through problems she had with her faith. The children affected by war weren't the only things she wrote about. There were notes about what she saw in her travels, funny stories of learning about the customs of other countries, all kinds of things. She smiled at the bright-pink journal that held the entries she'd made about Matthew when they were teenagers. She *had* to keep that one, she decided. Maybe she'd read it one night as she recovered from the surgery, just for the memories.

Her grandmother came in as she placed it on top of the others.

"My, you have a lot of journals."

"Been keeping them for a long time."

"I see."

Jenny saw that Phoebe had a faraway expression in her eyes. But when her grandmother realized she was looking at her, she smiled.

"Anything I can help with?"

Opening the last drawer of her dresser, Jenny found a ribbon-tied packet of letters and cards from her grandmothers. Her maternal grandmother had died when Jenny was twelve, so she cherished the ones her mother had saved for her. The letters from Phoebe were equally cherished for her support of Jenny through the sometimes lonely college years.

"You saved our letters, too?"

"Of course."

"You're a sweet, sentimental child," Phoebe said, hugging her.

"Letters mean a lot when you're away

269

from home."

Phoebe looked at the boxes. "Those are all you are sending to my house?"

When Jenny nodded, she held out her hand and led her to sit on the bed. "Are you sure that you can give up so much?"

"They're just things."

"Things that are important to you."

Jenny looked around her and then shook her head. "I was never interested in accumulating much. I went from a small dorm room at college to an apartment that wasn't much bigger. Even if I liked having a lot of things I wouldn't have had room."

She fell silent. "If you're worried that I'm giving up something, all I can tell you is I found something so much more important at your home. I was wavering in my faith and I found it again. I found a joy in simple things. And best of all, I got to renew my relationships with you and Matthew, and make new ones with the children and Hannah."

She held out her hands. "What would I have here that could match that?"

"How you doing, Jenny?" asked the anesthesiologist.

"Nice and floaty," she said, feeling the effects of the pre-op shot.

He chuckled.

"Wait," she said. "Mac?"

Her surgeon leaned over her. "Yes, Jenny, I'm here."

"Do a good job," she told him. "I want to walk without my cane when I'm married."

"Sure thing. See you later."

Before she'd left her hospital room that morning, she and her grandmother had prayed, but as the anesthesiologist held the mask over her face, Jenny said another prayer that all would go well.

She floated to the surface what felt like minutes later. Her grandmother was standing beside the bed. Then Jenny went under again. The lights were dim when she woke next. Someone was touching her wrist.

"How are you feeling?"

Jenny looked into the face of the nurse who was taking her blood pressure.

"Hurts."

The nurse adjusted the drip on the bag that hung by the bed. "You'll feel better soon."

"Grossmudder?"

"Excuse me?"

"Grandmother."

"Oh. I sent her to have something to eat. She'll be back soon. You rest now."

When she woke again, sunlight was pouring into the room. Her grandmother sat in a chair next to the window, looking tired.

"I better not find out you stayed all night," Jenny said.

Phoebe rose to walk over to the bed. "Good morning. What did you say?"

"I better not find out you stayed all night," she repeated. Her voice sounded rusty.

Phoebe smiled. "What would you do?"

"Be very unhappy with you."

Jenny moved her hand on top of the covers. The texture felt familiar. Looking down, she saw that she was covered with her grandmother's quilt, the same one she found when she was in the hospital the first time.

"You brought it with you?"

Her grandmother leaned down to kiss her forehead. "Of course." Then she smoothed Jenny's hair back from her face. "There now, no need for tears. I never got to spend as much time as I would have liked taking care of you when you were young. It is no hardship to watch over you now."

Several days later Jenny was sitting up in bed when her grandmother walked in. "Well, you're looking better. How are you feeling?"

"Okay," Jenny said, forcing a smile.

Phoebe walked toward her. "You're still in a lot of pain, aren't you? Do you want me to get the nurse?"

"Maybe in a minute. It'll get better. The doctor said it was an easier surgery than last time."

Her grandmother gave her an understanding smile. "Easier for him, eh?"

Jenny bit her lip. "Yeah."

"My, look at all the flowers," Phoebe said, looking around the room.

"David's family sent that one and my boss — my former boss — sent the big arrangement. He also sent a check to one of those children's organizations. Wasn't that nice, even after I went to see him and told him I was resigning?"

"Very nice."

Phoebe brought a long-stemmed rose from behind her back and gave it to Jenny.

"How sweet. Thank you."

"It's from Matthew. He gave me money to get you something since he couldn't be here."

"I miss him and the children." She glanced over at the cards they'd made and given to Phoebe for her.

"Just remember, the sooner you're better, the sooner we can go home."

Jenny stared at her feet covered with the quilt. "I wish I could click my heels and be back in Kansas right now." When Phoebe looked confused, she laughed. "I'm sorry, that's from a movie."

"I watched one on the television set in the waiting room while you had your surgery," Phoebe told her. "Strange how many different things can be put in boxes."

There was a commotion at the door and someone was making shushing noises. Then Sam poked his head in. "Jenny?"

"Sam!" Jenny held out her arms.

"Remember what I said," David told him as Sam bounded into the room. "You can give her a hug if you're very, very careful."

David walked over to kiss the top of Jenny's head. Picking up his son, he let him lean down to hug her neck.

"Oh, it's so good to see you! Where's Joy?"

"It's so good to see you — where's Joy?" David pretended to be offended. "She's right behind us."

He turned to Phoebe and gave her a quick hug. "How are you, Phoebe? Was the hotel okay?"

"Hotel?"

Her grandmother nodded. "David made arrangements for me to stay at the one next to the hospital."

David shrugged. "No big deal. Just makes it easier for her to come see you."

"It's a very big deal," Jenny said quietly. "Thank you."

"What are friends for?"

Joy walked in then with a small shopping bag. "For sneaking food in past the nurses," she said in a stage whisper.

"I'm allowed to have regular food now, Joy."

"It's more fun pretending I'm doing it on the sly," she told Jenny with a grin.

"Cheeseburgers!" cried Sam.

Joy clapped a hand over his mouth. "Sssh, you little snitch!" She looked at David. "You didn't tell her, did you? You said you wouldn't tell her."

David rolled his eyes. "I wouldn't dare."

"David and I arranged for a private plane to take you home as soon as you're ready."

"Guys, that's too expensive!"

"We want to do it," Joy said firmly. "We have just one request."

"Anything."

Joy and David exchanged a look. "Um, could we come to the wedding? Are outsiders okay?"

"You are not outsiders," Phoebe spoke up.

"No, you are not outsiders," Jenny affirmed. "You've been more than friends.

You've been my family."

She shifted to get more comfortable in bed. "I haven't sent out invitations yet because weddings are held in November, after the harvest."

"Jenny the Impatient can wait that long?" teased David.

"Jenny Banana," Sam corrected with his mouth full of fries.

They laughed. The adults opened their bags of food. Jenny sighed happily as Joy handed her a cheeseburger.

"It's Jenny's favorite fast food," Joy told Phoebe. "She doesn't cook much."

"Hey, I'm learning!"

They all munched as Sam stuffed more french fries in his mouth, and Jenny felt like she was floating on such a cloud of happiness that she wouldn't need her painkillers that night.

Home was just days away now. Home, and Matthew.

Joy was hiding the bags and drink containers in the shopping bag a half hour later when Jenny's doctor walked in. He hid his grin at her surreptitiously pushing the bag behind her, but his real expression was grave.

"Shall I come back?" he asked Jenny.

"We were just going," David assured him.

276

"Could I ask you for a ride back to the hotel?" Phoebe asked. "If you don't mind, Jenny, I think I'll take a nap and come back at dinnertime?"

"That would be great."

Everyone left after quick hugs and kisses. The doctor sat down heavily in the chair beside the bed, sighing.

A chill ran up Jenny's spine. "Something tells me you don't have good news," she said slowly, searching his face.

"I'm sorry. I don't."

12

"We've been getting some more information from military surgeons about problems associated with bomb victims overseas," he told her.

"What kind of problems?"

"There's a nasty little side effect to the bombing injuries. We saw some instances of it in earlier wars and conflicts but hadn't seen as much in the last few years."

"But now?"

"Now with our technology improving we're saving more soldiers, more victims, and we're starting to see more evidence of certain problems."

"What kind of problems?" When he hesitated, she felt the first flicker of fear. "Mac, you're scaring me."

"I'm sorry. I didn't tell you much about what I'd been hearing. There was no point in frightening you. As I mentioned, the bombers sometimes include contaminants in the bomb."

"Are you saying that you found some in the metal you took out of me?"

He looked at her. "I'm not sure. I saved the material from the first surgery and tested that with what I know now and I'm concerned."

Anxiety pressed on her chest. "Okay, spit it out, Mac."

"I want to run more tests. And I'm afraid you could be looking at more surgery."

It was getting harder to breathe. "Give me the bottom line. How bad is this?"

"I'm doing research, calling people I know." He reached over to grasp her hand. "Some victims have gotten sick." He paused. "Several died."

Jenny wondered if he knew that his hand had tightened almost painfully on hers.

"I felt I got all the metal out last time, but we know that's not really possible. Since you haven't reported any symptoms, I feel like you're probably in the clear. I'm having the metal retested as we speak."

He released her hand and then frowned. "I'm sorry. I didn't mean to hurt you."

Numb, she stared down at her hand. It was red where he held it so tightly, and now that he'd called attention to it, she felt the ache. "I don't know who was holding too tight — you or me."

"We'll start on the tests tomorrow." He got to his feet and patted her shoulder. "Hang in there. I'm sure everything will be all right."

She wasn't so sure, but she forced herself to smile at him and nod.

The minute he left the room, she burst into tears. She'd thought the worst of it was over, that she had come out on the other side. With her past surgeries, with the physical therapy, through sheer grit and determination, she was recovering. She could soon be walking without a cane. She was going to be married.

Fresh sobs shook her. This changed everything. Everything. What if the doctor found complications? What if she'd survived only to become sick, maybe die now?

This couldn't be happening.

Hailey, Jenny's favorite nurse, came and sat in the chair the doctor had just left. She did as he'd done — reached for her hand and simply held it.

"I know it's scary news," she told Jenny. "But try not to panic."

She handed her a box of tissues. "It's not good for you to be this upset, you're just recovering from surgery."

"How — how do you not get upset?"

Jenny asked her as she wiped at her tears with her free hand.

"By not thinking the worst until you have to," the nurse told her gently.

Jenny stared at Hailey. The woman had such kind eyes. "I'm — I'm trying. Really."

Hailey had been one of Jenny's nurses since she'd come down from recovery several days ago. She looked to be just a few years older than Jenny, but she cared for her with such skill, she seemed older. Whether it was placing pillows to support her just so or showing up just when she needed her, she had been one of the best nurses Jenny had had in her several hospital stays. Even now, the nurse held an injection in her free hand.

"The doctor left an order for a sedative if you want it," Hailey said when she saw Jenny's glance.

Jenny shook her head. "I don't want to be doped up when my grandmother comes back for dinner. She'd be suspicious that something's wrong. I don't want to tell her anything until — until we know."

"It's really mild, but I understand. Use the call button if you need me, okay?"

Jenny tried to sleep. Tried television. Tried not to cry again.

Finally, worn out with stress and worry,

she dozed off.

Jenny walked along the dusty road, wondering where everyone was. The sky was a bright-blue bowl overhead, the sun blazingly hot. Sweat ran down her face and dampened her shirt. She was thirsty, so thirsty she felt feverish.

A flock of birds flew out of the brush beside the road, as if something had flushed them out. Jenny pressed a hand to her heart, willing it to stop pounding.

It was too quiet. Snipers could be lurking in the bushes. A car could come along with Death at the wheel.

A branch snapped behind her. She spun around but didn't see anything. Turning back, she walked faster, faster, then started running.

A horse's hooves clip-clopped behind her. She glanced over her shoulder, and her eyes widened at the sight of the Amish buggy approaching. She couldn't see the driver in its dark depths but as it drew closer, she saw Matthew. She waved frantically and called his name.

To her utter shock, he frowned and waved, then returned his attention to the road.

The buggy passed her and proceeded down the road. Annie and Mary and Joshua peered from the back window at her, their sweet faces looking so sad.

She stretched out her hand to them, but the buggy speeded up and disappeared. Despairing, desolate, she sank down onto the road and wept.

Jenny woke with tears streaming down her cheeks. Her heart still pounded with the fear and drama of the nightmare.

"Jenny?" Her grandmother peered around the door. Then she caught sight of her granddaughter's face. "Oh, *liebschen,* are you all right?"

Jenny nodded and reached for the tissues. "I'm — fine."

Her grandmother drew the chair as close to the bed as possible, then she sat down and took Jenny's hands in hers. "Are you in pain? Shall I get the nurse?"

She was in pain now. When she nodded, her grandmother hurried out the door and soon returned with Hailey.

"Oh, sweetie, are you crying again?"

"Again?" Phoebe asked, looking from one to the other.

"I was really hurting earlier," Jenny rushed to say, giving Hailey a desperate glance. "But I thought the pain was easing."

"Sometimes it's that way," Hailey told her

as she checked the medication pump. "Some days it's two steps forward, one step back."

Jenny felt the blessed numbing begin spreading through her.

"Better?" Hailey asked her quietly. When Jenny nodded, she smiled. "When I looked in a while ago you were sleeping soundly."

Phoebe patted Jenny's hand. "Sleep's good for you. It'll help you heal."

"Dinner'll be here soon," Hailey told them as she walked to the door. "You're eating here like usual, Phoebe?"

"Yes, indeed." Phoebe smiled at the nurse and then, when she was gone, she turned back to Jenny. "You were crying *again?*"

Jenny shrugged. "I told you, I was in pain. And I'm missing Matthew and the children."

It was a lie, but surely a lie was acceptable in God's eyes when the alternative was to tell her grandmother that she was crying over fear of what the tests would reveal, wasn't it?

Dinner came a few minutes later. Jenny picked at it with little appetite.

"Don't know why you want to eat here," she told her grandmother when she realized she was staring at her in concern. "The food at the hotel must be better than this."

"I enjoy being here with you," Phoebe told

her. "Do you want me to get you something else from the cafeteria? Or maybe find one of the McDonalds you love?"

She smiled. "No, but thank you."

"I can't wait to get you home and fix your favorites and fatten you up," Phoebe told her.

Jenny couldn't help it. She broke down and cried again.

Matthew hung up the telephone and frowned.

He locked up the telephone shanty and went back into the house. Hannah looked up as he entered.

"What's wrong?"

He sat down heavily at the kitchen table. "Phoebe called me about Jenny."

"What did she say?" Hannah hurried over to sit next to him.

"She said Jenny is too quiet."

"I would imagine. She must be in a lot of pain since the surgery, poor thing. We must say a prayer for her."

"I think it's more than that." He didn't quite know what to say. He was afraid to put what he felt into words.

"Maybe you're worrying too much. Phoebe said that she came through the surgery well, didn't she?"

"*Ya.* Phoebe said she would take Jenny her cell phone so she could talk to me again this evening." He brooded as he stared into his coffee. "I wish I'd gone with them."

Then he realized that Hannah was talking to him. He raised his head. "What?"

"You still can."

"Still can what?"

She made an exasperated sound. "You can go there."

"*Ya.* I guess so."

"Well then?"

He lifted his eyes. "What if she's changed her mind about living here? About — about marrying me?"

"Why would you think that?"

"She's back in her own world," he said. "Maybe she's thinking she likes it there." He swallowed hard. "Why would she want to give all that up to be here?"

Hannah reached across to take his hand. "Because she wants to be with you and the *kinner.* She loves you. She loves them. And she told me how she felt she'd come home when she came here, Matthew."

Matthew stared at their joined hands. He wanted to believe what she was saying.

"Why do you doubt her now? Did she say anything that gave you cause to do so?"

Just that hesitation in her voice when

286

Phoebe had handed her the telephone . . . that quietness. It wasn't anything she'd said. Nothing he could put into words. But he'd so looked forward to talking to her and she'd answered him in monosyllables. He didn't want her to be unhappy away from him, but he had to admit to a selfish desire for her to be missing him. He hadn't heard that in her voice.

"You haven't changed your mind about her, have you? Matthew?"

He vehemently shook his head. "But maybe she has."

"Then go to her. Maybe she's sitting there miserable without you."

"And what if she isn't? What if the way she's behaving isn't because she's not feeling herself yet? What if she's changed her mind?"

Hannah sighed. "Then I guess you'll know. You could get your feelings hurt. But at least you won't sit here miserable, worrying. And you're forgetting one thing." She sat there, looking at him.

Now it was his turn to be exasperated. *"What?"*

"Maybe you'll find out that it was just your imagination. She'll be so happy to see you that you'll wonder what you were thinking . . ." She stood and kissed the top of his head. "And you'll feel like a *mopskopp.*"

Indignant, he glared at her. "I'm not a stupid fellow!"

She laughed and shot him a cocky grin as she stirred something that simmered on the back of the stove.

"No? I think you're stupid in love." Her grin faded. "You're just feeling insecure. But there's no need, Matthew. She loves you."

"Do you think Amelia would approve?"

"Amelia?"

"Ya."

She stopped stirring, and her expression was thoughtful. "Where did that come from?"

He shrugged, not wanting to tell her why. "I don't know. I've asked myself that question a couple of times since Jenny came back into my life."

"*Ya,* Matthew. Amelia loved you and would want you to be happy. And she would want the *kinner* to have a mother to love them."

She walked over and bent to put her arms around his neck. "Think about going to see Jenny, Matthew. Maybe the two of you need to see each other."

"I'll think about it," he said.

It wasn't just that he worried that Jenny

288

had changed her mind. But he felt Hannah wouldn't understand why he didn't want to go to see Jenny in New York City.

Finishing his coffee, he stood. "I'm going out to the barn to do some chores."

"Baked pork chops for supper."

"With applesauce?"

"*Ya.* With applesauce," she said with an indulgent smile.

He chuckled as he left the house. She always knew how to get him to remember to come back on time for supper.

The doctor walked into Jenny's room where she sat in a wheelchair looking out the window.

"Good, you're ready."

A nurse had come in and helped her to dress in the sweat suit she'd worn into the hospital the day of surgery, which included a roomy pair of pants with Velcro down the sides. She'd accomplished the task with a lot of patience. Still, this had almost been too much for Jenny, and they'd had to go slowly and let her rest for a few minutes several times.

The woman had been helpful, but she wouldn't say why Dr. Mac wanted her to dress.

Jenny looked at him. He was wearing jeans

and a polo shirt instead of the scrubs she always saw him in during his rounds. And he was carrying a big file. He handed it to her and began pushing her wheelchair out of the room.

"Are you discharging me today?"

"No. I have a surprise for you."

"I don't like surprises," she muttered darkly.

"I can imagine," he told her, punching the button on the elevator. "But this might be a good one."

A medical transport van was waiting at the hospital entrance. Jenny took a deep breath and exhaled. Even tinged with exhaust, it was nice to smell something other than the antiseptic smell of hospital air. But there would be nothing like the clean, fresh smell of the air back in Lancaster County. Sighing, she watched as the driver hooked her chair to the lift and tried not to wince when there was a small jolt as it settled inside the vehicle. Mac and the driver climbed in and soon they were off.

About ten minutes later, the van pulled into the driveway of a veterans' hospital.

"What are we doing here?"

Mac leaned around his seat. "I got a friend to consult with me about your case."

"I'm not a veteran."

"Well, you're pretty close to one, covering war overseas. But don't worry about it. She's doing it gratis."

"But why a veterans' hospital?"

"They're specialists in your type of injury here."

"What —"

"So many questions," Mac said, grinning at her.

"I'm a reporter. Questions are my life," she shot back.

Then she thought, *My old life.*

Once inside the hospital, Mac handed her the files and pushed her wheelchair down the hallways. Obviously, he knew his way.

Mac's friend, Lannie Barber, MD, turned out to be a pretty redhead with a long ponytail and inquisitive green eyes. She looked barely out of high school as she strode up to Jenny, shook her hand, and then seated herself behind her desk with an air of authority.

"Sorry I couldn't meet you at the hospital, but really, this is the best place for an exam."

She took the files Mac handed to her. Gesturing at him to sit, she began reading.

Jenny fidgeted in her wheelchair while she tried to decipher the other woman's expression. It was unnerving sitting here, feeling the anxiety build about what the doctor would say.

Finally, Dr. Barber looked up, only to fire off a barrage of questions at Mac. They engaged in a highly technical dialogue about tests and theories. The thick file was abandoned as they frowned over Jenny's x-rays and tossed around more mysterious jargon. She'd always considered herself a smart woman, but most of it was over her head.

Then Dr. Barber turned to her. "Would you mind if I examined you?"

Jenny had barely agreed when she was whisked to a room and lifted carefully onto an exam table.

"Nice work," Dr. Barber told Mac as she studied the surgical incision, then looked at the x-ray again.

"Thanks."

"Dr. Barber —"

"Lannie." She smiled at Jenny. "And I'm sorry, I haven't exactly been giving you my best bedside manner."

"It's okay. I just want to find out if I'm going to be okay."

"I want to run blood tests and then I'll be able to tell you more."

Mac wheeled her down to the lab and the blood was drawn.

"Can you wait here for a few minutes?" Mac asked her. "I want to check this out with Lannie."

"Sure."

He and Lannie disappeared with the technician, leaving Jenny in the hallway.

The place was a whirlwind of activity that swirled around her, patients being wheeled in and out of the lab, up and down the hallway to physical therapy. Unlike the hospital where her surgery had been performed, though, the patients at this one were mostly male, her age or younger.

But despite all of the people milling around, she felt as alone as she could ever remember.

Anxiety grew the longer she sat there. She talked to herself the way she had when she'd fallen on the road in the snow. How she wished Matthew would come find her, lifting her up and taking her back to his house to have dinner with his *kinner. It won't be much longer,* she told herself.

Someone dropped something metal near her — she shattered, crying out and covering her face with her hands.

"Miss? Miss? Are you all right?"

Shaking, she looked into the concerned face of a man who sat in a wheelchair in front of her.

"It's okay, it's not gunfire," he was saying. "We're here, in the hospital. You're safe."

She dropped her shaking hands into her lap and looked around, then back at him. "I — I know. I'm okay."

"Where'd you serve?"

"Serve?" She realized he thought she'd been in the military. "Oh, no. I was a civilian."

Recognition dawned in the kind blue eyes studying her. "I know you. I saw you on TV. I've watched a lot of it since I came to this hospital."

He gestured toward his heavily bandaged left leg, then held out his hand. "The name's Christopher Matlock. And you're Jenny Miller."

His hand was warm and strong and callused, like Matthew's. "I haven't seen you around here. I thought I knew everyone."

"I'm just here for a consultation. I had surgery and my doctor wanted me to see someone here."

"How many surgeries have you had so far?"

"Three."

"You're one up on me. Course, I saw what happened to you. I think you got it worse than I did."

So he'd been a bombing victim, too. No wonder he'd seemed to understand when she fell apart.

"I was just going to get coffee. Can I buy you a cup?"

He'd been through what she had and besides, he had such an appealing all-American boy-next-door look with blond hair cut military short, such sincere blue eyes, and an easy, engaging smile.

It was just a cup of coffee and some conversation about things they had in common. Maybe it was better than sitting alone getting anxious about the blood tests and consultation. And who knew how long the blood tests would take?

"That'd be nice, thanks. Just let me tell Mac where I'll be."

13

Matthew heard muffled crying as he passed Annie's room. He looked inside and saw that Annie had the covers pulled over her head. Sitting on the bed, he tugged at the quilt. "Annie? What's the matter, *liebschen?*"

Annie remained quiet under the quilt, but now he heard the hiccups she always got when she cried hard. He tugged again, and this time her tousled head was revealed.

"Tell *Daedi* what's wrong."

"I miss Jenny."

"I do, too."

Sitting up, she pushed her hair back from her face and knuckled away her tears. "She's not coming back. She went away just like *Mamm* and she's never coming back!"

"She's coming back, *liebschen.* She just needs to stay in the hospital a little longer."

Matthew didn't really understand why and he was getting worried, too. Phoebe had told him they were keeping Jenny there a few more days but didn't seem to know more.

But Annie couldn't be convinced. Tears started to flow again. "She's not coming back."

"She is. I promise." He hoped he could keep that promise.

"Let's go get her. I can take care of her."

Matthew hid his smile, gathering her into his arms. "I know you could. You'd do a good job. You take good care of your *dall*." He stroked her back.

"I'd bring her *supp* and *kichli* and loan her my *gwilde*."

Jenny might just feel better having a little girl who loved her serving her soup and cookies, tucked up with a warm quilt, he couldn't help thinking. The sooner they got Jenny back here, the better for all of them.

"Tell you what. We'll call her tomorrow, how about that?"

"Now." Annie, usually so sweet and amenable, folded her arms across her chest as her bottom lip jutted out.

"No, not now," he said firmly. "It's bedtime. She's sleeping like you should be. We'll call her as soon as Mary and Joshua come home from *schul* tomorrow afternoon. If Phoebe is there we'll talk to her, too."

"But *Daedi* —"

"But Annie!" he said, smiling in spite of himself. "Listen to *Daedi*."

She gave a dramatic sigh and nodded, then hugged him before she lay down and let him cover her tightly with her quilt. He leaned down to kiss her and left the room.

On his way to his own bed he looked in on Mary. She was turned toward the wall and her quilt — one her mother had made while she had chemotherapy — was pulled high up over her shoulder.

At first he thought she was sleeping, but then, just as he turned to go down the hallway to check on Joshua, he thought he heard sniffling. Glancing back, he saw that Mary's body was shaking.

"Mary?" he said softly, just in case he'd misheard and she was sleeping. A quiet sniffle came from under the quilt. When she didn't answer, he walked into the room and sat on her bed.

"Mary, is something wrong?" He prayed that she wasn't starting her woman time, dreaded that day,, glad that he could refer questions to Jenny or Hannah.

"I miss Jenny."

He nodded. "Me too."

"You don't think *Mamm* is upset that I said that?" she wanted to know as she sat up and looked at him, pushing away her tears. "I wouldn't want *Mamm* to be upset with me."

"She loves you. She would only look down on you with love," he told her. For the second time that night he gathered a daughter in his arms and tried to give her comfort, drawing the comfort he needed, too.

"I love her. Jenny, I mean. And *Mamm*, too." She was silent for a long moment. "She told me her *mamm* died when she was a girl."

"I know." He and Jenny had talked about it the first summer she'd come to visit her *grossmudder*. She felt she lost two parents — first her mother and then her father, who retreated into a world of his own, so grief-stricken he didn't realize that his daughter needed him.

Matthew had tried to remember not to do that when Amelia died but he didn't feel he'd succeeded. His children seemed well-adjusted, but he felt that was due more to Hannah than himself. She'd kept the whole family together.

"I promised Annie we'd call Jenny after you come home from *schul* tomorrow," he told her. "But you have to go to sleep now."

She opened her mouth to protest but the protest turned into a yawn.

299

"Right now," he said

"Okay. Night, *Daedi*."

He tucked her in and turned to leave the room.

Joshua stood there in the doorway, his eyes sad.

With a tired sigh, Matthew draped an arm around his son's shoulders. *The boy has grown another couple inches,* he thought.

"She'll be home soon, *Sohn*," he said as he guided Joshua toward his bedroom. He sat with him, quietly talking before Joshua pulled his quilt up to his chin and closed his eyes.

A few minutes later, Matthew approached his own bedroom.

This time of the day had always been his favorite. He'd so enjoyed this looking in on the *kinner*, tucked up safe and warm, sometimes smiling as they dreamed. He used to hold Amelia's hand as they performed this loving chore and then they'd walk into their own room and shut the door and have their together time. They loved their children, but their time alone as a couple was so special.

Now he was glad that they had made their time together special, for Amelia was gone but he had no regrets about making her know that he loved her.

Lying there alone in the big bed he'd built with his own hands, he thought about Jenny. He hoped that she wasn't in so much pain tonight, that she had cheered up, that she'd been told she was getting to go home soon. And he hoped that she was looking forward to coming home to him. With that thought, he laid his hand on the pillow beside his where he hoped she'd rest her head one day, and he slept.

"Shame on you, Doctor," Hailey chided Mac as she followed him into Jenny's room. "You've kept her out too long. Look at her; she's pale and obviously in pain. Did you think to give her something for it?"

He stood back as Hailey set the brake on the wheelchair and helped Jenny into bed, fussing over her, taking off her slippers, pulling the sheets over her. She reconnected the IV with the pain meds. "Let's let this take the edge off your pain before we get those clothes off you."

"Well, uh, since everything's under control here, I'll be going," Mac said, backing toward the door.

"Sure, make her have a setback then take no responsibility," Hailey muttered. "What were you thinking?"

Mac stiffened. "Hey, I'm a doctor; you

shouldn't be talking to me like that."

Having safely tucked her patient into bed, Hailey turned, put her hands on her hips, and gave him a fulminating glance.

"I — gotta go," he said. "We'll talk about this later."

"You bet we will!"

Jenny hid a smile and tried to get comfortable in bed. When her grandmother walked in a few minutes later, the medication was beginning to work and her head was nodding.

Hailey was holding the hanger with Jenny's clothes, about to put it into the closet.

"Does this mean she's getting discharged?" Phoebe wanted to know, her voice pitched higher with excitement.

"No, the doctor took Jenny out for a consultation. I was just hanging up her clothes."

"Consultation?" Phoebe looked from one to the other.

Jenny tried to think of a distraction. "Is that dinner?"

Hailey glanced toward the door. "I'm not sure. I'll go check."

Jenny sneaked a look at her grandmother and saw that she was staring at her intently.

"Your doctor took you for a consultation outside the hospital? What's going on,

Jenny? And don't tell me it's nothing."

"I'm just worrying. It's nothing."

"It's not nothing if it's worrying you, *kind*."

"I don't want to worry you."

"I won't worry," Phoebe said firmly. She took Jenny's hand and stroked it. "You won't worry me. Remember —"

"It's arrogant to worry when God knows what He's doing. He has a plan for you," Jenny quoted. "I remember."

So much has changed. What will happen now? She promptly burst into tears.

Phoebe sat on the bed and took Jenny into her arms. She patted her on the back and let her cry it out. "Ssh, *liebschen,* ssh, it's all right. Nothing can be this bad."

Jenny drew back to reach for a tissue and wipe away her tears. Taking a deep breath, she told her grandmother what had been happening, all in a rush so she wouldn't lose her nerve or start crying again.

"I can see why you're upset," Phoebe said gravely, taking Jenny's hands in hers. "You weren't expecting news like this."

"I thought things were going so well." Jenny's voice shook.

"They are."

"How can you say that?" She stared at her grandmother.

"Your doctor hasn't brought you bad news yet, has he? *Nee,*" she said when Jenny shook her head. "But if he does, you'll deal with it, Jenny, just as you have all that has happened to you — with grace, with faith. With hope. And you'll have Matthew and the *kinner* to help you through it."

Matthew. Tears rushed into Jenny's eyes again, and she blinked them back furiously. There had been too many tears for so long. Her grandmother was right — she had to wait to see what Mac and Lannie found out.

One of the nursing aides walked in with a dinner tray. Another aide followed, bringing Phoebe's tray.

Phoebe pulled the second bed table closer to Jenny's and then sat down there. They bent their heads in prayer for the meal.

Jenny poked at the contents of her plate. Tonight supper was ham, macaroni and cheese, and some limp brussels sprouts.

"You need to eat."

"I know." She cut a piece of ham. "I was just remembering the first time I made dinner — for Matthew and Hannah and the *kinner.* You told me how to bake a ham. Remember?"

"Yes, indeed."

She put a bite of ham in her mouth and chewed and then frowned at the funny noise she heard. Glancing over, she saw that her grandmother was pressing her lips together, trying not to laugh.

"The biscuits," they said at the same time, laughing.

"I looked the next day and even the wild animals weren't desperate enough to eat them," Jenny told her.

Phoebe pulled Jenny's cell phone from her pocket and handed it to Jenny. It vibrated in Jenny's hand as she looked to see who was calling.

"It's Matthew."

"He said he'd call tonight. I told him when I would be here to see you."

Jenny felt such a mix of emotions — pure, undiluted joy at his calling and then, just as quickly, trepidation about what she would say if he asked how she was doing. She hoped he wouldn't ask her anything she couldn't answer without worrying him. She flipped it open. "Hello."

"*Gut-n-owed,* Jenny."

"Matthew! How are you?"

"*Gut.* But I'm calling to see how you are." He stopped as Jenny heard Annie speaking in the background. "Wait a minute, Jenny, Annie is being very impatient."

She closed her eyes and bit her lip as he calmly reminded his daughter that she'd get to talk to Jenny in a minute.

The last time they'd talked, she had been feeling awful — full of pain from the surgery, full of fear at what the doctor had told her.

The pain was easing a little, and she still didn't know what Mac tell her in the next day or two. But her grandmother was right. She had to have faith. Hers had slipped, but somehow she had to find it again.

She hadn't thought she'd find love, not with her injuries. But Matthew had seen past them. She didn't want to lose him, didn't want to lose his precious children she'd fallen in love with as much as with him.

"Jenny? Are you still there?"

"I'm here. And yes, I'm feeling a little better. Thank you."

"Jenny, Jenny, Jenny," Annie sing-songed.

She laughed. What a darling little girl.

"Go tell Mary and Joshua to come," Matthew told her.

"I talk firwst."

"You get to go first," he agreed. "Go find Mary and Joshua."

"Jenny, Annie was upset last night," Matthew said quickly. "If you could reassure her that you're coming home soon, I'd appreciate it."

"Of course." She took a deep breath and then sighed. "Oh, I want to come home so badly."

"You've been away too long." His voice was low and fervent.

"It should be just a few more days," she told him and when she looked over at her grandmother, Jenny saw that she was smiling and nodding.

She heard a commotion over the phone line. Matthew was chuckling as Annie could be heard in the background.

"Annie's back. I'll let her talk now. Don't hang up when she's finished."

Jenny relaxed against her pillows and smiled. "I won't."

She heard Matthew gently reminding Annie not to talk too long, that Mary and Joshua wanted to talk, too.

A half hour later, after talking to each of the children and even Hannah, then saying good-bye to Matthew, Jenny handed the phone back to her grandmother.

"I don't know who talked more, them or me," she said, shaking her head. She fell silent.

"You didn't tell him."

She looked at her grandmother. "No. I don't really have anything to tell him yet."

"Lean on him," Phoebe said quietly. "He

loves you. He wants to marry you."

"I know. And I want to marry him."

"Want to? You *are* marrying him."

Jenny stared at her hands. She felt rather than saw her grandmother get up and come to sit on the bed.

"You haven't changed your mind." It was a statement, not a question.

"I will if the doctor says there's a problem. Matthew doesn't need another wife who has health problems and could — could —" She stopped, unable to finish.

"Hold on to your faith in God," Phoebe said, taking Jenny's hands and squeezing them. "He won't fail you."

A few minutes later, an announcement came over the p.a. system that visiting hours were over.

"I'm sure I can stay a while longer if you want me to."

Jenny shook her head. "No, but thank you. It's been a long day for both of us. You go back to the hotel. Promise me you'll take a taxi."

Phoebe smiled. "I will." She bent and kissed Jenny's forehead, then tucked the quilt around her. "Is there anything you want me to get for you before I leave?"

"You already have," Jenny murmured. "I don't know what I did without you before I came here."

Phoebe smiled. "You're a strong young woman. You managed just fine. But I'm happy you came to visit me. And I'm glad you decided to stay. Sleep now. We'll be back home soon."

Just as she reached the door, Jenny thought of something. "You know, I think I'd like to keep the cell phone tonight."

"*Schur.* But I don't have its charger with me."

"It'll be fine for a night without it."

Phoebe handed her the cell. "It'll be *gut* for you to have it if you want to talk to Matthew again."

After her grandmother left the room, Jenny got to work on her iPhone, looking up Web sites with information about bombing survivors. She knew she was fortunate in having Mac and Lannie on the job looking out for her. But she'd never been one to willingly be dependent on others, especially for something so important.

And she wasn't about to start now.

Mac came in bright and early the next morning. Hailey was right behind him.

Jenny waited for the fireworks.

"Nurse Hailey tells me I owe you an apology," he said, giving her a quick sidelong

309

glance. "She's right. I should have been more careful not to let you go without a pain injection. Once pain builds I know it can be hard to knock it back again. In my defense, you were having coffee with that soldier and I thought you were doing better than you were."

"It's not an apology if you defend what you did," Hailey muttered.

Mac grimaced. "Sorry, Jenny."

"It's okay. I should have spoken up."

With a brief glance at the nurse, Mac took a seat beside the bed. "Maybe you can help me work on my bedside manner."

"Maybe." Her voice was stern, but Jenny thought she detected a twinkle in the woman's eyes. She handed him Jenny's chart and left the room.

Is that a smile lurking around the corners of Mac's mouth? Jenny wondered. *Interesting.*

Mac studied his notes, then looked at her. "I don't want to keep you in suspense. Lannie and I didn't find any evidence of anything toxic in your blood work."

Jenny felt an initial burst of elation and then she realized that Mac was sitting there, silent, avoiding her eyes. "Do you know what I did last night, Mac?"

"Watched television?" he asked, glancing at her warily. "Went to bed early?"

310

She reached for her iPhone and held it out. "Great devices, these things. You can plan your day. Get concert tickets. Check your e-mail. And —"

"Do research on the Internet," he finished for her. He sighed heavily.

"I'm a reporter — used to be a reporter," she corrected. "I wanted to check things out for myself."

"I should have known." He sighed. "So what did you find out?"

"There've been some reports of toxicity appearing several years after the bombings. Victims have gotten sick."

"And most of the victims haven't."

"Ah, an optimist." Suddenly tired, she leaned back against the pillows.

Mac wrote more notes in her file. "I'm sending you home. Keep an eye on your temperature, and let me know right away if it goes up or you have any problems. I don't expect them." He closed the file and looked at her. "And send me a photo of you dancing at the wedding."

"No dancing. No photos."

"Huh. You don't say. Okay, well, then just enjoy yourself and have a happy life, Jenny." He shook her hand then strolled out of the room.

"Yeah," she sighed as she watched him leave. "I'll go do just that very thing."

14

"This feels familiar," Jenny said as Matthew carried her into Phoebe's house.

"Except I'm even happier to do it this time," he told her, gathering her closer.

Jenny pressed her cheek against his and sighed. "What a sweet thing to say."

"I missed you very much." He set her down carefully on the sofa. "How is the pain?"

"Better now." She reached for his hand and squeezed it. "I missed you, too, Matthew."

Phoebe bustled in. She'd shed her coat and now she helped Jenny take hers off. "How about a sandwich and a cup of tea?"

"That would be wonderful. And then you need to sit down. You've been buzzing around me like a busy bee all morning."

Jenny looked at Matthew. "*Grossmudder* made sure all our luggage got on the plane and took care of me on the flight. And that was no small task. I got sick when we went through a patch of bad weather."

Matthew took a seat in a chair next to the sofa and they talked while Phoebe fixed the simple lunch.

"You need to rest," he said later, after they'd eaten. "I can see you're trying to stay awake."

She wanted to protest, but her eyes wouldn't stay open. "Pain pills," she muttered. "I hate to take them." She remembered complaining about that very thing to David as he was bringing her here months ago.

"I'll stop by later with the *kinner*," Matthew told her, and she felt his kiss on her forehead as she drifted.

Phoebe patted her shoulder and covered her with a quilt. "Rest now. There will come a time very soon when you will not need them. And you will walk without pain to meet Matthew and become husband and wife."

She smiled, and then she slept.

Keeping his word, Matthew brought the children later that day. Annie wanted to climb into Jenny's lap, but he wouldn't let her.

"Remember, I told you we have to be

careful not to bump Jenny," he reminded her.

Leaning over as much as she could, Jenny held out her arms and Annie went into them, hugging her. She closed her eyes and inhaled the clean scent of Annie's hair, washed with baby shampoo. Hannah said Annie always insisted that she was a big girl, but complained that the other kind stung her eyes. It felt so good to hold the child that Jenny didn't want to let go. Tears rushed into her eyes as Joshua and Mary took their turns hugging her, telling her how much they'd missed her. All three held cards they'd made for her from construction paper and crayons and glitter that fell all over her lap and made her laugh.

Oh, how she loved them. How she'd missed them. It wasn't surprising to her how quickly she'd bonded with them, for they were such loving, wonderful children. But part of the bond had come from her knowing what it felt like to lose a parent so early in life. They had their father, but they longed for a mother's touch and found it again in her.

Mother. When she sat back she felt a rush of tears she had to blink away. How could she risk becoming their mother and leaving them, not just Matthew?

"*Daedi*, Jenny's crwying. Why is she crwying?" the always observant Annie asked.

"They're happy tears," she lied, wiping them away with her fingers. "Your *daedi* knows about happy tears, don't you, Matthew?" But when she looked up at him, she saw him watching her with a concerned frown.

Supper wore her out.

Jenny sat with her leg propped up on a chair and listened to the happy chatter of the children ranged around the kitchen table.

Hannah tried to stop them from talking with their mouths full but finally gave up the effort and grinned at Jenny. She reached over and squeezed Jenny's hand.

"It's so good to have you back. You've been missed."

Joshua turned to Phoebe. "What was the big city like?"

"Lots of people," she told him fondly, using his napkin to wipe a smear of gravy from his chin. "Lots of noise. Nothing like here."

"Did they give you ice cweam?" Annie asked Jenny.

"One of her friends had her tonsils out last year," Matthew told her. "Annie thinks everyone gets ice cream at the hospital."

Jenny smiled at Annie. "I had it some-times. My favorite's butter pecan. What's yours?"

"Stwahbewrry," Annie said, giving her a gap-toothed grin.

Instead of winding down as supper pro-gressed, the children seemed to get more animated. Jenny shifted in her seat several times until finally Matthew quietly asked her if she wanted to go into the other room. Grateful for the understanding, she nodded and he helped her up and back to the living room.

The children were disappointed, but Phoebe brought out ice cream and they put their dishes in the sink and were happily waiting for it to be served as Jenny left the kitchen.

Settled down on the sofa with a pillow and quilt, Jenny nodded when Matthew asked if she'd like some coffee. The last thing she remembered was watching him leave the room to get it.

This is the strangest thing, she thought drowsily, brushing at her cheek. What are but-terflies doing fluttering around my face at this time of the year? And since when did but-terflies giggle? She opened her eyes and stared into Annie's face. Annie's little mouth was still pursed in a kiss. She grinned at Jenny.

"*Kumm,* Annie, let Jenny sleep," her grandmother whispered. Smiling, Jenny dozed.

Waking a little while later, she blinked, wondering where she was and then realized. Sitting up carefully, she winced and glanced at the clock over the mantel. Time for another pain pill. She got to her feet, reached for the walker, and maneuvered carefully toward the kitchen.

Hannah was washing dishes as Matthew dried. She stood in the doorway for a moment and watched them, thinking how she loved this man. She'd come to love his sister like her own, too.

How was she going to tell him what Mac had said? She had to do it. There was no way she'd let him go into a marriage with her otherwise. What would his reaction be? Surely he would be afraid to become a widower again?

"Anyway, I wanted to talk to you about Jenny," Hannah was saying.

Jenny stopped dead in her tracks.

"When she first came, I told you that you shouldn't become interested in her."

Tears sprang into Jenny's eyes. Blindly, she turned to go back in the other room but moved awkwardly and her leg screamed in protest. She cried out and grabbed at the

318

doorframe, but her hand slipped and she started to fall.

A dish crashed to the floor as she heard Matthew shout her name. He grabbed her before she hit the floor and gathered her to his chest. "Are you okay?" he asked, stroking her hair. "Tell me you haven't hurt yourself!"

"Let me go!" She pushed at him and teetered for a moment. But he didn't let go and held on to her forearms, staring at her in concern. "Just let me go, please."

"What's wrong?" Matthew asked her.

Hannah rushed over. "Don't you understand? She heard what I was saying." She turned to Jenny and laid a hand on her arm. "Jenny, let me explain —"

"What's to explain?" She pulled away from them and moved into the other room, barely seeing her way through the blur of tears.

But leaving the room didn't help. They followed her as she sank down on the sofa again, keeping the walker between herself and them as if she needed a barrier to protect her.

"Jenny, what I was saying was how I felt before, when you first came here," Hannah told her. Her own eyes were filled with tears as she sank down on the sofa next to Jenny.

"Please, I feel terrible that I hurt you. I never meant for you to hear that. I love you like a sister."

Reaching into the pocket of her sweats, Jenny found a tissue and wiped her eyes. "Don't worry about it."

"I need to explain what you think you heard," Hannah insisted. "I didn't want Matthew to get involved with you because I was afraid he'd be hurt again. He'd lost one wife and here you were, so injured, hurting in your body and in your heart. I was afraid for him. I didn't want him to lose someone he loved again. But I was wrong."

"No, you weren't."

"What?"

Jenny wanted to pace but she couldn't. "I'm a bad prospect for marriage," she whispered, avoiding Matthew's intense scrutiny.

Matthew pulled the walker away from Jenny and set it aside. He knelt at her feet and took her hands in his. "What happened in New York City, Jenny?"

With an effort, she raised her eyes and looked at him. "Mac — my surgeon — he was worried that some of the metal they removed might be toxic, might cause me harm someday. Might even kill me."

"You said 'was.' "

"Mac said he can't be sure. I'm fine now but . . ." she trailed off, afraid to put it in words. "I can't marry you, Matthew."

"Have you changed your mind?"

She stared at him. "Didn't you hear what I said?"

"I heard you. Did you hear me? Did you change your mind because there's some difficulty, Jenny? Seems to me you go in saying it's for better or worse or it shouldn't be at all."

"But —"

"Did you change your mind about loving me?" he persisted. "Look me in the eye and tell me you don't love me."

"Of course I love you." Tears started sliding down her cheeks again. "I just can't saddle you with someone who might get sick, who might do just what Hannah said and make you a widower again."

"Amelia's dying like she did taught me something," Matthew told her quietly. "None of us knows when we'll join our heavenly Father. I might die before you. Besides, don't I get to have some say in this? I know you want to protect me just like Hannah. But I want you, Jenny. I want to marry you and be your husband and share my life and my *kinner* with you."

"I told you I don't know if I can have

children because of my injuries," she said. "Now, I'd be afraid to even try to have them with this hanging over me. I couldn't risk a baby's health —"

"We already talked about *kinner*," he reminded her. "I told you that I have three to share with you, Jenny. If it's God's will to have more, then it will be so."

"But —"

"I'm not losing you again, Jenny," he said. He took a seat next to her and gathered her into his arms.

Jenny realized that some time during their conversation Hannah had quietly gotten up and left them to talk privately.

"I don't know what to do," she told him, absorbing the strength and comfort of his arms.

"Trust in God, Jenny. He wouldn't have brought you back to me if we weren't supposed to be together again. Trust that we'll have a long, happy life together."

He brought out his pocket handkerchief and wiped away her tears. "I'm sure all of this has been hard on you. I should have gone there to the hospital with you, helped you through this. But you're home now. Everything will be fine again."

"You make it sound so easy," she murmured, exhausted from the day, from the worry.

"Rest now, dear one," Matthew told her as he stroked her hair. "Trust in Him that all is well."

Jenny woke when she heard the front door open and close.

Her grandmother came into the room. "Did you have a nice visit with Matthew and Hannah?"

Yawning, Jenny nodded. "It was nice of you to take the children home and put them to bed."

"I missed them."

"Me too. Then I fell asleep before it was even their bedtime."

"You've been through a lot. Your body needs sleep to heal." She gave Jenny a fond smile. "Are you ready to go to bed?"

"I shouldn't be, but I am." Jenny laughed and shook her head as she maneuvered herself up from the sofa. "I remember this funny writer, Erma Bombeck. She used to say that it was never too late to take a nap, that no one should have to go to bed tired."

"Sounds very wise," her grandmother said. She sighed. "It'll be good to sleep in our own beds tonight, *ya?*"

"*Ya.*"

Jenny used the time recuperating to study to join the church, to write in her journal, and to read. She was impatient as always but now felt content.

So much in her had healed in the last months — her spirit as well as her body. Even though a surgeon had had to hurt her again to help her, Jenny felt so different emotionally that it wasn't long before she was taking her first steps with a cane instead of the walker, then walking more and more.

Matthew came to visit one afternoon and found her writing in her journal. She made room for him to sit on the sofa beside her.

"Mary loves writing in the journal you gave her."

"I started writing in one when I was about her age." Jenny looked sternly at Matthew. "I hope that you don't read her journal or let Joshua tease her about it. She'd be devastated if she thought anyone read it."

China crashed to the floor.

Matthew jumped up. "Phoebe? Are you all right? Did you burn yourself?"

Phoebe stared down at the spreading stain on her long apron. "I'm fine. I'll get the broom."

"You go change. I'll sweep it up."

Is it my imagination or did Grandmother look strange as she left the room? Jenny wondered.

Then Matthew returned with a broom and dustpan and swept up the shards of the teapot and cups Phoebe had been carrying. "I'll go put more water on to boil," he told her.

When he returned, he saw that Jenny was staring pensively at the fire.

"What is it?"

"Is it my imagination or was my grandmother upset when she heard us talking about journals?"

"It was just an accident."

Jenny thought about it, then nodded. "Maybe you're right."

Matthew gestured at the laptop that sat on the table beside her. "What are you writing on your machine?"

"Oh, just some notes about my time overseas. Doodling, really."

"You said once I could see the television interview David did with you. Without my *kinner,* since they're too young. But then you left for the surgery and we didn't do it. Can we look at it now?"

Surprised, she nodded. "If you want to. The DVD is on my desk in my room."

325

He rose. "I'll see if Phoebe will get it for me."

When he returned with it, Jenny put it in the computer. "Have you ever watched a DVD?"

He shook his head. "I saw a movie once, with friends. During my rumschpringe."

"Sometime I'd like to hear all about that time," she teased him.

"There isn't much to tell," he assured her. "I didn't have much interest in exploring outside my community and got baptized soon after."

Jenny started the DVD. Even after the interview ended, Matthew wore a troubled expression as he stared at the blank screen.

"Now you know why I didn't want the children to see it," she said.

Turning to her, he lifted her hand, kissed it, and held it to his cheek.

"It hurts to see what happened to you. I don't know how you survived it." He sighed. "God didn't want you to join Him yet."

He lapsed into thought for a long moment. "I'm glad you went to do the interview with David," he said finally. "He was right to get you to do it. There's been a peace about you since you came back from that trip, even though you had bad news about needing more surgery."

"I know."

She closed the lid on the laptop. "I thought I had to go back overseas and I knew I couldn't, not with my problems recovering from my injuries. But when David showed the organizations that help children and asked viewers to contribute, I realized that I didn't have to feel like I was the only one who could try to make people care."

Matthew linked his fingers with hers. "Jenny, sometimes when a person gets a second chance at life I wonder if it isn't because they're supposed to do something more with their life. It occurs to me that you could make people care in a different way."

He gestured at the laptop. "Write about the children, Jenny," he told her. "Write so that people will care. Maybe it's time for you to do a book about the children, about what you saw, about what you wish people would do for them. Write from your heart, Jenny, and the people will hear."

How have I been so lucky — no, blessed — to meet someone who so truly understands me? she wondered.

"You have the time now," he continued. "You should use it."

She looked at him doubtfully. "I don't know if I can do that. I wrote for a newspaper before I joined the network, and of course, I wrote what I was going to say on the air. *But a book?* I don't know." Laughing, she shook her head. "Every journalist I know says they have a book in them, that they'll write it when they get time. But few ever do."

"You can do it, Jenny," he said. "You can do anything."

Jenny brought his hand to her lips and kissed it. "Thank you for saying that."

She thought about it after he left. Maybe she *should* try writing a book. If nothing else, she certainly did have the time and something she wanted to say so much.

Flipping through her big yellow legal pad, she read what she'd written that morning: *He was a little boy. Maybe six years old. He didn't know how old he was. No one had ever told him. He was lucky. He had a big sister who tried to take care of him after their parents were killed when a mortar fell on their home.*

Phoebe brought her tea and set it on the table near the sofa. Jenny murmured a thank you, but kept writing. When she looked up a little while later, Phoebe was sitting quietly in the chair near the fire, staring into the flames.

"Grandmother?"

Phoebe turned. "Yes?"

"Are you okay?"

"Yes. I told you that I didn't burn myself."

"You seem quiet." Jenny set the laptop aside and reached for her cup.

"It would be rude to talk when you're writing."

Jenny smiled. "It's okay. I'm just fooling around a little with an idea. Matthew seems to think I should write it."

"What is the idea?"

"There was this little boy I met overseas. He lost his parents when a bomb hit their house."

"When you make someone care about one, you make them care about many."

Jenny stared at her, surprised. "I heard that once. Someone said it about Anne Frank, a young Jewish girl who wrote in a journal during World War II. The journal was found after she died, and it was published."

Phoebe looked again at the fire. "No one thought it was wrong to publish it without her permission?"

Jenny shook her head. "It made people care about those who were put to death by the Nazis just because they were Jewish. Someone had hidden Anne and her family, but the Nazis found them and sent them to a concentration camp — a prison camp. Yet even when bad things were happening to people around her, Anne wrote that she still believed that people were good."

"What happened to Anne?"

"She died in the camp."

Phoebe sighed and shook her head. "I think Matthew has a good idea. Perhaps what you write about the children will make people care."

"Maybe."

"Well, I've sat long enough. I think I will go start supper."

"But we just ate —" Jenny began.

Phoebe had already hurried from the room.

Shrugging, Jenny put down her cup and picked up her laptop.

Matthew looked grim when he stopped by several days later.

"Josiah has been complaining again," he told Jenny and Phoebe. "Seems he objects to Jenny being baptized."

"But he can't stop it, can he?"

Phoebe shook her head. "No. Benjamin and Isaac made a point of talking to me last Sunday. They said good things about you and the articles that you gave them to read. I'm sure they'll speak to the bishop if it's necessary."

"I didn't tell you to worry you," Matthew told Jenny. "If we don't get approval, we'll be married anyway."

Jenny frowned. "How would you —" she stopped and stared at him. "No, Matthew! I won't have you go outside your church to marry me."

"And I won't let anything or anyone stand in the way of marrying you," he said simply but firmly.

He left to go do some chores, promising to return to take Jenny to her first physical therapy appointment since the surgery.

"Well," said Phoebe. "Matthew has spoken."

Jenny laughed. "He is a very determined man, isn't he?"

Phoebe's smiled and she nodded. "Now, I was thinking that we could do two different things this afternoon. We could discuss the *Ordnung* some more together, or we could do something about the wedding."

"Hmm," Jenny mused. "Studying the rules or planning my wedding? Guess which one I'll choose?"

Weddings were simple in the community, as Jenny expected. She would be married here, in her grandmother's home. Her dress wouldn't be white, and it wouldn't be fancy.

Instead, the usual color was a shade of blue. The dress, unlike those in *Englisch* weddings, would be one she'd wear when she was buried.

"How well do you sew?" Phoebe asked.

"As well as I cook." She looked at her grandmother. "Don't say it."

"Say what?"

But Phoebe was trying hard not to smile. "I'll help you make your dress."

It wasn't the dress Jenny had thought she would wear in her wedding. When she was a little girl she'd fantasized about a long white dress that glistened with crystals and pearls and a flowing white veil on her hair.

But when she thought about the man who would stand beside her and make vows with her, when she thought about the precious children who would be her family afterward, what she wore held little importance to her.

The meal after the wedding would be a feast, enough to make the tables groan with abundance: roast chicken and its filling, mashed potatoes and gravy, vegetables, and dessert upon dessert. All of it was to be prepared by the bride's family, so Hannah had offered to help her.

"I can help," Jenny told her. "Maybe I should make apple crisp. It was the one thing that turned out well when I cooked."

"When you're better you'll be cooking more. It just takes practice."

"I hope so. I sincerely hope so. Otherwise we'll all starve unless you invite us over to dinner every night."

She frowned as she stretched her leg to ease a slight cramp. "I need to talk to Hannah. Matthew says she is insisting that she will move out after he and I marry."

"That's as it should be."

"But that's been her home since Amelia died. I don't want her to feel like she's being pushed out."

"I know Hannah. She won't feel pushed out. She'll want you to be the woman of the house."

Jenny sighed. "So much to think about. And the book keeps pulling at me. I think I'll go work on it for a while until Matthew comes for me."

"Look, there's a crocus pushing out of the snow," Jenny cried as they drove to her appointment. "Spring is truly here. Some trees even have buds." She sighed. "I feel like I've had to hibernate in the house for so long."

"When you're feeling better we'll do something."

Jenny seized on his words. "What? What?"

He chuckled. "It'll be a surprise. And a

reward to you for getting better."

"I'm not looking forward to therapy again. But Mac, my surgeon, thinks it should be easier this time. He better be right, or he'll hear about it."

The ride in the buggy was the first time they'd been alone since she'd come home. She held hands with him and cherished spending this time alone. They talked about the coming months, what Matthew would plant in the fields, about the children and about the wedding planning she and her grandmother had been doing.

"And the book?"

"The book is going well."

He nodded, as if that was to be understood.

"I wrote David what I was doing and he sent me the name of an agent to represent the book to a publisher when I'm ready." She fell silent.

"You miss him and his wife and son."

She nodded. "They're such good friends. They did so much for me both times I was in the hospital. Joy said they're looking forward to coming to the wedding."

"It'll be good to have them here as friends who have become family for you."

He was silent for so long, she touched his hand so he'd look at her.

"Is something bothering you, Matthew?"

"I wish that my parents had been able to meet you."

"I wish that my parents had met you, too."

"Actually, I met your father once," he admitted after a long moment.

"You did? When?"

"When he came to get you that last summer."

She blinked. "I didn't know. He never said anything."

Matthew hesitated. "I don't think he liked me, Jenny."

"Oh, I doubt that, Matthew. It was probably just that fathers never like the boys who pay attention to their daughters."

He shot her a rueful look. "If you say so."

Something bright golden yellow distracted her. "Oh, look! Daffodils! I love daffodils! They're my favorite."

She turned to him. "Except for that beautiful rose Phoebe brought to me in the hospital from you."

"I wish that I could have gone there to be with you."

"You needed to stay here. And I wasn't away long."

"It felt like months," he told her.

She slipped her arm through his and hugged it. "What a sweet thing to say. But it was enough that my grandmother came with me. It's been good to spend time with her after us not being seeing each other much through the years."

"And she'll be close by when you move into my house."

"I told her she may need to invite us over often until my cooking gets better."

"Your cooking is good."

"You have an iron stomach and a forgiving nature," she told him with a wry smile. "Oh, here we are."

The therapy was painful and hard, as it always was the first visit after surgery. If Mac thought it would be different, he was wrong. But Jenny was even more determined than last time. "I want to walk without a cane when I get married," she told the therapist.

"Oh, wow, you're engaged! That's wonderful!"

The woman looked at Jenny's left hand. "You didn't get your ring yet? Oh, wait, are you engaged to that handsome Amish guy who brings you? They don't do engagement or wedding rings, do they? Well, finding the right man is the most important part, right? You know what I mean."

Jenny smiled. "Right."

There were familiar-looking paper bags sitting in the buggy when Jenny came out.

"McDonalds? Did my grandmother tell you it's my weakness?"

"She said your friend Joy made you happy sneaking their food into the hospital."

Jenny nodded. Looking at the bag again, she laughed. "Now that's a picture I never visualized. Did you go through the drive-through?"

Smiling, he shook his head. "No, I went inside. There's a spot nearby where I thought we could park and eat."

When he pulled the buggy over a short time later, she saw that he'd found a place where daffodils had sprung up.

"How thoughtful," she whispered. "Thank you."

"You're welcome." Reaching into one of the bags, he brought out a cheeseburger and handed it to her.

Jenny looked into the bag next to her. "Oh, good, french fries. If you hadn't gotten fries, I'd have to reevaluate whether you were the right man for me."

He laughed. "If Annie finds out that we had McDonalds without her, she'll be unhappy with both of us," he told her, biting into his Big Mac.

"Hannah invited me to come over tomorrow and talk about the routine at your house." Jenny squeezed some ketchup on her fries. "Matthew, I wish she would reconsider her decision to move out when we're married."

"There is no arguing with Hannah about this." He finished his fries and reached over to steal one of hers. "She feels you need to be the woman of the house, the mother the children are expecting."

"Mother," she said softly. "I like the sound of that."

"I'll remind you of that when they're not on their best behavior."

"Be careful how you talk about my children," she admonished. "And don't try to steal any more of my fries."

"Look at that!" he exclaimed. "I have never seen one of those come out before spring is here."

Jenny turned to look. "I don't see anything."

But, out of the corner of her eye, she saw movement. When she turned back, he was popping several fries into his mouth.

"Matthew! I didn't know you were a french fry thief!" She eyed him. "What else don't I know about you?"

His grin faded. "Jenny? Are you having second thoughts?"

"Well, I don't know. A french fry thief. I'll have to think about this."

"A woman who would not share a few french fries with her hard-working husband-to-be," he said soberly. "Perhaps I should think about this, too."

He was the first to laugh and with a jerk of the reins, he set the buggy moving.

"Can I drive?"

"Have you ever done it before?" He stopped at what he said and chuckled as he shook his head. "Of course not. There are no buggies in New York City, are there?"

She bit her lip, suppressing her smile. "But it's something I need to learn to do, right?"

He looked pointedly at her fries.

"You drive a hard bargain." She handed him the box.

He showed her how to indicate direction to Pilot, his horse. It was surprisingly easy and very calming to drive the buggy. Matthew sat beside her munching his fries — hers, really — and nodding approvingly when she looked over to see how she was doing.

"Life's funny, don't you think?" she asked

as she gazed out at the fields beside the road.

"Funny?"

"I could never have imagined what's happening to my life now," she said. "Not in a million years."

"That is what is amazing about God," he told her. "He can imagine better things, bigger things for us than we can." He thought for a moment. "In Corinthians, it says we can't know what God has prepared for those who love Him."

When they arrived at her grandmother's house, a moving van was just leaving.

"My things!" Jenny cried. She got out of the buggy before Matthew could help her and pushed her walker ahead of her.

Phoebe looked up when Jenny opened the door. "You just missed the moving men. I told them to put the boxes in your room. I hope you can still get in there to sleep."

"I didn't pack that much."

Her grandmother smiled. "I didn't think so until they put them in that room."

"I need to get back home," Matthew told them.

"That sounds like you don't want to help me unpack."

"It would not be seemly to visit your bedroom," he said, backing toward the door.

"Men are the same no matter where you find them," Jenny said wryly as he left.

"I'll help you unpack. Sit and rest for a few minutes before you do it. You look tired."

"Therapy wore me out." She pushed the walker out of the way as she sat down at the table. "I was just joking with Matthew. I can unpack the boxes myself."

Phoebe brought two mugs of coffee to the table. "So, are you looking forward to having your things around you?"

Jenny nodded. "I was thinking about that. The things I had sent, I mean. I know that brides here take many things to their new home. Linens and house goods they've embroidered and that family members have given them for their future home. I don't have any of that. I suppose I could have brought more things from my apartment but they didn't seem right here."

"Where you sent them, the women's shelter, that was a good place for them, a good thing to do. You have a generous heart. Besides, I can't think of anything Matthew's home needs that it does not have. Once you move in as his wife, you'll see what you need and we'll make it or shop for it."

Jenny went to her room and as her grandmother had warned, there wasn't much space to navigate. She lay down on the bed, grateful for a place to rest until she could begin unpacking. Therapy had been painful, but the memory of how it had helped in the past made her hopeful. Mac had promised she would walk at her wedding if she worked hard at therapy.

She found herself thinking about what Matthew had said earlier about Josiah objecting to her joining the church. It troubled her that she'd made an enemy in him. Matthew had been upset about it enough to say he'd go outside the church to marry her. He was a calm, rational man, her Matthew; if he was reacting the way he was, it made her worry. This was a time when they should have been happily making plans to marry, getting to know each other better, doing fun things together as a couple and with the children. Instead, they had to be concerned with whether their union would, in effect, be blessed by the church, which Matthew had made a part of his everyday life.

Exhausted, she fell asleep, only to toss and turn. She dreamed of trying to run from something, but her balky legs wouldn't co-operate. She heard footsteps behind her, someone running and coming closer and closer, and when she turned to look, she saw Josiah picking up stones and throwing them after her. They struck her in the back, hurting, slowing her, and she called for Matthew to help.

She woke to find her cheeks wet with tears. Sleep was such a blessing, but would the nightmares end after she'd proved herself in the community?

15

Waiting.

Jenny had never been good at it. Having to sit around and heal for months so far hadn't helped. Perhaps she should have learned patience from the experience. But once she'd started feeling better, once she knew she had a future with Matthew, she just wanted to get on with it.

She had to admit to herself that once or twice she thought about what he'd said about their getting married outside the church. The trouble was, she knew his faith was too important to him and it had become important to her. She told herself that good things were worth waiting for.

So she tried to be patient and focus on each day and enjoy it.

Matthew's suggestion that she write a book had been brilliant. Writing was cathartic for her. The words seemed to pour out, and for the time she was writing, she didn't think of anything else. What she was saying was too important.

But when the intensity got to her, when her body was resisting hours spent sitting, writing, she found herself feeling restless and directionless. She'd always known where she was going and depended on herself for what she wanted. Now it felt that things were out of her hands.

Her grandmother noticed and, bless her, kept suggesting things Jenny could do that wouldn't tax her. One day, Hannah even came by to invite her to see Matthew's home.

Jenny had barely had time to knock when Hannah opened the door.

Hannah smiled. "Welcome home." She leaned forward to kiss Jenny's cheek.

Touched, Jenny kissed her future sister-in-law's cheek. "What a sweet thing to say."

"It *will* be your home," Hannah told her. "I thought you might want to know more about the children, about the house, about the daily routine." She shut the door and then turned to search Jenny's face. "Jenny, I hope that there are no hard feelings between us for what you overheard the day you came home."

"We're fine," Jenny told her without reservation. She hugged Hannah and then stood back, smiling. "I feel like you're the *schweschder* I never had."

"I feel that way, too."

They took a tour of the comfortable old farmhouse, which was scrupulously clean. Mary and Annie shared a room where their beds were neatly made, covered with colorful quilts their mother had sewn for them. Annie's favorite bedtime storybook lay on hers. Joshua's room was next door, and it was as neat as the girls' room, his bed covered with a quilt of many shades of blue.

Hannah's room was small, not much bigger than the children's rooms. It was plain in *Englisch* standards, but Hannah had added a bright quilt in the star pattern and she'd put a vase of daffodils on the dresser. Afternoon light filtered in through a large window and gave it such a peaceful air.

"This could be a room for another *kind,*" she told Jenny a little shyly. "Maybe a *sohn* since Joshua feels a little overwhelmed by two *schweschders.*"

Jenny bit her lip, and she took a deep breath. "I'm not sure that will happen, Hannah. I had some internal damage. The doctor says —"

"They don't know everything," Hannah interjected. "God *knows*. It doesn't matter what the doctors say. If it is God's will for

346

you to have a *kind,* you and Matthew will have a *kind.*"

"I hope you're right." Jenny glanced around the room.

Finally, Hannah showed Jenny Matthew's room. A big bed with a hand-carved headboard dominated the room; there were three matching dressers as well. Jenny asked if Matthew had carved them as some of the men did here during times when they weren't busy with farming or other occupations, especially during the quiet winter months, and Hannah nodded.

Jenny knew not to expect photographs of the children, but having been to the home of her friends David and Joy where framed photos of Sam were everywhere, she still noticed it. She knew the cultures were different and she respected that.

They returned to the kitchen, the room in Matthew's house that Jenny had grown to love for the wonderful memories.

"I made tea and some blueberry friendship bread," Hannah told Jenny as she served the bread with pots of fruit preserves.

"Mmm, this is delicious," Jenny told her after sampling it. "Why's it called friendship bread?"

"A friend gave me a loaf of the bread and the recipe with a crock of starter," she said.

"Sort of like the kind of starter stuff that sourdough bread is made with?"

"Yes. So then you have what you need to make the bread for yourself and for friends. And it gets passed down and down through friends and family."

She handed Jenny a napkin-wrapped loaf of the bread with a small crock.

"Oh, but you can't give me yours."

"This is a new crock, with some of my starter, just for you. So you can make the friendship bread, too."

Jenny took the crock and stared at it for a moment, then she looked at Hannah. More than a recipe was being given, and Jenny wasn't sure she could tell Hannah how much it meant to her.

"You've been such a good friend to me," Jenny said quietly. "No, more than a friend. You've welcomed me and never thought about what would happen to you if Matthew and I decided to marry."

Hannah smiled. "I like you for yourself, Jenny, but I love you for what you've brought out in my brother. You're good for him. You're good for the children."

"I know what it's like to have your mother die when you're young. I know what it's like to feel that pain."

"This house is filled with love and laughter

again, and it's because of you. I can move now and know that I'm leaving a happy family."

"But I feel like I'm pushing you out," Jenny said. "I want you to stay and be part of our family. You're a wonderful woman, Hannah. Surely the loving sacrifice you made will be rewarded."

"*Lieb* is never a sacrifice," Hannah told her with a smile. She hesitated for a moment. "Jenny, Phoebe and I have been friends for many years. She asked me if I wanted to move into her house, and I've decided to accept her generous offer."

"Oh, my!" Jenny stared at her. "What a wonderful idea!"

"You don't mind?"

"Mind? I think it's the perfect solution!" She threw her arms around Hannah. "Just think, both my grandmother and my best friend right next door. What could be better?" She glanced at the window. "Have you told Matthew?"

"Not yet. I wanted to make sure you didn't mind."

Jenny smiled. "Let's tell him at supper. I know he and the children will be delighted you'll be so close."

"*Allrecht,*" Hannah said, nodding.

"Can I ask you something?"

"Schur."

"It's very personal."

Hannah touched her hand lying on the table. "I've asked you enough questions. What is it you want to know?"

"Did you not marry because you've been so busy helping Matthew with the house and children?"

Conflicting emotions chased across Hannah's face. "I told you, love isn't a sacrifice. I told you that before. I just haven't found the right *mann*."

"What are you looking for?"

Hannah laughed. "You make it sound like I should make a list."

"Why not?" Jenny asked. She propped her elbow on the table and cupped her cheek in her hand as she studied Hannah's blushing face. "I have friends who've done that then found the man they married." She glanced at the pad of paper held by a magnetic clip on the refrigerator. "Grab that pad and find a pencil."

"This is silly." But as Jenny continued to stare at her, Hannah got up to do as she was asked. She took her seat at the table again.

"Okay. The right *mann* loves God as much as I do and makes Him the Head of our household. He's honest and kindhearted and generous. He loves me and the *kinner* we'll have. He's a hard worker and . . ." She looked up at Jenny. "What else?"

"He's handsome and makes your heart flutter."

Hannah's laugh filled the kitchen. "Well, I don't think my heart has ever fluttered. That sounds like it might be hazardous."

Jenny smiled. "I assure you it's a wonderful feeling. Mine flutters every time I look at Matthew."

"I like the way the two of you look at each other. When you talk about each other."

"Me too," Jenny confessed, knowing she probably looked goofy in love.

Hannah chewed on her lip as she reread the list she'd been composing. Then she glanced back up at Jenny, her eyes twinkling. "You know who this reminds me of?"

"Matthew," they said at the same time and laughed.

"You couldn't do better than to find a man like him," Jenny said.

"Did you make a list?"

Jenny shook her head. "No, all I did was visit my grandmother and there he was, right next door." She stopped and laughed. "He was the boy next door." When her future sister-in-law looked blank, she explained what that meant.

"So even though some of your friends write wish lists, you let God bring you the man he set aside for you?"

"I guess I did. Huh," Jenny said, thinking about it.

"And then God brought you back here at the right time, for you to be with Matthew forever."

Forever. Jenny liked the sound of that.

Matthew was stepping out of the barn when he saw Jenny enter his home.

Their home soon.

He wanted to go say hello, to have his day brightened by her smile. But he also wanted to let the two women he loved talk about the time when Jenny would come to this house to live and Hannah would go on to her own life.

When Jenny had first returned, Hannah had spoken against her, he remembered. She'd felt she needed to warn him about why he should not renew his relationship with Jenny. He'd been unhappy with her for being so uncharacteristically judgmental and had feared that she would not be friendly. But Hannah's reservations had seemed to evaporate almost immediately. She'd been happy at the news they were to be wed, too. In fact, more than once he'd seen her exchanging a look with Phoebe.

Matthew stopped in his tracks. *Had Hannah and Phoebe been guilty of matchmaking?* He would have to ask them, although if they had, he wondered if they'd admit it.

There was plenty to do as he waited so that he wouldn't look as though he was some lovesick youth, unable to be away from the woman he loved. Then Jenny saved him when she came out to the barn to find him. She must have really wanted to see him since she moved slowly across the yard with her walker.

"We thought you might like to stop for coffee. If you have time."

He nodded. "I have time. How is it going, this talk the two of you are having?"

"Wonderful," she said. "She went over the children's routine and gave me some of their favorite recipes."

"Joshua likes food, period," he told her. "Much like me. The girls are a little more particular, but they eat almost anything Hannah makes."

"That's because she's a great cook."

Pilot whinnied and stuck his head out of his stall.

"Hi, boy." Jenny walked slowly over to him and stroked his head.

"He's probably hoping we'll go for a ride today."

"Not today," Jenny told the horse. "But I'll bring you an apple before I leave."

She looked around the interior of the barn. It was, like everything else on the farm, neat and well cared for.

Matthew shut the barn door after they walked outside. She watched him look out at the fields. Slipping her arm through his, she did the same.

"Bet you can't wait to get to the planting."

"I admit to being a little restless."

She'd come to know that he was a man of action, one who loved the hard work of this farm. Thankfully, she didn't shy from work either. Although Plain children grew up knowing they were expected to do chores every day — and not to get allowances — Jenny knew even before she'd talked to Hannah that taking care of a family on this farm would be a lot of work.

But she couldn't imagine anything she looked forward to more.

"Jenny, there's something I want to say to you."

She stopped and looked at him.

"I want you to be comfortable here, to feel that it's your home," he said quietly.

354

"Every woman should have her home the way she wants it. You and I could pick out new paint and wallpaper, and I'll do the work before you come here."

"Matthew, no! I wouldn't want to upset the children by making them think I'm taking over, that I'm pushing their mother away."

"They won't think that. They love you and want you to live here. And you shouldn't feel that you're taking over their mother's home. The children understand that she lives in heaven now and you'll be their mother here on earth."

She was humbled by his saying that. Smiling at him, she squeezed his arm.

"Let me tell you how they behaved when you didn't come home on the day we expected."

He sat her down on a bale of hay and told her about the night all three children had been upset and he'd had to calm then down. Tears threatened her own eyes as she listened.

"I am so blessed," she whispered. "They are such wonderful children."

"What about me?" he asked, pretending to sulk "Maybe I cried, too."

She stood and kissed his cheek. "I doubt that."

He wrapped his arms around her. "I missed you so. I should have gone with you."

"It's just as well you didn't," she said, standing in his embrace. "I think I needed to face it myself. And it was important for you to be here with the children." Moving back, she looked up at him as she found her own handkerchief to wipe way her tears.

She wanted to tell him Hannah's news but that was for her future sister-in-law to tell. So, instead Jenny said, "Come inside and have some coffee and the treat Hannah baked."

There was one more snow after those first daffodils, and then spring was very much in evidence with its sweet promise of new leaves on the trees and men plowing and planting the fields.

Though the air still held a nip, children ran barefoot and enjoyed being outdoors. There was more work for everyone.

Jenny helped with spring cleaning as her grandmother swept through the house looking for every speck of dirt. Even when she didn't find it, she cleaned some more.

Shaking her head as the older woman made her sit and rest while she carried rugs outside to beat the dust — what dust? — from them, Jenny hoped one day when she

356

was fully recovered that she would have such energy.

Now that she had made the commitment to stay, Jenny joined her grandmother in attending Sunday services at the various homes in their community. She could move about better in the kitchen afterward, helping the women to set out the food while the older girls watched the children and the men tended the horses, although she still had to sit down often. And the cane she hated so much was always at hand. But it was better than the walker she'd been able to give up.

As they saw that she was not just Phoebe's visiting granddaughter but a woman who had come to join them and marry one of their favorite sons, she felt the other women warming to her.

One day they surprised her with a quilting at her grandmother's home.

"We thought we'd make a quilt for you," one of the women said. "For you and Matthew. For your bed."

For our marriage bed, thought Jenny.

One older woman showed her how to cut squares of different fabrics to begin a quilt. Although she'd been watching Phoebe, this was the first time she'd tried it for herself.

Naomi, a woman about Jenny's age,

showed Jenny a quilt she'd made of scraps of material she'd had left from making clothes for her children.

"Whenever I look at my favorite quilt, it helps me remember the dress I made for Anna Mae or the shirt Amos loved," Esther said.

Jenny found herself remembering the brightly colored head scarf a young Afghan girl had once given her. Maybe one day she'd make a quilt with a design incorporating that and some clothing she'd bought overseas, she thought, moving some squares around on the table. The task reminded her of how hard she'd worked to pick up the pieces of her life again, make some sense of it, gain some order. Find peace and faith in her God.

Maybe this is *why women love quilting.* It isn't just a way to make something beautiful and creative as well as the all-important *useful.* It's a way to sit and think about the order and purpose in one's life.

Now she had purpose, she realized. She was regaining her mobility with more of the hated physical therapy, writing her book, and learning about the ways of the community. Soon, she'd become a new wife to Matthew and a stepmother to his kinner. She was meeting more of the people in the community and finding herself embraced by a growing group of friends, such as these women who sat around in a circle and showed such willingness to welcome her — and show her how to make the things they loved, like their precious quilts.

Well, it seemed she was welcomed by so many — but not everyone was friendly. Josiah popped into her thoughts. He remained distant and suspicious.

But Jenny was a veteran of TV news and that job was not for the fainthearted. When she got her first nasty letter at the network, David had told her everyone got them and she'd need to develop a thicker skin. After all, no one was liked by everyone. He said a psychologist friend had told him that a person was lucky if half the people who met them liked them.

Perhaps she wasn't doing so badly if Josiah was the only one who didn't seem to like her here. Then again, she had no idea if other people were merely being polite.

Enough, she told herself. What a silly thing to waste time on. It was a relief finally not to be so housebound. People in the community began to approach her, and she was enjoying things like this quilting circle and work frolics and all the other functions where she wasn't sure if the fun of socializing was more important or the work.

The nicer weather brought out the tourists. They passed the house often each day and milled about in town. Jenny came to accept them as part of life and ignored the occasional questions about why she wasn't "dressed Amish" when she was with her grandmother or Matthew and the *kinner.*

She'd enjoyed taking over the reins when Matthew let her drive, so Phoebe showed her how to hitch up her horse to the buggy and encouraged her to take it out if she liked. After all, if Jenny was ever to get around by herself she would have to learn.

Daisy, her grandmother's horse, was patient as Jenny struggled to do the hitching up by herself. She was feeling pretty good when she drove up to the road in front of her grandmother's house and looked both ways for traffic.

Just then, she saw Josiah going past in his buggy. Jenny lifted her hand in greeting and he turned his head to regard her with a stony face, then stared ahead.

Shaking her head, wondering if he would ever change his mind about her, she called to Daisy and gave the reins a shake.

Daisy stepped onto the road and then hesitated. She cocked her ear and stopped.

"C'mon, Daisy, let's go!" Jenny called to

her. *Cars don't do this,* she thought. "Go, horsie! Now!"

Shaking her head, Daisy moved forward, entering the road.

It happened so suddenly, Jenny would think later.

A speeding car came out of nowhere. The driver honked the horn and brakes squealed as the car tried to avoid the buggy entering the road.

Jenny tried desperately to get out of its way, pulling at the reins, but Daisy reared up in panic and jerked the opposite way, and the buggy skidded and toppled over.

Jenny screamed as she slid across the seat and threw out her arms to break her fall. Her head hit the side of the buggy, and she blacked out.

Matthew heard a car horn and the scream of brakes. He dropped the bag of seed he was holding and rushed out to look down the road.

Josiah was turning his buggy around.

"What happened?"

"Accident. Get in."

But Matthew ran, too terrified to ride. There was an overturned buggy down by Phoebe's house. *What if it is her — or Jenny — in it?*

A car was parked beside the road. He looked further and saw Daisy struggling to get free of the buggy that lay on its side.

"Dear God," he cried. "Please, let Jenny and Phoebe be all right."

He ran past the *Englisch* woman who had been driving the car. She had a cell phone in her hand.

"I called 911," she called to him. "Someone's hurt in the buggy."

Phoebe rushed out of the house. "Matthew? What happened?"

His steps faltered and his heart leaped into his throat. "It's Jenny? Jenny's in the buggy?"

He ran and peered into the buggy. Jenny lay crumpled on her side in the wreckage. Grabbing Daisy's bridle, he worked to restrain her from pulling at the buggy and further injuring Jenny. The horse's eyes were wide and wild.

"Phoebe, see how badly Jenny is hurt."

Frantically, he freed the horse.

Josiah took her reins and led her away, talking quietly to calm her.

Phoebe looked up from where she knelt beside Jenny's prone body. Her face was white and her eyes were filled with fear. "Matthew, she's unconscious."

He checked for a pulse but it felt weak.

"She's breathing."

"I don't know where she's hurt." Tears ran down Phoebe's cheeks. "Oh, I feel so helpless!"

Then, just as she said the words, she took a deep breath and Matthew could see her willing herself to calm.

"God is in charge," she said, as if reminding herself. "There is no place He is not." She began praying as she stroked the hair back from Jenny's pale face.

"They said the ambulance is on the way," said the driver. "We're not supposed to move her."

The sound of sirens grew louder as emergency vehicles came up the road.

Jenny was carefully lifted from the wreckage and placed on a board. The paramedics carried her to the waiting ambulance and put her inside.

"You her husband?" a paramedic asked Matthew.

He knew they were asking so that they could let him ride with her to the hospital. For a moment, he was tempted to say yes, but he couldn't lie.

"Not yet," he said. "This is her grandmother."

The paramedic turned to Phoebe. "Do you want to ride with us, ma'am?"

"Yes, please."

They helped her into the ambulance. The doors shut, the siren started, and the ambulance took off in a burst of speed.

Matthew realized that Josiah was speaking to him.

"Get in the buggy," the older man said. "I'll drive you to the hospital.

Matthew hesitated.

"Please. Get in the buggy. I've already taken the horse to Phoebe's barn."

He climbed inside, and Josiah jerked the reins, urging his horse to a gallop.

"She will be all right," he told Matthew. "She's a strong woman. You and I have seen that, have we not?"

Surprised, Matthew glanced over at him. He didn't know what to say so he said nothing.

"We must do as Phoebe did," the older man said. "We must pray."

Matthew nodded and asked God to take care of Jenny. The moment Josiah pulled up to the hospital's emergency entrance, Matthew jumped out of the buggy.

"Thank you," he managed to say before he bolted into the hospital.

Phoebe was in the waiting room. He went to sit with her, and they held hands while they waited.

"Jenny woke up in the ambulance," she told him. "She was talking to the paramedics, and they said that was good."

An eternity seemed to pass. Matthew smelled the disinfectant smells and watched the nurses taking patients behind the closed doors. Other people sat in the waiting room, wearing worried expressions. Everyone looked up expectantly each time a doctor or nurse entered. Tension filled the room, a familiar tension and dread.

"You can see her now," the nurse came to tell them.

Phoebe got up and turned to him when he didn't follow. "Matthew?"

But he couldn't make himself move. "I —" He shook his head. "You go first."

"You know that you'll just sit here and worry. And she'll want to see you."

Matthew got to his feet. He fought the sense of panic as they walked down the hallway behind the nurse.

Jenny was sitting up on a gurney in a cubicle, looking unhappy as she held an ice bag on her wrist. There was bruising on her forehead, and a small bandage covered one eyebrow. "I can't believe what happened," she said when she saw them. "Please tell me that driver got a speeding ticket!"

"I don't know," Phoebe told her as she

bent to hug her. "I rode in the ambulance with you. What did the doctor say?"

"I have a sprained wrist," she said, holding it up for them to see how swollen it was. Then she was staring at him. "Matthew?"

Her voice echoed in his ears as if he stood in a tunnel. "I — I'll be right back."

He stumbled out of the room and down the hallway, nearly running someone over in his rush to get outside. There, he took several deep breaths to steady himself.

What must Jenny have thought? he asked himself. Had he offered her comforting words, or said he was glad she was not seriously injured? No, he'd stood there, silent, and then had rushed out of the room.

He felt a hand on his shoulder and turned to see Josiah.

"How is she?"

"She'll be fine," he said and his voice sounded shaky. "Just some bruising and — a sprained wrist."

Josiah nodded. He stroked his beard as he stared at Matthew.

They watched another ambulance pull up at the emergency entrance.

"But being here makes you remember those last days with Amelia?"

"Ya." And there'd been the recent worries when Jenny had to have surgery. He'd failed

366

her, not stood by her for the surgery or when she'd been worried about the extra tests. Matthew told himself that he hadn't been there to share her worries.

But Josiah didn't need to know all that. Matthew nodded, unable to speak.

"I don't like this place, either," Josiah said after a moment.

Matthew looked at him. "What?"

"My Ruth —" he stopped and stared at the hat he held in his hands.

"I'm sorry," Matthew said, feeling chastened. Josiah's wife had spent her last days here. It had to be as hard for him, too. But he'd only thought of himself. Not of Jenny. Not of this man who'd driven him here. Josiah might be a grumpy old man determined to cling to the way things had always been. He might have resisted Jenny being part of the community. But when Matthew needed a ride, Josiah had immediately given it to him.

"I need to go back in," Matthew said. He took a deep breath, let it out. Jenny might be frightened, too, being in a hospital after all she'd been through. He hadn't been there in New York. But he could be there for her now.

And just because he'd lost one wife early didn't mean that he'd lose another so soon.

All was in God's plan, and he had to accept even as he didn't understand.

Straightening, he said, "I'll go back now."

"*Gut.* Do you want me to wait and give you a ride home?"

Matthew shook his head. "I'm hoping that they won't keep her. But thank you. Thank you for everything." He watched the older man open his mouth, then shut it.

"Is there something you wanted to say?"

"You can tell Phoebe to send me those articles she seemed to think I should read. That Jenny wrote."

"Okay," Matthew said slowly. "I'll do that."

"Doesn't mean that I think it's a good idea for you to be marrying an *Englischer.* Our worlds just don't mix."

"I guess we just have to agree to disagree."

Josiah nodded and turned to leave.

"Oh, Josiah?"

"Yes?" He turned back.

"If you could stop by my place and tell Hannah what happened and that I'll be home soon, I would appreciate it."

"*Ya,* I'll do that."

When Matthew walked back to see Jenny again, a nurse was explaining how she was to care for her wrist.

"The doctor is discharging her," Phoebe

told him. "He doesn't think she has a concussion, but I'm to watch her tonight and call if I notice any symptoms." She held up the printed sheet of instructions.

When he continued to look at Jenny, she eyed him closely. "Are you all right?"

He took a deep breath. "I am now."

Moving to the gurney, he bent to give her a hug, careful not to hold her too tightly. "I was so frightened when I saw you lying there."

"I'm sorry. I'm all right. But I want to go home. Please, can we go home now?"

"Let me go get us transportation." He cradled her cheeks in his hands and bent to kiss her. "I love you."

"I love you, too."

Spring seemed over in a flash.

The season was so short in this part of the country, it seemed to Jenny, and then summer was upon them with a golden haze of heat.

She wiped the back of her hand over her forehead as she helped Phoebe with canning one afternoon.

"Hot work," Phoebe said, seeming unfazed by the heat. She lovingly lined up jars filled with summer's bounty — strawberry preserves, blackberry and blueberry jam, watermelon pickles, chowchow, bread and butter pickles, tomatoes, and more.

When they were finished, they sat and rewarded themselves with glasses of iced tea.

"What's your favorite season?" she asked her grandmother.

"The fall," Phoebe said instantly. "I love the colors of the leaves, the cooler weather. Looking at a harvest moon and knowing that soon the time of rest will come after all the hard work of harvesting has been done."

She took a sip of tea and smiled at Jenny. "What's your favorite?"

"I've always loved fall for the colors and the cooler weather. But I think I'll like this fall most of all."

"And would the reason be that you will be marrying Matthew?" Phoebe asked with a twinkle in her eyes.

Jenny laughed. "Of course."

She thought about how bitterly cold it had been when she came here. The weather had seemed to match her inner chill and misery.

The summer weather now reminded Jenny of when she'd visited her grandmother and developed a crush on Matthew. But this summer, when they went blueberry picking, they'd been a couple out with their children.

"What are you thinking about?"

"I've been here three seasons now," Jenny told her thoughtfully. "Each has had something good and something that has been a challenge." She was silent for a moment. "Like the passage from Ecclesiastes: 'To every thing there is a season, and a time to every purpose under the heavens.'"

Jenny tried to smother a yawn. She was not about to look tired when her grandmother still appeared to have the energy to go for hours.

"You should go rest," Phoebe told her. "We had a long morning."

"I'm not resting unless you do."

Phoebe chuckled. "You are a stubborn young woman."

"Hmm," said Jenny. "I wonder where I got that?"

"Fine, we'll have a rest." Phoebe got to her feet and started toward her room.

Jenny stood and stretched. The ache in her lower back was a good ache, from standing and working, not from injuries and surgeries. Still, it would be good to take a rest.

She got as far as her room when she heard the knock on the door.

"I'll get it," Jenny called to her grandmother.

She'd been getting stronger and stronger

and taking more and more steps without her cane. So she started for the kitchen, and though her legs trembled with the effort, and she reached now and then to steady herself on furniture, she was elated when she reached the door without incident.

The man she loved stood on the porch.

"Matthew! I thought you wouldn't be by until much later. Come in."

He stepped inside, took off his straw hat, and hung it on the peg as she closed the door.

"Would you like some iced tea?"

"In a little while." He took her hands in his. "Jenny, I went to speak to the bishop."

Her heart stopped, then started again. She searched his face. "What did he say?"

"You may be baptized next month."

"Baptized? Really?" She held her breath.

He nodded and smiled. "And we'll be married the first Tuesday in November."

With a joyful cry Jenny threw her arms around him and held him. His arms came around her. They stood there for a long moment.

When she pulled back, she smiled up at him. "You said it would be worth the wait. You were right." Suddenly she swayed and reached for a nearby chair. "Oh, I think I need to sit down."

He pulled out a chair and helped her to sit, then took a seat himself. Frowning, he looked around. "Jenny, where's your cane?"

"In the other room," she told him, grinning. "I told you that I'm determined to walk without it at our wedding."

"I know you will," he told her quietly. "I know you will."

He kissed her and then he smiled. "Now, shall we share our good news with our family?"

16

Jenny woke before dawn on her wedding day.

Lying in her grandmother's house, she thought about how much her life was going to change after today. In a matter of hours, she'd be married to Matthew and become a wife and a mother all at the same time. She'd move into his house and into a life different from anything she'd imagined.

She fairly jumped out of bed with excitement.

The sudden move caused her hip to scream in protest. Reaching behind her, she felt for the bed and lowered herself to it. She took a deep breath, rubbed at her hip, and told herself to be careful. She'd worked too hard to get to this point, to be able to walk without her cane. *Now isn't the time to be careless and hurt myself and have to use that hated cane. Not today.* She wanted to walk with Matthew at their wedding.

So she sat there and let her hip rest until the pain subsided. She said her morning prayer and thanked God for this day, and then she got up slowly and went about getting dressed.

When she was a little girl she'd played Getting Married just like a lot of other little girls and worn a costume of a white satin dress and veil. She'd carried a bouquet of dandelions and persuaded a boy who lived next door to stand in as a groom. It wasn't hard to get him to participate when he found out she'd made a little chocolate cake with chocolate frosting in her Easy Bake oven.

Today, she combed her hair, parting it in the middle, then fastened it at the nape of her neck, and placed the black *kapp* worn for weddings on her head. Next she lifted the dress she and her grandmother had made, the fabric the color of morning glories, and slipped it over her head. The immaculate white organdy cape and apron that had been so carefully ironed were next. The outfit was Sunday best, in the tradition of *demut* — humility — not a fancy one like *Englischers* wore in weddings.

She stared at her reflection in the mirror over the chest of drawers. No feeling like a princess dressed in a billowy white dress and veil. No flowers. No wedding planners or near-hysteria about details.

She felt quietly content when she reflected on the preparations going on without her, what was happening just hours from now.

There was a knock on the door and her grandmother called her name. "Come in."

"Lieblich!" she murmured as she walked into the room.

"I'm hardly lovely," Jenny said with a self-deprecating laugh. "But I hope Matthew likes how I look."

"Don't argue with me," Phoebe told her with some asperity. But Jenny saw the twinkle in her eyes. "He would love you if you wore a flour sack, but happily, that's not necessary." She stood there studying Jenny for a long moment. "How I wish your parents could be here." Then tears welled up in her eyes, and she shook her head. "But your father —" she stopped and pressed her hands against her mouth.

"My father what?" When her grandmother didn't speak, she touched her arm. "What about Dad?"

Shaking her head, Phoebe searched in her pocket for her handkerchief and wiped the tears away. "Never mind."

She embraced Jenny carefully so she wouldn't wrinkle the delicate organdy fabric of the cape and apron, then stepped away. "I just wanted to come up and see if you needed any help dressing. But since you're ready, let's just say a prayer, shall we?"

Jenny nodded. "That would be wonderful."

After they finished, Phoebe squeezed Jenny's hands. "See you downstairs." And she was gone in a flurry of skirts, closing the door behind her.

Jenny looked in the mirror one more time, then she smiled and with a deep breath, left the room, carefully descending the wooden stairs.

Matthew stood waiting. He looked so handsome in his wedding clothes, the black suit, the white shirt, and black bow-tie accenting his tanned skin and deep blue eyes.

"You look beautiful," he said softly, and his eyes were warm on hers as he drew her to him for a kiss. It lasted for only seconds since they could feel the eyes of their family looking on, but it was warm enough to be an unspoken promise of time together later. "I love you."

For a moment, it felt like they were alone in a world that contained only their love. As always, tears threatened to flood Jenny's eyes. "I love you, too."

He took her hand and led her to the table

— but she wasn't allowed to sit yet. Hannah swooped in, her eyes sparkling with tears. She hugged them, absorbing their love and support.

When she felt arms clutching her legs, Jenny looked down to see Annie looking up at her adoringly. Jenny leaned down to hug her and then held out her arms for Mary and Joshua.

Breakfast was just a quick bite since so much food was being prepared for all the feasting that would take place that day. Jenny had already attended several weddings and had eaten so much she'd wondered if she'd have to adjust her own wedding garments.

The aromas of food cooking wafted up from the basement: the rich scents of roasted chicken with bread stuffing that was traditional for a wedding — along with creamed celery, mashed potatoes and gravy, and all the vegetables and breads and desserts. After days of preparation, these scents clung to the air.

After breakfast, Matthew drew Jenny outside to the porch for a quiet word together.

"Should we be seen out here?" she protested, but he didn't have to convince her. She followed him, her heart beating fast.

"You look so beautiful," he said and then his lips swooped in for another kiss. She laughed, happier than she could ever remember being. Then she glanced around.

"What?"

"I keep wondering if Josiah will pop up and frown at us."

He chuckled and shook his head. "I think he's finally accepted you. I think he came to see how much I loved you after your accident. He understood that I was afraid I would lose you. I'm not saying he's still not the stern, traditional Old Order Amish *mann* who's concerned about change happening in the community or that he'll be here today. But I know his opinion of you has softened."

Matthew lifted her chin with his hand. "But it doesn't matter. Only God's opinion matters. And I believe He brought us together again." He embraced her, and then, when she shivered in a brisk autumn breeze, they went inside.

Soon helpers arrived to assist with the food and the seating. Jenny and Matthew greeted their guests before the service and the ceremony, a custom she thought was incredibly sweet. Acknowledging her pleasure at their attendance was so important

— especially when she saw three of the first arrivals.

"Jenny!" The young boy's high squeal was a delightful surprise.

"Sam!" Jenny cried, reaching for him. "David! Joy! You came!"

The three of them took turns hugging Jenny and shaking Matthew's hand.

Joy moved closer and whispered, "Am I dressed okay? I didn't want to offend anyone."

Jenny stared straight into Joy's eyes, not even bothering to check out the outfit. "You're dressed just fine, and no one will judge you. I'm so happy you're here!"

"Sam promised he'll behave," David inserted, glancing at his son who was staring wide-eyed at the people milling about the crowded kitchen.

"Sam always behaves," Jenny said firmly. "I warned you that the service is long so if he gets restless, as children do, no one will think anything of you going outside for a few minutes. Just don't miss the big moment!"

"We won't," Joy promised. "David, let's go find a seat and get out of the way."

Church service started a short time later. The house was packed with friends and family from the community. Jenny and Matthew were seated together at the front with the ministers and the bishop, leaving for a brief time to meet with one of them about their marriage. Though her back ached a little from the hours of sermon and singing, she felt a sense of wonder that today, this service would end with a beginning — of her walking into a life with Matthew, a life with these people surrounding her, who had become as close as family.

And then it was time for her to join Matthew in a vow before God.

Jenny rose from her seat and, for a moment, wished she'd not been so caught up with the service that she forgot she still got stiff from sitting so long. She straightened, and as her friends and family watched, she walked slowly with Matthew to stand before the bishop.

Matthew glanced at the woman beside him and thought about how beautiful she looked, how radiant, in the traditional wedding clothes of his church.

Until today . . . well, if he were honest, until this moment, he wondered if Jenny would go through with it. Not because he didn't have faith in her or in his God. No, he had been afraid to believe he'd get this second chance at happiness with her.

He'd tried to assure himself that from the time she'd come home, broken in body and questioning everything she believed in, something seemed to be part of God's greater plan for them. But still, it was much like the work he did with his farm. He believed that all would be well when he planted and nurtured and prayed over his crop, but he still felt better when the harvest was safely in.

And so, as they stood side by side and were questioned about their marriage that was to be, he felt a peace settling over his heart.

There was a slight commotion and a gentle wave of laughter swept the room. When he looked to his side, he saw that Annie was bouncing on her toes as she watched the ceremony. Of all his children, she was the one who had fallen in love with Jenny first. Perhaps it was because she was too young to remember her own *mamm.* But he also thought it was because she and Jenny shared a difficulty in expressing themselves verbally. Both had improved so much since they worked hard with their speech therapy.

Now, when they were asked if they would love and honor each other in marriage, Jenny's voice was clear and fluid. *"Ya,"* she said, and she looked at him with love.

As he stood beside her and received this gift of her love from God, he thanked Him as a final prayer was said to bless their union. They faced the congregation as husband and wife — he felt the love of everyone in the room. He hoped that Jenny felt it too.

Married.

Jenny told herself to remember each and every moment of every minute that passed so she could tell her grandchildren what it was like the day she, a woman who'd come here as an *Englischer* and become one of the Plain People, had married their grandfather who was Amish.

But the day was long, filled with not one but two sumptuous meals and laughter and stories, and everything became a big happy blur. She smiled as she glimpsed young women seated at a table on one side of the room looking across at the young men on the opposite. She wondered if they dreamed of their own weddings. She and Matthew played matchmaker and paired couples up to sit at tables for the evening meal, a traditional wedding activity.

Jenny frowned when she looked for Hannah and didn't find her. Then, moments after the couples were seated, Hannah was once again in the room, but there was no one to pair her with. *Strange,* thought Jenny, wanting to ask Hannah where she'd gone. Then Hannah was moving away and the opportunity to ask her where she'd gone had passed.

Children raced around playing games, and it was nearly ten that night before things began to wind down. Hannah and Phoebe took Joshua and Mary and a very tired Annie to their home next door.

Since it was traditional for the newly married couple to stay at the bride's home, Jenny wondered if her new sister-in-law and grandmother were giving them privacy.

David and Joy and Sam left for a bed and breakfast. Some of the women stored leftovers and cleaned up the kitchen, then climbed into buggies with their families to leave.

"Are you tired, *mei fraa?*" Matthew asked as they stood in the doorway and watched their guests leaving.

Jenny watched the line of old-fashioned buggies rolling down the road. Only the twentieth-century addition of fluorescent triangle signs made it obvious that they weren't something out of time.

"I should be," she said. "It's been a long

day." She smiled at him. "But I'm not tired at all."

He closed the door and she picked up the propane-powered lantern. Hand in hand, they climbed the stairs to their room.

GLOSSARY

aenti — aunt
allrecht — all right
boppli — baby or babies
bruder — brother
daedi — daddy
dall — doll
danki — thanks
du bischt willkumm — you are welcome
eldre — parents, in addition to common usage
Englisch or Englischer — a non-Amish person
fiewer — fever
fraa — wife
gebet — prayer
gem gschehne — You are welcome
gwilde — quilt
grossdochder — granddaughter
grossmudder — grandmother
gut-n-owed — good evening
guder mariye — good morning

gut — good

gut nacht — good night

haus — house

hungerich — hungry

kaffi — coffee

kapp — prayer covering or cap

kich — kitchen

kichli — cookies

kind, kinner — child, children

kumm — come

lieb — love

liebschen — dearest or dear one

mamm — mom

mann — husband

mariyefrieh — tomorrow morning

mopskopp — stupid fellow

mammi — grandmother

mei — my

nachtesse — supper

naerfich — nervous

nee — no

onkel — uncle

Ordnung — The rules of the Amish both written and unwritten. Certain behavior has been expected within the Amish community for many, many years. These rules vary from community to community, but the most common are to not have electricity in the home, to not own or drive an automobile, and to dress in a certain way.

Pennsylvania Deitsch — Pennsylvania German

redd-up — clean up

ruck — dress

rumschpringe — time period when teenagers are allowed to experience the Englisch world while deciding whether to join the church

schul — school

schur — sure

schweschder — sister

supp — soup

sohn — son

wasser — water

Wie geht's — Good day! How are you?

willkumm — welcome

wunderbaar — wonderful

ya — yes

DISCUSSION QUESTIONS

Caution: Please don't read before completing the book as questions contain spoilers!

1. Jenny experiences a mixture of emotions about being seriously injured. While she's grateful to be alive, she wonders why God allowed her to be hurt when she feels she was doing His work. Have you ever wondered why bad things happen to good people?

2. When Jenny wakes in a hospital, she finds herself tucked in a quilt her grandmother sent. "Come. Heal" reads the accompanying note. What is your special place you retreat to when you're hurting?

3. Jenny and Matthew fell in love when they were teenagers, but she left and he married another. What do you think might have happened

if they had been married back then?

4. Someone once said that pain softens the soul. If that's true, Jenny's soul is certainly softened by all the pain she endures from her injuries. Do you think pain softens the soul?

5. Jenny's father was born Amish but he chose to leave before being baptized. As she visited her grandmother during summers, Jenny realized that the Plain life felt very comfortable and "right" for her. Do you share the same religious and spiritual beliefs as your parents? Why, or why not?

6. Amish religious services are held in the homes of its worshippers. Have you ever attended a service in a church very different from the kind you are accustomed to? How was it?

7. A man from the community disapproves of Jenny. Have you ever felt unjustly accused? What was the situation? How did you handle it?

8. The Amish believe that children are gifts from God and that the number of children a couple has is determined by God's will. Do you agree with this? Explain.

9. Just when Jenny feels that her life is on track and everything is going well, she encounters another challenge. Sometimes people say that God never gives you more than you can handle. How do you feel about this statement?

10. We are God's children and, thus, beautiful to Him. Yet Jenny struggles with self-esteem issues because she is scarred. What would you say to someone who feels that they are less than beautiful in the eyes of the one they love?

11. Jenny is sad that she can't continue the work she loves but then she finds a way to do something different to accomplish the same goal. Have you ever felt a door close because another is opening with a new opportunity? Explain.

12. In Ecclesiastes, we read that there is a time to every purpose under heaven . . . a time to be born and a time to die . . . a time to weep and a time to love. Jenny feels that because she may not be able to have children she should not marry Matthew. What would you tell Jenny?

AMISH PRETZELS

I tested this recipe given to me by an Amish friend and ate entirely too many pretzels. You can make these traditionally, with just a sprinkling of kosher salt, OR you can roll them in sesame or poppy seeds or garlic or onion powder before baking for a savory version.

If you have a sweet tooth, after baking, try rolling plain pretzels in cinnamon sugar or a simple glaze made with confection sugar and water.

1 tablespoon plus 1/4 teaspoon yeast
1/4 warm water (make sure it's warm, not hot)
3-3/4 cups all-purpose flour
3/4 cup plus two tablespoons powdered sugar
1-1/4 teaspoon salt
2 teaspoons vegetable oil
1-1/4 cups baking soda

4 cups warm (not hot) water
nonstick baking spray
1/4 cup melted butter

Dissolve yeast in warm water in a small bowl and let sit for a few minutes. Combine flour, sugar, and salt in a large bowl. Add water and oil. Stir until blended, then form dough into a ball. Knead dough on floured board for five or six minutes. Using a paper towel and some vegetable oil, coat the inside of a big bowl with oil and place dough in it. Cover, set in a warm (not hot) place to rise for about forty-five minutes.

Preheat oven to 425 degrees. Combine baking soda with the four cups of warm water and stir. Put dough on clean kitchen counter (don't use any flour) and cut into eight portions. Roll each until it's about three-feet long. Pick up each end of the dough and twist in pretzel shape, flipping around so the middle is wrapped twice.

Dip pretzels in the warm baking soda and water mixture, and blot any excess moisture before placing on two baking sheets sprayed lightly with nonstick baking spray. Now season them as you have decided — sprinkle with kosher salt or with the seeds or flavored onion or garlic powder. If you're planning on having sweet pretzels, you should not add salt before baking.

Bake pretzels for approximately four minutes. Don't walk away from the oven! If it looks like they're browning unevenly, you may need to turn the pans around. Remove when the pretzels are a nice golden color. Top with a little melted butter and eat immediately.

If you want the sweet kind, you can use the premixed cinnamon sugar or combine two teaspoons cinnamon with a half cup sugar. Spread melted butter on the pretzels, then sprinkle the cinnamon sugar over them and enjoy!

For some extra fun, get children to help you form the dough into stick shapes or alphabet letters before baking.

ABOUT THE AUTHOR

Barbara Cameron is the author of 21 fiction and nonfiction books, three nationally televised movies (HBO-Cinemax), and the winner of the first Romance Writers of America Golden Heart Award. When a relative took her to visit the Amish community in Lancaster, Pennsylvania, she felt led to write about the spiritual values and simple joys she witnessed there. She currently resides in Edgewater, Florida. Find out more about Barbara at www.barbara cameron.com, www.amishhearts.com, and www.amishliving.com.